The Haunted Hotel

and

The Dream-Woman

WILKIE COLLINS

The Haunted Hotel
A Mystery of Modern Venice

and

The Dream-Woman

ZULMA
classics

ZULMA *classics*

JANE AUSTEN
Northanger Abbey
and Love and Freindship

WILKIE COLLINS
The Haunted Hotel
and The Dream-Woman

THOMAS HARDY
The Well-Beloved
and Alicia's Diary

NATHANIEL HAWTHORNE
Lady Eleanore's Mantle
and Other Tales of Mystery

HENRY JAMES
Italian Tales

SHERIDAN LE FANU
Carmilla

ROBERT LOUIS STEVENSON
Strange Case of Dr. Jekyll and Mr. Hyde
and Essays in the Art of Writing

OSCAR WILDE
The Picture of Dorian Gray
and The Decay of Lying

∽∽∽

Typeset in Minion and Bauer Bodoni.
Cover design: David Lee Fong.
Cover painting: *Una tormenta inesperada*, by Raúl Agrán (Picture Alain Mangin).
Printed in France.

ISBN 2-84304-284-4

CONTENTS

CONTENTS

FOREWORD

PLAGUED by the ramifications of her crimes, a woman wanders the shadowy and deserted streets of Venice. A crumbling palace hastily made over as a luxury hotel, a man gone missing, and an anonymous letter help to set the scene for *The Haunted Hotel: A Mystery of Modern Venice,* published in 1879 towards the end of Collins' prolific career. While less intimidating in length, it shares the characteristic features of Collins' most important novels *Armadale, The Woman in White,* and *The Moonstone.* The features, and the dramatic effects: premonitions, dizzy fits, unexplained disappearances, and also more horror-story devices than Collins was in the habit of using. This can be seen from the masterly opening scene in which an agonised Countess Narona consults a Harley Street doctor on the eve of her wedding to Lord Montbarry. Is she insane, or are the premonitions haunting her really going to occur? In two marvellous pages, by turns ironic and melo-dramatic, Collins introduces his character—a woman teetering on the edge of the law, at war with society and with herself, an out-sider heralding misfortune; as such, Countess Narona has much in common with the heroine of *Armadale,* Lydia Gwilt. *The Dream-Woman,* a short story which complements the present title, con-tinues to explore this theme of the criminal woman.

William Wilkie Collins' style and legacy single him out as perhaps the most modern of all the Victorian novelists. He died in 1889 at the age of 65, prematurely haggard from the abuse of laudanum. He is the undisputed inventor of the sensation novel and one might say also of the detective novel; he certainly pioneered the hybrid romantic and procedural style that would later give rise to the thriller. The son of a well-known painter, Collins made a living from his work from an early age. He and Dickens were friends, and travelled to Italy—notably Venice—together in 1853. He also maintained a most unusual personal life, living openly and officially with Mrs. Caroline Graves but never marrying her, and also keeping a mistress, Miss Martha Rudd, with whom he had three children. Illegitimate characters play a major role in his work; they are always unconventional, with their strangeness revealed in a physical characteristic: Countess Narona is unusually pallid; the devilish Miss Gwilt is a redhead; the opium-addicted doctor who solves the mystery in *The Moonstone* is a half-caste whose hair is streaked with white; and Miserrimus Dexter, the eccentric collector in *The Law and the Lady,* is born without legs. Those who are new to Collins would do well to pay particular attention to the outsiders, for it is they who shape the stories . . .

Collins' contemporaries loved his work for the intriguing plots—*The Woman in White* was first published in serial form and readers used to queue at the news stand for the next instalment. Today's reader might derive more pleasure from the psychological complexity of his troubled characters, and his sharp sense for different narrative voices and styles. Collins loved the theatre and like his friend Dickens was a semi-professional actor; many of his stories and novels were adapted for the stage. Set in a remarkably topical, somewhat noxious Venice just starting to be affected by modern tourism, *The Haunted Hotel*—with its apparitions, olfactory hallucinations and secret passages—is itself like one of those shadowy chambers in which life's mysteries unfold.

The text of *The Haunted Hotel* reproduced here is that of the first British book edition published by Chatto & Windus in 1879. A few errors in spelling and punctuation have been silently corrected or modernized.

The Haunted Hotel

THE FIRST PART

CHAPTER I

IN the year 1860, the reputation of Doctor Wybrow as a London physician reached its highest point. It was reported on good authority that he was in receipt of one of the largest incomes derived from the practice of medicine in modern times.

One afternoon, towards the close of the London season, the Doctor had just taken his luncheon after a specially hard morning's work in his consulting-room, and with a formidable list of visits to patients at their own houses to fill up the rest of his day—when the servant announced that a lady wished to speak to him.

"Who is she?" the Doctor asked. "A stranger?"

"Yes, sir."

"I see no strangers out of consulting-hours. Tell her what the hours are, and send her away."

"I have told her, sir."

"Well?"

"And she won't go."

"Won't go?" The Doctor smiled as he repeated the words. He was a humourist in his way; and there was an absurd side to the situation which rather amused him. "Has this obstinate lady given you her name?" he inquired.

"No, sir. She refused to give any name—she said she wouldn't keep you five minutes, and the matter was too important to wait till to-morrow. There she is in the consulting-room; and how to get her out again is more than I know."

Doctor Wybrow considered for a moment. His knowledge of

women (professionally speaking) rested on the ripe experience of more than thirty years; he had met with them in all their varieties—especially the variety which knows nothing of the value of time, and never hesitates at sheltering itself behind the privileges of its sex. A glance at his watch informed him that he must soon begin his rounds among the patients who were waiting for him at their own houses. He decided forthwith on taking the only wise course that was open under the circumstances. In other words, he decided on taking to flight.

"Is the carriage at the door?" he asked.

"Yes, sir."

"Very well. Open the house-door for me without making any noise, and leave the lady in undisturbed possession of the consulting-room. When she gets tired of waiting, you know what to tell her. If she asks when I am expected to return, say that I dine at my club, and spend the evening at the theatre. Now then, softly, Thomas! If your shoes creak, I am a lost man."

He noiselessly led the way into the hall, followed by the servant on tip-toe.

Did the lady in the consulting-room suspect him? or did Thomas's shoes creak, and was her sense of hearing unusually keen? Whatever the explanation may be, the event that actually happened was beyond all doubt. Exactly as Doctor Wybrow passed his consulting-room, the door opened—the lady appeared on the threshold—and laid her hand on his arm.

"I entreat you, sir, not to go away without letting me speak to you first."

The accent was foreign; the tone was low and firm. Her fingers closed gently, and yet resolutely, on the Doctor's arm.

Neither her language nor her action had the slightest effect in inclining him to grant her request. The influence that instantly stopped him, on the way to his carriage, was the silent influence of her face. The startling contrast between the corpse-like pallor of her complexion and the overpowering life and light, the glittering metallic brightness in her large black eyes, held him literally spell-bound. She was dressed in dark colours, with perfect taste; she was of middle height, and (apparently) of middle age—say a year or two over thirty. Her lower features—the nose, mouth, and chin—possessed the fineness and delicacy of form which is oftener seen among women of foreign races than among women of English birth. She was unquestionably a handsome person—with the one serious drawback of her ghastly complexion, and with the less noticeable defect of a total want of tenderness in the expression of her eyes. Apart from his first emotion of surprise, the feeling she produced in the Doctor may be described as an overpowering feeling of professional curiosity. The case might prove to be something entirely new in his professional experience. "It looks like it," he thought; "and it's worth waiting for."

She perceived that she had produced a strong impression of some kind upon him, and dropped her hold on his arm.

"You have comforted many miserable women in your time," she said. "Comfort one more, to-day."

Without waiting to be answered, she led the way back into the room.

The Doctor followed her, and closed the door. He placed her in the patients' chair, opposite the windows. Even in London the sun, on that summer afternoon, was dazzlingly bright. The radiant light flowed in on her. Her eyes met it unflinchingly, with the steely steadiness of the eyes of an eagle. The smooth pallor of her unwrinkled skin looked more fearfully white than ever. For the first time, for many a long year past, the Doctor felt his pulse quicken its beat in the presence of a patient.

Having possessed herself of his attention, she appeared, strangely enough, to have nothing to say to him. A curious apathy seemed to have taken possession of this resolute woman. Forced to speak first, the Doctor merely inquired, in the conventional phrase, what he could do for her.

The sound of his voice seemed to rouse her. Still looking straight at the light, she said abruptly: "I have a painful question to ask."

"What is it?"

Her eyes travelled slowly from the window to the Doctor's face. Without the slightest outward appearance of agitation, she put the "painful question" in these extraordinary words:

"I want to know, if you please, whether I am in danger of going mad?"

Some men might have been amused, and some might have been alarmed. Doctor Wybrow was only conscious of a sense of disappointment. Was this the rare case that he had anticipated, judging rashly by appearances? Was the new patient only a hypochondriacal woman, whose malady was a disordered stomach and whose misfortune was a weak brain? "Why do you come to *me?*" he asked sharply. "Why don't you consult a doctor whose special employment is the treatment of the insane?"

She had her answer ready on the instant.

"I don't go to a doctor of that sort," she said, "for the very reason that he *is* a specialist: he has the fatal habit of judging everybody by lines and rules of his own laying down. I come to *you*, because my case is outside of all lines and rules, and because you are famous in your profession for the discovery of mysteries in disease. Are you satisfied?"

He was more than satisfied—his first idea had been the right idea, after all. Besides, she was correctly informed as to his professional position. The capacity which had raised him to fame and fortune was his capacity (unrivalled among his brethren) for the discovery of remote disease.

"I am at your disposal," he answered. "Let me try if I can find out what is the matter with you."

He put his medical questions. They were promptly and plainly answered; and they led to no other conclusion than that the strange lady was, mentally and physically, in excellent health. Not satisfied with questions, he carefully examined the great organs of life. Neither his hand nor his stethoscope could discover anything that was amiss. With the admirable patience and devotion to his art which had distinguished him from the time when he was a student, he still subjected her to one test after another. The result was always the same. Not only was there no tendency to brain disease—there was not even a perceptible derangement of the nervous system. "I can find nothing the matter with you," he said. "I can't even account for the extraordinary pallor of your complexion. You completely puzzle me."

"The pallor of my complexion is nothing," she answered a little impatiently. "In my early life I had a narrow escape from death by poisoning. I have never had a complexion since—and my skin is so delicate, I cannot paint without producing a hideous rash. But that is of no importance. I wanted your opinion given positively. I believed in you, and you have disappointed me." Her head dropped on her breast. "And so it ends!" she said to herself bitterly.

The Doctor's sympathies were touched. Perhaps it might be more correct to say that his professional pride was a little hurt. "It may end in the right way yet," he remarked, "if you choose to help me."

She looked up again with flashing eyes. "Speak plainly," she said. "How can I help you?"

"Plainly, madam, you come to me as an enigma, and you leave me to make the right guess by the unaided efforts of my art. My art will do much, but not all. For example, something must have occurred—something quite unconnected with the state of your bodily health—to frighten you about yourself, or you would never have come here to consult me. Is that true?"

She clasped her hands in her lap. "That is true!" she said eagerly. "I begin to believe in you again."

"Very well. You can't expect me to find out the moral cause which has alarmed you. I can positively discover that there is no physical cause of alarm; and (unless you admit me to your confidence) I can do no more."

She rose, and took a turn in the room. "Suppose I tell you?" she said. "But, mind, I shall mention no names!"

"There is no need to mention names. The facts are all I want."

"The facts are nothing," she rejoined. "I have only my own impressions to confess—and you will very likely think me a fanciful fool when you hear what they are. No matter. I will do my best to content you—I will begin with the facts that you want. Take my word for it, *they* won't do much to help you."

She sat down again. In the plainest possible words, she began the strangest and wildest confession that had ever reached the Doctor's ears.

CHAPTER II

"IT is one fact, sir, that I am a widow," she said. "It is another fact, that I am going to be married again."

There she paused, and smiled at some thought that occurred to her. Doctor Wybrow was not favourably impressed by her smile— there was something at once sad and cruel in it. It came slowly, and it went away suddenly. He began to doubt whether he had been wise in acting on his first impression. His mind reverted to the commonplace patients and the discoverable maladies that were waiting for him, with a certain tender regret.

The lady went on.

"My approaching marriage," she said, "has one embarrassing circumstance connected with it. The gentleman whose wife I am to be, was engaged to another lady when he happened to meet with me, abroad: that lady, mind, being of his own blood and family, related to him as his cousin. I have innocently robbed her of her lover, and destroyed her prospects in life. Innocently, I say— because he told me nothing of his engagement until after I had accepted him. When we next met in England—and when there was danger, no doubt, of the affair coming to my knowledge—he told me the truth. I was naturally indignant. He had his excuse ready; he showed me a letter from the lady herself, releasing him from his engagement. A more noble, a more high-minded letter, I never read in my life. I cried over it—I who have no tears in me for sorrows of my own! If the letter had left him any hope of being forgiven, I would have positively refused to marry him. But the firmness of it—without anger, without a word of reproach, with heartfelt wishes even for his happiness—the firmness of it, I say, left him no hope. He appealed to my compassion; he appealed to his love for me. You know what women are. I too was soft-hearted—I said, Very well; yes! In a week more (I tremble as I think of it) we are to be married."

She did really tremble—she was obliged to pause and compose herself, before she could go on. The Doctor, waiting for more facts, began to fear that he stood committed to a long story. "Forgive me for reminding you that I have suffering persons waiting to see me," he said. "The sooner you can come to the point, the better for my patients and for me."

The strange smile—at once so sad and so cruel—showed itself again on the lady's lips. "Every word I have said is to the point," she answered. "You will see it yourself in a moment more."

She resumed her narrative.

"Yesterday—you need fear no long story, sir; only yesterday — I was among the visitors at one of your English luncheon parties. A lady, a perfect stranger to me, came in late—after we had left the table, and had retired to the drawing-room. She happened to take a chair near me; and we were presented to each other. I knew her by name, as she knew me. It was the woman whom I had robbed of her lover, the woman who had written the noble letter. Now listen! You were impatient with me for not interesting you in what I said just now. I said it to satisfy your mind that I had no enmity of feeling towards the lady, on my side. I admired her, I felt for her— I had no cause to reproach myself. This is very important, as you will presently see. On her side, I have reason to be assured that the circumstances had been truly explained to her, and that she understood I was in no way to blame. Now, knowing all these necessary things as you do, explain to me, if you can, why, when I rose and met that woman's eyes looking at me, I turned cold from head to foot, and shuddered, and shivered, and knew what a deadly panic of fear was, for the first time in my life."

The Doctor began to feel interested at last.

"Was there anything remarkable in the lady's personal appearance?" he asked.

"Nothing whatever!" was the vehement reply. "Here is the true description of her:—The ordinary English lady; the clear cold blue eyes, the fine rosy complexion, the inanimately polite manner, the large good-humoured mouth, the too plump cheeks and chin: these, and nothing more."

"Was there anything in her expression, when you first looked at her, that took you by surprise?"

"There was natural curiosity to see the woman who had been preferred to her; and perhaps some astonishment also, not to see a more engaging and more beautiful person; both those feelings restrained within the limits of good breeding, and both not lasting for more than a few moments—so far as I could see. I say, "so far," because the horrible agitation that she communicated to me disturbed my judgment. If I could have got to the door, I would have run out of the room, she frightened me so! I was not even able to stand up—I sank back in my chair; I stared horror-struck at the calm blue eyes that were only looking at me with a gentle surprise. To say they affected me like the eyes of a serpent is to say nothing. I felt her soul in them, looking into mine—looking, if such a thing can be, unconsciously to her own mortal self. I tell you my impression, in all its horror and in all its folly! That woman is destined (without knowing it herself) to be the evil genius of my life. Her innocent eyes saw hidden capabilities of wickedness in me that I was not aware of myself, until I felt them stirring under her look. If I commit faults in my life to come—if I am even guilty of crimes—she will bring the retribution, without (as I firmly believe) any conscious exercise of her own will. In one indescribable moment I felt all this—and I suppose my face showed it. The good artless creature was inspired by a sort of gentle alarm for me. "I am afraid the heat of the room is too much for you; will you try my smelling bottle?" I heard her say those kind words; and I remember nothing else—I fainted. When I recovered my senses, the company had all gone; only the lady of the house was with me. For the moment I could say nothing to her; the dreadful impression that I have tried to describe to you came back to me with the coming back of my life. As soon I could speak, I implored her to tell me the whole truth about the woman whom I had supplanted. You see, I had a faint hope that her good character might not really be deserved, that her noble letter was a skilful piece of hypocrisy—in short, that she secretly hated me, and was cunning enough to hide it. No! the lady had been her friend from her girlhood, was as familiar with her as if they had been sisters—

knew her positively to be as good, as innocent, as incapable of hating anybody, as the greatest saint that ever lived. My one last hope, that I had only felt an ordinary forewarning of danger in the presence of an ordinary enemy, was a hope destroyed for ever. There was one more effort I could make, and I made it. I went next to the man whom I am to marry. I implored him to release me from my promise. He refused. I declared I would break my engagement. He showed me letters from his sisters, letters from his brothers, and his dear friends—all entreating him to think again before he made me his wife; all repeating reports of me in Paris, Vienna, and London, which are so many vile lies. "If you refuse to marry me," he said, "you admit that these reports are true—you admit that you are afraid to face society in the character of my wife." What could I answer? There was no contradicting him—he was plainly right: if I persisted in my refusal, the utter destruction of my reputation would be the result. I consented to let the wedding take place as we had arranged it—and left him. The night has passed. I am here, with my fixed conviction—that innocent woman is ordained to have a fatal influence over my life. I am here with my one question to put, to the one man who can answer it. For the last time, sir, what am I—a demon who has seen the avenging angel? or only a poor mad woman, misled by the delusion of a deranged mind?"

Doctor Wybrow rose from his chair, determined to close the interview.

He was strongly and painfully impressed by what he had heard. The longer he had listened to her, the more irresistibly the conviction of the woman's wickedness had forced itself on him. He tried vainly to think of her as a person to be pitied—a person with a morbidly sensitive imagination, conscious of the capacities for evil which lie dormant in us all, and striving earnestly to open her heart to the counter-influence of her own better nature; the effort was beyond him. A perverse instinct in him said, as if in words, Beware how you believe in her!

"I have already given you my opinion," he said. "There is no sign of your intellect being deranged, or being likely to be deranged, that medical science can discover—as *I* understand it.

As for the impressions you have confided to me, I can only say that yours is a case (as I venture to think) for spiritual rather than for medical advice. Of one thing be assured: what you have said to me in this room shall not pass out of it. Your confession is safe in my keeping."

She heard him, with a certain dogged resignation, to the end. "Is that all?" she asked.

"That is all," he answered.

She put a little paper packet of money on the table. "Thank you, sir. There is your fee."

With those words she rose. Her wild black eyes looked upward, with an expression of despair so defiant and so horrible in its silent agony that the Doctor turned away his head, unable to endure the sight of it. The bare idea of taking anything from her—not money only, but anything even that she had touched—suddenly revolted him. Still without looking at her, he said, "Take it back; I don't want my fee."

She neither heeded nor heard him. Still looking upward, she said slowly to herself, "Let the end come. I have done with the struggle: I submit."

She drew her veil over her face, bowed to the Doctor, and left the room.

He rang the bell, and followed her into the hall. As the servant closed the door on her, a sudden impulse of curiosity—utterly unworthy of him, and at the same time utterly irresistible—sprang up in the Doctor's mind. Blushing like a boy, he said to the servant, "Follow her home, and find out her name." For one moment the man looked at his master, doubting if his own ears had not deceived him. Doctor Wybrow looked back at him in silence. The submissive servant knew what that silence meant—he took his hat and hurried into the street.

The Doctor went back to the consulting-room. A sudden revulsion of feeling swept over his mind. Had the woman left an infection of wickedness in the house, and had he caught it? What devil had possessed him to degrade himself in the eyes of his own servant? He had behaved infamously—he had asked an honest man, a man who had served him faithfully for years, to turn spy!

Stung by the bare thought of it, he ran out into the hall again, and opened the door. The servant had disappeared; it was too late to call him back. But one refuge from his contempt for himself was now open to him—the refuge of work. He got into his carriage and went his rounds among his patients.

If the famous physician could have shaken his own reputation, he would have done it that afternoon. Never before had he made himself so little welcome at the bedside. Never before had he put off until to-morrow the prescription which ought to have been written, the opinion which ought to have been given, to-day. He went home earlier than usual—unutterably dissatisfied with himself.

The servant had returned. Doctor Wybrow was ashamed to question him. The man reported the result of his errand, without waiting to be asked.

"The lady's name is the Countess Narona. She lives at——"

Without waiting to hear where she lived, the Doctor acknowledged the all-important discovery of her name by a silent bend of the head, and entered his consulting-room. The fee that he had vainly refused still lay in its little white paper covering on the table. He sealed it up in an envelope; addressed it to the "Poor-box" of the nearest police-court; and, calling the servant in, directed him to take it to the magistrate the next morning. Faithful to his duties, the servant waited to ask the customary question, "Do you dine at home to-day, sir?"

After a moment's hesitation he said, "No: I shall dine at the club."

The most easily deteriorated of all the moral qualities is the quality called "conscience." In one state of a man's mind, his conscience is the severest judge that can pass sentence on him. In another state, he and his conscience are on the best possible terms with each other in the comfortable capacity of accomplices. When Doctor Wybrow left his house for the second time, he did not even attempt to conceal from himself that his sole object, in dining at the club, was to hear what the world said of the Countess Narona.

CHAPTER III

~~~~~~~~

THERE was a time when a man in search of the pleasures of gossip sought the society of ladies. The man knows better now. He goes to the smoking-room of his club.

Doctor Wybrow lit his cigar, and looked round him at his brethren in social conclave assembled. The room was well filled; but the flow of talk was still languid. The Doctor innocently applied the stimulant that was wanted. When he inquired if anybody knew the Countess Narona, he was answered by something like a shout of astonishment. Never (the conclave agreed) had such an absurd question been asked before! Every human creature, with the slightest claim to a place in society, knew the Countess Narona. An adventuress with a European reputation of the blackest possible colour—such was the general description of the woman with the deathlike complexion and the glittering eyes.

Descending to particulars, each member of the club contributed his own little stock of scandal to the memoirs of the Countess. It was doubtful whether she was really, what she called herself, a Dalmatian lady. It was doubtful whether she had ever been married to the Count whose widow she assumed to be. It was doubtful whether the man who accompanied her in her travels (under the name of Baron Rivar, and in the character of her brother) was her brother at all. Report pointed to the Baron as a gambler at every "table" on the Continent. Report whispered that his so-called sister had narrowly escaped being implicated in a famous trial for poisoning at Vienna—that she had been known at Milan as a spy in the interests of Austria—that her "apartment" in Paris had been denounced to the police as nothing less than a private gambling-house—and that her present appearance in England was the natural result of the discovery. Only one member of the assembly in the smoking-room took the part of this much-abused woman, and declared that her character had been most cruelly and most unjustly assailed. But as the man was a lawyer, his interference went for nothing: it was naturally attributed to the spirit of contradiction inherent in his profession. He was asked derisively what he thought of the circumstances under which the Countess had become engaged to be married; and he made the characteristic answer, that he thought the circumstances highly creditable to both parties, and that he looked on the lady's future husband as a most enviable man.

Hearing this, the Doctor raised another shout of astonishment by inquiring the name of the gentleman whom the Countess was about to marry.

His friends in the smoking-room decided unanimously that the celebrated physician must be a second "Rip-van-Winkle," and that he had just awakened from a supernatural sleep of twenty years. It was all very well to say that he was devoted to his profession, and that he had neither time nor inclination to pick up fragments of gossip at dinner-parties and balls. A man who did not know that the Countess Narona had borrowed money at Homburg of no less a person than Lord Montbarry, and had then deluded him into making her a proposal of marriage, was a man who had probably never heard of Lord Montbarry himself. The younger members of the club, humouring the joke, sent a waiter for the "Peerage," and read aloud the memoir of the nobleman in question, for the Doctor's benefit—with illustrative morsels of information interpolated by themselves.

"Herbert John Westwick. First Baron Montbarry, of Montbarry, King's County, Ireland. Created a Peer for distinguished military services in India. Born, 1812. Forty-eight years old, Doctor, at the present time. Not married. Will be married next week, Doctor, to the delightful creature we have been talking about. Heir presumptive, his lordship's next brother, Stephen Robert, married to Ella, youngest daughter of the Reverend Silas Marden, Rector of Runnigate, and has issue, three daughters. Younger brothers of his lordship, Francis and Henry, unmarried. Sisters of his lordship, Lady Barville, married to Sir Theodore Barville, Bart.; and Anne, widow of the late Peter Norbury, Esq., of

Norbury Cross. Bear his lordship's relations well in mind, Doctor. Three brothers Westwick, Stephen, Francis, and Henry; and two sisters, Lady Barville and Mrs. Norbury. Not one of the five will be present at the marriage; and not one of the five will leave a stone unturned to stop it, if the Countess will only give them a chance. Add to these hostile members of the family another offended relative not mentioned in the "Peerage," a young lady———"

A sudden outburst of protest in more than one part of the room stopped the coming disclosure, and released the Doctor from further persecution.

"Don't mention the poor girl's name; it's too bad to make a joke of that part of the business; she has behaved nobly under shameful provocation; there is but one excuse for Montbarry—he is either a madman or a fool." In these terms the protest expressed itself on all sides. Speaking confidentially to his next neighbour, the Doctor discovered that the lady referred to was already known to him (through the Countess's confession) as the lady deserted by Lord Montbarry. Her name was Agnes Lockwood. She was described as being the superior of the Countess in personal attraction, and as being also by some years the younger woman of the two. Making all allowance for the follies that men committed every day in their relations with women, Montbarry's delusion was still the most monstrous delusion on record. In this expression of opinion every man present agreed—the lawyer even included. Not one of them could call to mind the innumerable instances in which the sexual influence has proved irresistible in the persons of women without even the pretension to beauty. The very members of the club whom the Countess (in spite of her personal disadvantages) could have most easily fascinated, if she had thought it worth her while, were the members who wondered most loudly at Montbarry's choice of a wife.

While the topic of the Countess's marriage was still the one topic of conversation, a member of the club entered the smoking-room whose appearance instantly produced a dead silence. Doctor Wybrow's next neighbour whispered to him, "Montbarry's brother —Henry Westwick!"

The new-comer looked round him slowly, with a bitter smile.

"You are all talking of my brother," he said. "Don't mind me. Not one of you can despise him more heartily than I do. Go on, gentlemen—go on!"

But one man present took the speaker at his word. That man was the lawyer who had already undertaken the defence of the Countess.

"I stand alone in my opinion," he said, "and I am not ashamed of repeating it in anybody's hearing. I consider the Countess Narona to be a cruelly-treated woman. Why shouldn't she be Lord Montbarry's wife? Who can say she has a mercenary motive in marrying him?"

Montbarry's brother turned sharply on the speaker. "*I* say it!" he answered.

The reply might have shaken some men. The lawyer stood on his ground as firmly as ever.

"I believe I am right," he rejoined, "in stating that his lordship's income is not more than sufficient to support his station in life; also that it is an income derived almost entirely from landed property in Ireland, every acre of which is entailed."

Montbarry's brother made a sign, admitting that he had no objection to offer so far.

"If his lordship dies first," the lawyer proceeded, "I have been informed that the only provision he can make for his widow consists in a rent-charge on the property of no more than four hundred a year. His retiring pension and allowances, it is well known, die with him. Four hundred a year is therefore all that he can leave to the Countess, if he leaves her a widow."

"Four hundred a year is *not* all," was the reply to this. "My brother has insured his life for ten thousand pounds; and he has settled the whole of it on the Countess, in the event of his death."

This announcement produced a strong sensation. Men looked at each other, and repeated the three startling words, "Ten thousand pounds!" Driven fairly to the wall, the lawyer made a last effort to defend his position.

"May I ask who made that settlement a condition of the marriage?" he said. "Surely it was not the Countess herself?"

Henry Westwick answered, "It was the Countess's brother"; and added, "which comes to the same thing."

After that, there was no more to be said—so long, at least, as Montbarry's brother was present. The talk flowed into other channels; and the Doctor went home.

But his morbid curiosity about the Countess was not set at rest yet. In his leisure moments he found himself wondering whether Lord Montbarry's family would succeed in stopping the marriage after all. And more than this, he was conscious of a growing desire to see the infatuated man himself. Every day during the brief interval before the wedding, he looked in at the club, on the chance of hearing some news. Nothing had happened, so far as the club knew. The Countess's position was secure; Montbarry's resolution to be her husband was unshaken. They were both Roman Catholics, and they were to be married at the chapel in Spanish Place. So much the Doctor discovered about them—and no more.

On the day of the wedding, after a feeble struggle with himself, he actually sacrificed his patients and their guineas, and slipped away secretly to see the marriage. To the end of his life, he was angry with anybody who reminded him of what he had done on that day!

The wedding was strictly private. A close carriage stood at the church door; a few people, mostly of the lower class, and mostly old women, were scattered about the interior of the building. Here and there Doctor Wybrow detected the faces of some of his brethren of the club, attracted by curiosity, like himself. Four persons only stood before the altar—the bride and bridegroom and their two witnesses. One of these last was an elderly woman, who might have been the Countess's companion or maid; the other was undoubtedly her brother, Baron Rivar. The bridal party (the bride herself included) wore their ordinary morning costume. Lord Montbarry, personally viewed, was a middle-aged military man of the ordinary type: nothing in the least remarkable distinguished him either in face or figure. Baron Rivar, again, in his way was another conventional representative of another well-known type. One sees his finely-pointed moustache, his bold eyes, his crisply-curling hair, and his dashing carriage of the head, repeated hundreds of times over on the Boulevards of Paris. The only noteworthy point about him was of the negative sort—he was not in the least like his sister. Even the officiating priest was only a harmless, humble-looking old man, who went through his duties resignedly, and felt visible rheumatic difficulties every time he bent his knees. The one remarkable person, the Countess herself, only raised her veil at the beginning of the ceremony, and presented nothing in her plain dress that was worth a second look. Never, on the face of it, was there a less interesting and less romantic marriage than this. From time to time the Doctor glanced round at the door or up at the galleries, vaguely anticipating the appearance of some protesting stranger, in possession of some terrible secret, commissioned to forbid the progress of the service. Nothing in the shape of an event occurred—nothing extraordinary, nothing dramatic. Bound fast together as man and wife, the two disappeared, followed by their witnesses, to sign the registers; and still Doctor Wybrow waited, and still he cherished the obstinate hope that something worth seeing must certainly happen yet.

The interval passed, and the married couple, returning to the church, walked together down the nave to the door. Doctor Wybrow drew back as they approached. To his confusion and surprise, the Countess discovered him. He heard her say to her husband, "One moment; I see a friend." Lord Montbarry bowed and waited. She stepped up to the Doctor, took his hand, and wrung it hard. He felt her overpowering black eyes looking at him through her veil. "One step more, you see, on the way to the end!" She whispered those strange words, and returned to her husband. Before the Doctor could recover himself and follow her, Lord and Lady Montbarry had stepped into their carriage, and had driven away.

Outside the church door stood the three or four members of the club who, like Doctor Wybrow, had watched the ceremony out of curiosity. Near them was the bride's brother, waiting alone. He was evidently bent on seeing the man whom his sister had spoken to, in broad daylight. His bold eyes rested on the Doctor's face, with a momentary flash of suspicion in them. The cloud suddenly cleared away; the Baron smiled with charming courtesy, lifted his hat to his sister's friend, and walked off.

The members constituted themselves into a club conclave on the church steps. They began with the Baron. "Damned ill-looking rascal!" They went on with Montbarry. "Is he going to take that horrid woman with him to Ireland?" "Not he! he can't face the tenantry; they know about Agnes Lockwood." "Well, but where *is* he going?" "To Scotland." "Does *she* like that?" "It's only for a fortnight; they come back to London, and go abroad." "And they will never return to England, eh?" "Who can tell? Did you see how she looked at Montbarry, when she had to lift her veil at the beginning of the service? In his place, I should have bolted. Did *you* see her, Doctor?" By this time, Doctor Wybrow had remembered his patients, and had heard enough of the club gossip. He followed the example of Baron Rivar, and walked off.

"One step more, you see, on the way to the end," he repeated to himself, on his way home. "What end?"

CHAPTER IV

ON the day of the marriage Agnes Lockwood sat alone in the little drawing-room of her London lodgings, burning the letters which had been written to her by Montbarry in the bygone time.

The Countess's maliciously smart description of her, addressed to Doctor Wybrow, had not even hinted at the charm that most distinguished Agnes—the artless expression of goodness and purity which instantly attracted everyone who approached her. She looked by many years younger than she really was. With her fair complexion and her shy manner, it seemed only natural to speak of her as "a girl," although she was now really advancing towards thirty years of age. She lived alone with an old nurse devoted to her, on a modest little income which was just enough to support the two. There were none of the ordinary signs of grief in her face, as she slowly tore the letters of her false lover in two, and threw the pieces into the small fire which had been lit to consume them. Unhappily for herself, she was one of those women who feel too deeply to find relief in tears. Pale and quiet, with cold trembling fingers, she destroyed the letters one by one without daring to read them again. She had torn the last of the series, and was still shrinking from throwing it after the rest into the swiftly destroying flame, when the old nurse came in, and asked if she would see "Master Henry,"—meaning that youngest member of the Westwick family, who had publicly declared his contempt for his brother in the smoking-room of the club.

Agnes hesitated. A faint tinge of colour stole over her face.

There had been a long past time when Henry Westwick had owned that he loved her. She had made her confession to him, acknowledging that her heart was given to his eldest brother. He had submitted to his disappointment; and they had met thenceforth as cousins and friends. Never before had she associated the idea of him with embarrassing recollections. But now, on the very day when his brother's marriage to another woman had consummated his brother's treason towards her, there was something vaguely repellent in the prospect of seeing him. The old nurse (who remembered them both in their cradles) observed her hesitation; and sympathising of course with the man, put in a timely word for Henry. "He says, he's going away, my dear; and he only wants to shake hands, and say good-bye." This plain statement of the case had its effect. Agnes decided on receiving her cousin.

He entered the room so rapidly that he surprised her in the act of throwing the fragments of Montbarry's last letter into the fire. She hurriedly spoke first.

"You are leaving London very suddenly, Henry. Is it business? or pleasure?"

Instead of answering her, he pointed to the flaming letter, and to some black ashes of burnt paper lying lightly in the lower part of the fireplace.

"Are you burning letters?"

"Yes."

"*His* letters?"

"Yes."

He took her hand gently. "I had no idea I was intruding on you, at a time when you must wish to be alone. Forgive me, Agnes—I shall see you when I return."

She signed to him, with a faint smile, to take a chair.

"We have known one another since we were children," she said. "Why should I feel a foolish pride about myself in your presence? Why should I have any secrets from you? I sent back all your brother's gifts to me some time ago. I have been advised to do more, to keep nothing that can remind me of him—in short, to burn his letters. I have taken the advice; but I own I shrank a little from destroying the last of the letters. No—not because it was the last, but because it had this in it." She opened her hand, and showed him a lock of Montbarry's hair, tied with a morsel of golden cord. "Well! well! let it go with the rest."

She dropped it into the flame. For awhile, she stood with her back to Henry, leaning on the mantel-piece, and looking into the fire. He took the chair to which she had pointed, with a strange contradiction of expression in his face: the tears were in his eyes, while the brows above were knit close in an angry frown. He muttered to himself, "Damn him!"

She rallied her courage, and looked at him again when she spoke. "Well, Henry, and why are you going away?"

"I am out of spirits, Agnes, and I want a change."

She paused before she spoke again. His face told her plainly that he was thinking of *her* when he made that reply. She was grateful to him, but her mind was not with him: her mind was still with the man who had deserted her. She turned round again to the fire.

"Is it true," she asked, after a long silence, "that they have been married to-day?"

He answered ungraciously in the one necessary word:—'Yes."

"Did you go to the church?"

He resented the question with an expression of indignant surprise. "Go to the church?" he repeated. "I would as soon go to——" He checked himself there. "How can you ask?" he added in lower tones. "I have never spoken to Montbarry, I have not even seen him, since he treated you like the scoundrel and the fool that he is."

She looked at him suddenly, without saying a word. He understood her, and begged her pardon. But he was still angry. "The reckoning comes to some men," he said, "even in this world. He will live to rue the day when he married that woman!"

Agnes took a chair by his side, and looked at him with a gentle surprise.

"Is it quite reasonable to be so angry with her, because your brother preferred her to me?" she asked.

Henry turned on her sharply. "Do *you* defend the Countess, of all the people in the world?"

"Why not?" Agnes answered. "I know nothing against her. On the only occasion when we met, she appeared to be a singularly timid, nervous person, looking dreadfully ill; and *being* indeed so ill that she fainted under the heat of the room. Why should we not do her justice? We know that she was innocent of any intention to wrong me; we know that she was not aware of my engagement——"

Henry lifted his hand impatiently, and stopped her. "There is such a thing as being *too* just and *too* forgiving!" he interposed. "I can't bear to hear you talk in that patient way, after the scandalously cruel manner in which you have been treated. Try to forget them both, Agnes. I wish to God I could help you to do it!"

Agnes laid her hand on his arm. "You are very good to me, Henry; but you don't quite understand me. I was thinking of myself and my trouble in quite a different way, when you came in. I was wondering whether anything which has so entirely filled my heart, and so absorbed all that is best and truest in me, as my feeling for your brother, can really pass away as if it had never existed. I have destroyed the last visible things that remind me of him. In this world I shall see him no more. But is the tie that once bound us, completely broken? Am I as entirely parted from the good and evil fortune of his life as if we had never met and never loved? What do *you* think, Henry? I can hardly believe it."

"If you could bring the retribution on him that he has deserved," Henry Westwick answered sternly, "I might be inclined to agree with you."

As that reply passed his lips, the old nurse appeared again at the door, announcing another visitor.

"I'm sorry to disturb you, my dear. But here is little Mrs. Ferrari wanting to know when she may say a few words to you."

Agnes turned to Henry, before she replied. "You remember Emily Bidwell, my favourite pupil years ago at the village school, and afterwards my maid? She left me, to marry an Italian courier, named Ferrari—and I am afraid it has not turned out very well. Do you mind my having her in here for a minute or two?"

Henry rose to take his leave. "I should be glad to see Emily again at any other time," he said. "But it is best that I should go now. My mind is disturbed, Agnes; I might say things to you, if I stayed here any longer, which—which are better not said now. I shall cross the Channel by the mail to-night, and see how a few weeks' change will help me." He took her hand. "Is there anything in the world that I can do for you?" he asked very earnestly. She thanked him, and tried to release her hand. He held it with a tremulous lingering grasp. "God bless you, Agnes!" he said in faltering tones, with his eyes on the ground. Her face flushed again, and the next instant turned paler than ever; she knew his heart as well as he knew it himself—she was too distressed to speak. He lifted her hand to his lips, kissed it fervently, and, without looking at her again, left the room. The nurse hobbled after him to the head of the stairs: she had not forgotten the time when the younger brother had been the unsuccessful rival of the elder for the hand of Agnes. "Don't be down-hearted, Master Henry," whispered the old woman, with the unscrupulous common sense of persons in the lower rank of life. "Try her again, when you come back!"

Left alone for a few moments, Agnes took a turn in the room, trying to compose herself. She paused before a little water-colour drawing on the wall, which had belonged to her mother: it was her own portrait when she was a child. "How much happier we should be," she thought to herself sadly, "if we never grew up!'"

The courier's wife was shown in—a little meek melancholy woman, with white eyelashes, and watery eyes, who curtseyed deferentially and was troubled with a small chronic cough. Agnes shook hands with her kindly. "Well, Emily, what can I do for you?"

The courier's wife made rather a strange answer: "I'm afraid to tell you, Miss."

"Is it such a very difficult favour to grant? Sit down, and let me hear how you are going on. Perhaps the petition will slip out while we are talking. How does your husband behave to you?"

Emily's light grey eyes looked more watery than ever. She shook her head and sighed resignedly. "I have no positive complaint to make against him, Miss. But I'm afraid he doesn't care about me; and he seems to take no interest in his home—I may almost say he's tired of his home. It might be better for both of us, Miss, if he went travelling for awhile—not to mention the money, which is beginning to be wanted sadly." She put her handkerchief to her eyes, and sighed again more resignedly than ever.

"I don't quite understand," said Agnes. "I thought your husband had an engagement to take some ladies to Switzerland and Italy?"

"That was his ill-luck, Miss. One of the ladies fell ill—and the others wouldn't go without her. They paid him a month's salary as compensation. But they had engaged him for the autumn and winter—and the loss is serious."

"I am sorry to hear it, Emily. Let us hope he will soon have another chance."

"It's not his turn, Miss, to be recommended when the next applications come to the couriers' office. You see, there are so many of them out of employment just now. If he could be privately recommended——" She stopped, and left the unfinished sentence to speak for itself.

Agnes understood her directly. "You want my recommendation," she rejoined. "Why couldn't you say so at once?"

Emily blushed. "It would be such a chance for my husband," she answered confusedly. "A letter, inquiring for a good courier (a six months' engagement, Miss!) came to the office this morning. It's another man's turn to be chosen—and the secretary will recommend him. If my husband could only send his testimonials by the same post—with just a word in your name, Miss—it might turn the scale, as they say. A private recommendation between gentlefolks goes so far." She stopped again, and sighed again, and looked down at the carpet, as if she had some private reason for feeling a little ashamed of herself.

Agnes began to be rather weary of the persistent tone of mystery in which her visitor spoke. "If you want my interest with any friend of mine," she said, "why can't you tell me the name?"

The courier's wife began to cry. "I'm ashamed to tell you, Miss."

For the first time, Agnes spoke sharply. "Nonsense, Emily! Tell me the name directly—or drop the subject—whichever you like best."

Emily made a last desperate effort. She wrung her handkerchief hard in her lap, and let off the name as if she had been letting off a loaded gun:—"Lord Montbarry!"

Agnes rose and looked at her.

"You have disappointed me," she said very quietly, but with a look which the courier's wife had never seen in her face before. "Knowing what you know, you ought to be aware that it is impossible for me to communicate with Lord Montbarry. I always supposed you had some delicacy of feeling. I am sorry to find that I have been mistaken."

Weak as she was, Emily had spirit enough to feel the reproof. She walked in her meek noiseless way to the door. "I beg your pardon, Miss. I am not quite so bad as you think me. But I beg your pardon, all the same."

She opened the door. Agnes called her back. There was something in the woman's apology that appealed irresistibly to her just and generous nature. "Come," she said; "we must not part in this way. Let me not misunderstand you. What is it that you expected me to do?"

Emily was wise enough to answer this time without any reserve. "My husband will send his testimonials, Miss, to Lord Montbarry in Scotland. I only wanted you to let him say in his letter that his wife has been known to you since she was a child, and that you feel some little interest in his welfare on that account. I don't ask it now, Miss. You have made me understand that I was wrong."

Had she really been wrong? Past remembrances, as well as present troubles, pleaded powerfully with Agnes for the courier's wife. "It seems only a small favour to ask," she said, speaking under the impulse of kindness which was the strongest impulse in her nature. "But I am not sure that I ought to allow my name to be mentioned in your husband's letter. Let me hear again exactly what he wishes to say." Emily repeated the words—and then offered one of those suggestions, which have a special value of their own to persons unaccustomed to the use of their pens. "Suppose you try, Miss, how it looks in writing?" Childish as the idea was, Agnes tried the experiment. "If I let you mention me," she said, "we must at least decide what you are to say." She wrote the words in the briefest and plainest form:—"I venture to state that my wife has been known from her childhood to Miss Agnes Lockwood, who feels some little interest in my welfare on that account." Reduced to this one sentence, there was surely nothing in the reference to her name which implied that Agnes had permitted it, or that she was even aware of it. After a last struggle with herself, she handed the written paper to Emily. "Your husband must copy it exactly, without altering anything," she stipulated. "On that condition, I grant your request." Emily was not only thankful—she was really touched. Agnes hurried the little woman out of the room. "Don't give me time to repent and take it back again," she said. Emily vanished.

"Is the tie that once bound us completely broken? Am I as entirely parted from the good and evil fortune of his life as if we had never met and never loved?" Agnes looked at the clock on the mantel-piece. Not ten minutes since, those serious questions had been on her lips. It almost shocked her to think of the common-place manner in which they had already met with their reply. The mail of that night would appeal once more to Montbarry's remembrance of her—in the choice of a servant.

Two days later, the post brought a few grateful lines from Emily. Her husband had got the place. Ferrari was engaged, for six months certain, as Lord Montbarry's courier.

THE SECOND PART

CHAPTER V

AFTER only one week of travelling in Scotland, my lord and my lady returned unexpectedly to London. Introduced to the mountains and lakes of the Highlands, her ladyship positively declined to improve her acquaintance with them. When she was asked for her reason, she answered with a Roman brevity, "I have seen Switzerland."

For a week more, the newly-married couple remained in London, in the strictest retirement. On one day in that week the nurse returned in a state of most uncustomary excitement from an errand on which Agnes had sent her. Passing the door of a fashionable dentist, she had met Lord Montbarry himself just leaving the house. The good woman's report described him, with malicious pleasure, as looking wretchedly ill. "His cheeks are getting hollow, my dear, and his beard is turning grey. I hope the dentist hurt him!"

Knowing how heartily her faithful old servant hated the man who had deserted her, Agnes made due allowance for a large infusion of exaggeration in the picture presented to her. The main impression produced on her mind was an impression of nervous uneasiness. If she trusted herself in the streets by daylight while Lord Montbarry remained in London, how could she be sure that his next chance-meeting might not be a meeting with herself? She waited at home, privately ashamed of her own undignified conduct, for the next two days. On the third day the fashionable intelligence of the newspapers announced the departure of Lord and Lady Montbarry for Paris, on their way to Italy.

Mrs. Ferrari, calling the same evening, informed Agnes that her husband had left her with all reasonable expression of conjugal kindness; his temper being improved by the prospect of going abroad. But one other servant accompanied the travellers—Lady Montbarry's maid, rather a silent, unsociable woman, so far as Emily had heard. Her ladyship's brother, Baron Rivar, was already on the Continent. It had been arranged that he was to meet his sister and her husband at Rome.

One by one the dull weeks succeeded each other in the life of Agnes. She faced her position with admirable courage, seeing her friends, keeping herself occupied in her leisure hours with reading and drawing, leaving no means untried of diverting her mind from the melancholy remembrance of the past. But she had loved too faithfully, she had been wounded too deeply, to feel in any adequate degree the influence of the moral remedies which she employed. Persons who met with her in the ordinary relations of life, deceived by her outward serenity of manner, agreed that "Miss Lockwood seemed to be getting over her disappointment." But an old friend and school companion who happened to see her during a brief visit to London, was inexpressibly distressed by the change that she detected in Agnes. This lady was Mrs. Westwick, the wife of that brother of Lord Montbarry who came next to him in age, and who was described in the "Peerage" as presumptive heir to the title. He was then away, looking after his interests in some mining property which he possessed in America. Mrs. Westwick insisted on taking Agnes back with her to her home in Ireland. "Come and keep me company while my husband is away. My three little girls will make you their playfellow, and the only stranger you will meet is the governess, whom I answer for your liking beforehand. Pack up your things, and I will call for you to-morrow on my way to the train." In those hearty terms the invitation was given. Agnes thankfully accepted it. For three happy months she lived under the roof of her friend. The girls hung round her in tears at her departure; the youngest of them wanted to go back with Agnes to London. Half in jest, half in earnest, she said to her old friend at parting, "If your governess leaves you, keep the place open for me." Mrs. Westwick laughed.

The wiser children took it seriously, and promised to let Agnes know.

On the very day when Miss Lockwood returned to London, she was recalled to those associations with the past which she was most anxious to forget. After the first kissings and greetings were over, the old nurse (who had been left in charge at the lodgings) had some startling information to communicate, derived from the courier's wife.

"Here has been little Mrs. Ferrari, my dear, in a dreadful state of mind, inquiring when you would be back. Her husband has left Lord Montbarry, without a word of warning—and nobody knows what has become of him."

Agnes looked at her in astonishment. "Are you sure of what you are saying?" she asked.

The nurse was quite sure. "Why, Lord bless you! the news comes from the couriers' office in Golden Square—from the secretary, Miss Agnes, the secretary himself!" Hearing this, Agnes began to feel alarmed as well as surprised. It was still early in the evening. She at once sent a message to Mrs. Ferrari, to say that she had returned.

In an hour more the courier's wife appeared, in a state of agitation which it was not easy to control. Her narrative, when she was at last able to speak connectedly, entirely confirmed the nurse's report of it.

After hearing from her husband with tolerable regularity from Paris, Rome, and Venice, Emily had twice written to him afterwards—and had received no reply. Feeling uneasy, she had gone to the office in Golden Square, to inquire if he had been heard of there. The post of the morning had brought a letter to the secretary from a courier then at Venice. It contained startling news of Ferrari. His wife had been allowed to take a copy of it, which she now handed to Agnes to read.

The writer stated that he had recently arrived in Venice. He had previously heard that Ferrari was with Lord and Lady Montbarry, at one of the old Venetian palaces which they had hired for a term. Being a friend of Ferrari, he had gone to pay him a visit. Ringing at the door that opened on the canal, and failing to make anyone hear him, he had gone round to a side entrance opening on one of the narrow lanes of Venice. Here, standing at the door (as if she was waiting for him to try that way next), he found a pale woman with magnificent dark eyes, who proved to be no other than Lady Montbarry herself.

She asked, in Italian, what he wanted. He answered that he wanted to see the courier Ferrari, if it was quite convenient. She at once informed him that Ferrari had left the palace, without assigning any reason, and without even leaving an address at which his monthly salary (then due to him) could be paid. Amazed at this reply, the courier inquired if any person had offended Ferrari, or quarrelled with him. The lady answered, "To my knowledge, certainly not. I am Lady Montbarry; and I can positively assure you that Ferrari was treated with the greatest kindness in this house. We are as much astonished as you are at his extraordinary disappearance. If you should hear of him, pray let us know, so that we may at least pay him the money which is due."

After one or two more questions (quite readily answered) relating to the date and the time of day at which Ferrari had left the palace, the courier took his leave.

He at once entered on the necessary investigations—without the slightest result so far as Ferrari was concerned. Nobody had seen him. Nobody appeared to have been taken into his confidence. Nobody knew anything (that is to say, anything of the slightest importance) even about persons so distinguished as Lord and Lady Montbarry. It was reported that her ladyship's English maid had left her, before the disappearance of Ferrari, to return to her relatives in her own country, and that Lady Montbarry had taken no steps to supply her place. His lordship was described as being in delicate health. He lived in the strictest retirement— nobody was admitted to him, not even his own countrymen. A stupid old woman was discovered who did the housework at the palace, arriving in the morning and going away again at night. She had never seen the lost courier—she had never even seen Lord Montbarry, who was then confined to his room. Her ladyship, "a most gracious and adorable mistress," was in constant attendance on her noble husband. There was no other servant then in the house (so far as the old woman knew) but herself. The meals were sent in from a restaurant. My lord, it was said, disliked strangers. My lord's brother-in-law, the Baron, was generally shut up in a remote part of the palace, occupied (the gracious mistress said) with experiments in chemistry. The experiments sometimes made a nasty smell. A doctor had latterly been called in to his lordship—an Italian doctor, long resident in Venice. Inquiries being addressed to this gentleman (a physician of undoubted capacity and respectability), it turned out that he also had never seen Ferrari, having been summoned to the palace (as his memorandum book showed) at a date subsequent to the courier's disappearance. The doctor described Lord Montbarry's malady as bronchitis. So far, there was no reason to feel any anxiety, though the attack was a sharp one. If alarming symptoms should appear, he had arranged with her ladyship to call in another physician. For the rest, it was impossible to speak too highly of my lady; night and day, she was at her lord's bedside.

With these particulars began and ended the discoveries made by Ferrari's courier-friend. The police were on the look-out for the lost man—and that was the only hope which could be held forth for the present, to Ferrari's wife.

"What do you think of it, Miss?" the poor woman asked eagerly. "What would you advise me to do?"

Agnes was at a loss how to answer her; it was an effort even to listen to what Emily was saying. The references in the courier's letter to Montbarry—the report of his illness, the melancholy picture of his secluded life—had reopened the old wound. She was not even thinking of the lost Ferrari; her mind was at Venice, by the sick man's bedside.

"I hardly know what to say," she answered. "I have had no experience in serious matters of this kind."

"Do you think it would help you, Miss, if you read my husband's letters to me? There are only three of them—they won't take long to read."

Agnes compassionately read the letters.

They were not written in a very tender tone. "Dear Emily," and

"Yours affectionately"—these conventional phrases, were the only phrases of endearment which they contained. In the first letter, Lord Montbarry was not very favourably spoken of:—"We leave Paris to-morrow. I don't much like my lord. He is proud and cold, and, between ourselves, stingy in money matters. I have had to dispute such trifles as a few centimes in the hotel bill; and twice already, some sharp remarks have passed between the newly-married couple, in consequence of her ladyship's freedom in purchasing pretty tempting things at the shops in Paris. 'I can't afford it; you must keep to your allowance.' She has had to hear those words already. For my part, I like her. She has the nice, easy foreign manners—*she* talks to me as if I was a human being like herself."

The second letter was dated from Rome.

"My lord's caprices" (Ferrari wrote) "have kept us perpetually on the move. He is becoming incurably restless. I suspect he is uneasy in his mind. Painful recollections, I should say—I find him constantly reading old letters, when her ladyship is not present. We were to have stopped at Genoa, but he hurried us on. The same thing at Florence. Here, at Rome, my lady insists on resting. Her brother has met us at this place. There has been a quarrel already (the lady's maid tells me) between my lord and the Baron. The latter wanted to borrow money of the former. His lordship refused in language which offended Baron Rivar. My lady pacified them, and made them shake hands."

The third, and last letter, was from Venice.

"More of my lord's economy! Instead of staying at the hotel, we have hired a damp, mouldy, rambling old palace. My lady insists on having the best suites of rooms wherever we go—and the palace comes cheaper for a two months' term. My lord tried to get it for longer; he says the quiet of Venice is good for his nerves. But a foreign speculator has secured the palace, and is going to turn it into an hotel. The Baron is still with us, and there have been more disagreements about money matters. I don't like the Baron—and I don't find the attractions of my lady grow on me. She was much nicer before the Baron joined us. My lord is a punctual paymaster; it's a matter of honour with him; he hates parting with his money, but he does it because he has given his word. I receive my salary regularly at the end of each month—not a franc extra, though I have done many things which are not part of a courier's proper work. Fancy the Baron trying to borrow money of *me*! he is an inveterate gambler. I didn't believe it when my lady's maid first told me so—but I have seen enough since to satisfy me that she was right. I have seen other things besides, which—well! which don't increase my respect for my lady and the Baron. The maid says she means to give warning to leave. She is a respectable British female, and doesn't take things quite so easily as I do. It is a dull life here. No going into company—no company at home—not a creature sees my lord—not even the consul, or the banker. When he goes out, he goes alone, and generally towards nightfall. Indoors, he shuts himself up in his own room with his books, and sees as little of his wife and the Baron as possible. I fancy things are coming to a crisis here. If my lord's suspicions are once awakened, the consequences will be terrible. Under certain provocations, the noble Montbarry is a man who would stick at nothing. However, the pay is good—and I can't afford to talk of leaving the place, like my lady's maid."

Agnes handed back the letters—so suggestive of the penalty paid already for his own infatuation by the man who had deserted her!—with feelings of shame and distress, which made her no fit counsellor for the helpless woman who depended on her advice.

"The one thing I can suggest," she said, after first speaking some kind words of comfort and hope, "is that we should consult a person of greater experience than ours. Suppose I write and ask my lawyer (who is also my friend and trustee) to come and advise us to-morrow after his business hours?"

Emily eagerly and gratefully accepted the suggestion. An hour was arranged for the meeting on the next day; the correspondence was left under the care of Agnes; and the courier's wife took her leave.

Weary and heartsick, Agnes lay down on the sofa, to rest and compose herself. The careful nurse brought in a reviving cup of tea. Her quaint gossip about herself and her occupations while Agnes had been away, acted as a relief to her mistress's overburdened mind. They were still talking quietly, when they were startled by a loud knock at the house door. Hurried footsteps ascended the stairs. The door of the sitting-room was thrown open violently; the courier's wife rushed in like a mad woman. "He's dead! they've murdered him!" Those wild words were all she could say. She dropped on her knees at the foot of the sofa—held out her hand with something clasped in it—and fell back in a swoon.

The nurse, signing to Agnes to open the window, took the necessary measures to restore the fainting woman. "What's this?" she exclaimed. "Here's a letter in her hand. See what it is, Miss."

The open envelope was addressed (evidently in a feigned handwriting) to "Mrs. Ferrari." The post-mark was "Venice." The contents of the envelope were a sheet of foreign note-paper, and a folded enclosure.

On the note-paper, one line only was written. It was again in a feigned handwriting, and it contained these words:

"*To console you for the loss of your husband.*"

Agnes opened the enclosure next.

It was a Bank of England note for a thousand pounds.

CHAPTER VI

THE next day, the friend and legal adviser of Agnes Lockwood, Mr. Troy, called on her by appointment in the evening.

Mrs. Ferrari—still persisting in the conviction of her husband's death—had sufficiently recovered to be present at the consultation. Assisted by Agnes, she told the lawyer the little that was known relating to Ferrari's disappearance, and then produced the correspondence connected with that event. Mr. Troy read (first) the three letters addressed by Ferrari to his wife; (secondly) the letter written by Ferrari's courier-friend, describing his visit to the palace and his interview with Lady Montbarry; and (thirdly) the one line of anonymous writing which had accompanied the extraordinary gift of a thousand pounds to Ferrari's wife.

Well known, at a later period, as the lawyer who acted for Lady Lydiard, in the case of theft, generally described as the case of "My Lady's Money," Mr. Troy was not only a man of learning and experience in his profession—he was also a man who had seen something of society at home and abroad. He possessed a keen eye for character, a quaint humour, and a kindly nature which had not been deteriorated even by a lawyer's professional experience of mankind. With all these personal advantages, it is a question, nevertheless, whether he was the fittest adviser whom Agnes could have chosen under the circumstances. Little Mrs. Ferrari, with many domestic merits, was an essentially commonplace woman. Mr. Troy was the last person living who was likely to attract her sympathies—he was the exact opposite of a commonplace man.

"She looks very ill, poor thing!" In these words the lawyer opened the business of the evening, referring to Mrs. Ferrari as unceremoniously as if she had been out of the room.

"She has suffered a terrible shock," Agnes answered.

Mr. Troy turned to Mrs. Ferrari, and looked at her again, with the interest due to the victim of a shock. He drummed absently with his fingers on the table. At last he spoke to her.

"My good lady, you don't really believe that your husband is dead?"

Mrs. Ferrari put her handkerchief to her eyes. The word "dead" was ineffectual to express her feelings. "Murdered!" she said sternly, behind her handkerchief.

"Why? And by whom?" Mr. Troy asked.

Mrs. Ferrari seemed to have some difficulty in answering. "You have read my husband's letters, sir," she began. "I believe he discovered——" She got as far as that, and there she stopped.

"What did he discover?"

There are limits to human patience—even the patience of a bereaved wife. This cool question irritated Mrs. Ferrari into expressing herself plainly at last.

"He discovered Lady Montbarry and the Baron!" she answered, with a burst of hysterical vehemence. "The Baron is no more that vile woman's brother than I am. The wickedness of those two wretches came to my poor dear husband's knowledge. The lady's maid left her place on account of it. If Ferrari had gone away too, he would have been alive at this moment. They have killed him. I say they have killed him, to prevent it from getting to Lord Montbarry's ears." So, in short sharp sentences, and in louder and louder accents, Mrs. Ferrari stated *her* opinion of the case.

Still keeping his own view in reserve, Mr. Troy listened with an expression of satirical approval.

"Very strongly stated, Mrs. Ferrari," he said. "You build up your sentences well; you clinch your conclusions in a workmanlike manner. If you had been a man, you would have made a good lawyer—you would have taken juries by the scruff of their necks. Complete the case, my good lady—complete the case. Tell us next who sent you this letter, enclosing the bank-note. The 'two wretches' who murdered Mr. Ferrari would hardly put their hands in their pockets and send you a thousand pounds. Who is it—eh? I see the post-mark on the letter is 'Venice.' Have you any friend in that interesting city, with a large heart, and a purse to correspond, who has been let into the secret and who wishes to console you anonymously?"

It was not easy to reply to this. Mrs. Ferrari began to feel the first inward approaches of something like hatred towards Mr. Troy. "I don't understand you, sir," she answered. "I don't think this is a joking matter."

Agnes interfered, for the first time. She drew her chair a little nearer to her legal counsellor and friend.

"What is the most probable explanation, in your opinion?" she asked.

"I shall offend Mrs. Ferrari if I tell you," Mr. Troy answered.

"No, sir, you won't!" cried Mrs. Ferrari, hating Mr. Troy undisguisedly by this time.

The lawyer leaned back in his chair. "Very well," he said, in his most good-humoured manner. "Let's have it out. Observe, madam, I don't dispute your view of the position of affairs at the palace in Venice. You have your husband's letters to justify you; and you have also the significant fact that Lady Montbarry's maid did really leave the house. We will say, then, that Lord Montbarry has presumably been made the victim of a foul wrong—that Mr. Ferrari was the first to find it out—and that the guilty persons had reason to fear, not only that he would acquaint Lord Montbarry with his discovery, but that he would be a principal witness against them if the scandal was made public in a court of law. Now mark! Admitting all this, I draw a totally different conclusion from the conclusion at which you have arrived. Here is your husband left in this miserable household of three, under very awkward circumstances for *him*. What does he do? But for the bank-note and the written message sent to you with it, I should say that he had wisely withdrawn himself from association with a disgraceful discovery and exposure, by taking secretly to flight. The money modifies this view—unfavourably so far as Mr. Ferrari is concerned. I still believe he is keeping out of the way. But I now say he is *paid* for keeping out of the way—and that bank-note there on the table is the price of his absence, sent by the guilty persons to his wife."

Mrs. Ferrari's watery grey eyes brightened suddenly; Mrs. Ferrari's dull drab-coloured complexion became enlivened by a glow of brilliant red.

"It's false!" she cried. "It's a burning shame to speak of my husband in that way!"

"I told you I should offend you!" said Mr. Troy.

Agnes interposed once more—in the interests of peace. She took the offended wife's hand; she appealed to the lawyer to reconsider that side of his theory which reflected harshly on Ferrari. While she was still speaking, the servant interrupted her by entering the room with a visiting-card. It was the card of Henry Westwick; and there was an ominous request written on it in pencil. "I bring bad news. Let me see you for a minute downstairs." Agnes immediately left the room.

Alone with Mrs. Ferrari, Mr. Troy permitted his natural kindness of heart to show itself on the surface at last. He tried to make his peace with the courier's wife.

"You have every claim, my good soul, to resent a reflection cast upon your husband," he began. "I may even say that I respect you for speaking so warmly in his defence. At the same time, remember, that I am bound, in such a serious matter as this, to tell you what is really in my mind. I can have no intention of offending you, seeing that I am a total stranger to you and to Mr. Ferrari. A thousand pounds is a large sum of money; and a poor man may excusably be tempted by it to do nothing worse than to keep out of the way for awhile. My only interest, acting on your behalf, is to get at the truth. If you will give me time, I see no reason to despair of finding your husband yet."

Ferrari's wife listened, without being convinced: her narrow little mind, filled to its extreme capacity by her unfavourable opinion of Mr. Troy, had no room left for the process of correcting its first impression. "I am much obliged to you, sir," was all she said. Her eyes were more communicative—her eyes added, in *their* language, "You may say what you please; I will never forgive you to my dying day."

Mr. Troy gave it up. He composedly wheeled his chair around, put his hands in his pockets, and looked out of window.

After an interval of silence, the drawing-room door was opened.

Mr. Troy wheeled round again briskly to the table, expecting to see Agnes. To his surprise there appeared, in her place, a perfect stranger to him—a gentleman, in the prime of life, with a marked expression of pain and embarrassment on his handsome face. He looked at Mr. Troy, and bowed gravely.

"I am so unfortunate as to have brought news to Miss Agnes Lockwood which has greatly distressed her," he said. "She has retired to her room. I am requested to make her excuses, and to speak to you in her place."

Having introduced himself in those terms, he noticed Mrs. Ferrari, and held out his hand to her kindly. "It is some years since we last met, Emily," he said. "I am afraid you have almost forgotten the 'Master Henry' of old times." Emily, in some little confusion, made her acknowledgments, and begged to know if she could be of any use to Miss Lockwood. "The old nurse is with her," Henry answered; "they will be better left together." He turned once more to Mr. Troy. "I ought to tell you," he said, "that my name is Henry Westwick. I am the younger brother of the late Lord Montbarry."

"The *late* Lord Montbarry!" Mr. Troy exclaimed.

"My brother died at Venice yesterday evening. There is the telegram." With that startling answer, he handed the paper to Mr. Troy.

The message was in these words:

"Lady Montbarry, Venice. To Stephen Robert Westwick, Newbury's Hotel, London. It is useless to take the journey. Lord Montbarry died of bronchitis, at 8.40 this evening. All needful details by post."

"Was this expected, sir?" the lawyer asked.

"I cannot say that it has taken us entirely by surprise," Henry answered. "My brother Stephen (who is now the head of the family) received a telegram three days since, informing him that alarming symptoms had declared themselves, and that a second physician had been called in. He telegraphed back to say that he had left Ireland for London, on his way to Venice, and to direct that any further message might be sent to his hotel. The reply came in a second telegram. It announced that Lord Montbarry was in a state of insensibility, and that, in his brief intervals of consciousness, he recognised nobody. My brother was advised to wait in London for later information. The third telegram is now in your hands. That is all I know, up to the present time."

Happening to look at the courier's wife, Mr. Troy was struck by the expression of blank fear which showed itself in the woman's face.

"Mrs. Ferrari," he said, "have you heard what Mr. Westwick has just told me?"

"Every word of it, sir."

"Have you any questions to ask?"

"No, sir."

"You seem to be alarmed," the lawyer persisted. "Is it still about your husband?"

"I shall never see my husband again, sir. I have thought so all along, as you know. I feel sure of it now."

"Sure of it, after what you have just heard?"

"Yes, sir."

"Can you tell me why?"

"No, sir. It's a feeling I have. I can't tell why."

"Oh, a feeling?" Mr. Troy repeated, in a tone of compassionate contempt. "When it comes to feelings, my good soul——!" He left the sentence unfinished, and rose to take his leave of Mr. Westwick. The truth is, he began to feel puzzled himself, and he did not choose to let Mrs. Ferrari see it. "Accept the expression of my sympathy, sir," he said to Mr. Westwick politely. "I wish you good evening."

Henry turned to Mrs. Ferrari as the lawyer closed the door. "I have heard of your trouble, Emily, from Miss Lockwood. Is there anything I can do to help you?"

"Nothing, sir, thank you. Perhaps, I had better go home after what has happened? I will call to-morrow, and see if I can be of any use to Miss Agnes. I am very sorry for her." She stole away, with her formal curtsey, her noiseless step, and her obstinate resolution to take the gloomiest view of her husband's case.

Henry Westwick looked round him in the solitude of the little drawing-room. There was nothing to keep him in the house, and yet he lingered in it. It was something to be even near Agnes—to see the things belonging to her that were scattered about the room. There, in the corner, was her chair, with her embroidery on the work-table by its side. On the little easel near the window was her last drawing, not quite finished yet. The book she had been reading lay on the sofa, with her tiny pencil-case in it to mark the place at which she had left off. One after another, he looked at the objects that reminded him of the woman whom he loved—took them up tenderly—and laid them down again with a sigh. Ah, how far, how unattainably far from him, she was still! "She will never forget Montbarry," he thought to himself as he took up his hat to go. "Not one of us feels his death as she feels it. Miserable, miserable wretch—how she loved him!"

In the street, as Henry closed the house-door, he was stopped by a passing acquaintance—a wearisome inquisitive man—doubly unwelcome to him, at that moment. "Sad news, Westwick, this about your brother. Rather an unexpected death, wasn't it? We never heard at the club that Montbarry's lungs were weak. What will the insurance offices do?"

Henry started; he had never thought of his brother's life insurance. What could the offices do but pay? A death by bronchitis, certified by two physicians, was surely the least disputable of all deaths. "I wish you hadn't put that question into my head!" he broke out irritably. "Ah!" said his friend, "you think the widow will get the money? So do I! so do I!"

CHAPTER VII

~~~~~~~~

SOME days later, the insurance offices (two in number) received the formal announcement of Lord Montbarry's death, from her ladyship's London solicitors. The sum insured in each office was five thousand pounds—on which one year's premium only had been paid. In the face of such a pecuniary emergency as this, the Directors thought it desirable to consider their position. The medical advisers of the two offices, who had recommended the insurance of Lord Montbarry's life, were called into council over their own reports. The result excited some interest among persons connected with the business of life insurance. Without absolutely declining to pay the money, the two offices (acting in concert) decided on sending a commission of inquiry to Venice, "for the purpose of obtaining further information."

Mr. Troy received the earliest intelligence of what was going on. He wrote at once to communicate his news to Agnes; adding, what he considered to be a valuable hint, in these words:

"You are intimately acquainted, I know, with Lady Barville, the late Lord Montbarry's eldest sister. The solicitors employed by her husband are also the solicitors to one of the two insurance offices. There may possibly be something in the report of the commission of inquiry touching on Ferrari's disappearance. Ordinary persons would not be permitted, of course, to see such a document. But a sister of the late lord is so near a relative as to be an exception to general rules. If Sir Theodore Barville puts it on that footing, the lawyers, even if they do not allow his wife to look at the report, will at least answer any discreet questions she may ask referring to it. Let me hear what you think of this suggestion, at your earliest convenience."

The reply was received by return of post. Agnes declined to avail herself of Mr. Troy's proposal.

"My interference, innocent as it was," she wrote, "has already been productive of such deplorable results, that I cannot and dare not stir any further in the case of Ferrari. If I had not consented to let that unfortunate man refer to me by name, the late Lord Montbarry would never have engaged him, and his wife would have been spared the misery and suspense from which she is suffering now. I would not even look at the report to which you allude if it was placed in my hands—I have heard more than enough already of that hideous life in the palace at Venice. If Mrs. Ferrari chooses to address herself to Lady Barville (with your assistance), that is of course quite another thing. But, even in this case, I must make it a positive condition that my name shall not be mentioned. Forgive me, dear Mr. Troy! I am very unhappy, and very unreasonable—but I am only a woman, and you must not expect too much from me."

Foiled in this direction, the lawyer next advised making the attempt to discover the present address of Lady Montbarry's English maid. This excellent suggestion had one drawback: it could only be carried out by spending money—and there was no money to spend. Mrs. Ferrari shrank from the bare idea of making any use of the thousand-pound note. It had been deposited in the safe keeping of a bank. If it was even mentioned in her hearing, she shuddered and referred to it, with melodramatic fervour, as "my husband's blood-money!"

So, under stress of circumstances, the attempt to solve the mystery of Ferrari's disappearance was suspended for awhile.

It was the last month of the year 1860. The commission of inquiry was already at work; having begun its investigations on

December 6. On the 10th, the term for which the late Lord Montbarry had hired the Venetian palace, expired. News by telegram
reached the insurance offices that Lady Montbarry had been
advised by her lawyers to leave for London with as little delay as
possible. Baron Rivar, it was believed, would accompany her to
England, but would not remain in that country, unless his services
were absolutely required by her ladyship. The Baron, "well known
as an enthusiastic student of chemistry," had heard of certain
recent discoveries in connection with that science in the United
States, and was anxious to investigate them personally.

These items of news, collected by Mr. Troy, were duly communicated to Mrs. Ferrari, whose anxiety about her husband
made her a frequent, a too frequent, visitor at the lawyer's office.
She attempted to relate what she had heard to her good friend
and protectress. Agnes steadily refused to listen, and positively
forbade any further conversation relating to Lord Montbarry's
wife, now that Lord Montbarry was no more. "You have Mr. Troy
to advise you," she said; "and you are welcome to what little
money I can spare, if money is wanted. All I ask in return is
that you will not distress me. I am trying to separate myself
from remembrances—" her voice faltered; she paused to control
herself——"from remembrances," she resumed, "which are sadder
than ever since I have heard of Lord Montbarry's death. Help
me by your silence to recover my spirits, if I can. Let me hear
nothing more, until I can rejoice with you that your husband is
found."

Time advanced to the 13th of the month; and more information of the interesting sort reached Mr. Troy. The labours of the
insurance commission had come to an end—the report had been
received from Venice on that day.

CHAPTER VIII

~~~~~~~~~~

ON the 14th the Directors and their legal advisers met for the reading of the report, with closed doors. These were the terms in which the Commissioners related the results of their inquiry:

"*Private and confidential.*

"We have the honour to inform our Directors that we arrived in Venice on December 6, 1860. On the same day we proceeded to the palace inhabited by Lord Montbarry at the time of his last illness and death.

"We were received with all possible courtesy by Lady Montbarry's brother, Baron Rivar. 'My sister was her husband's only attendant throughout his illness,' the Baron informed us. 'She is overwhelmed by grief and fatigue—or she would have been here to receive you personally. What are your wishes, gentlemen? and what can I do for you in her ladyship's place?'

"In accordance with our instructions, we answered that the death and burial of Lord Montbarry abroad made it desirable to obtain more complete information relating to his illness, and to the circumstances which had attended it, than could be conveyed in writing. We explained that the law provided for the lapse of a certain interval of time before the payment of the sum assured, and we expressed our wish to conduct the inquiry with the most respectful consideration for her ladyship's feelings, and for the convenience of any other members of the family inhabiting the house.

"To this the Baron replied, 'I am the only member of the family living here, and I and the palace are entirely at your disposal.' From first to last we found this gentleman perfectly straightforward, and most amiably willing to assist us.

"With the one exception of her ladyship's room, we went over the whole of the palace the same day. It is an immense place only partially furnished. The first floor and part of the second floor were the portions of it that had been inhabited by Lord Montbarry and the members of the household. We saw the bedchamber, at one extremity of the palace, in which his lordship died, and the small room communicating with it, which he used as a study. Next to this was a large apartment or hall, the doors of which he habitually kept locked, his object being (as we were informed) to pursue his studies uninterruptedly in perfect solitude. On the other side of the large hall were the bedchamber occupied by her ladyship, and the dressing-room in which the maid slept previous to her departure for England. Beyond these were the dining and reception rooms, opening into an antechamber, which gave access to the grand staircase of the palace.

"The only inhabited rooms on the second floor were the sitting-room and bedroom occupied by Baron Rivar, and another room at some distance from it, which had been the bedroom of the courier Ferrari.

"The rooms on the third floor and on the basement were completely unfurnished, and in a condition of great neglect. We inquired if there was anything to be seen below the basement— and we were at once informed that there were vaults beneath, which we were at perfect liberty to visit.

"We went down, so as to leave no part of the palace un-explored. The vaults were, it was believed, used as dungeons in the old times—say, some centuries since. Air and light were only partially admitted to these dismal places by two long shafts of winding construction, which communicated with the back yard of the palace, and the openings of which, high above the ground, were protected by iron gratings. The stone stairs leading down into the vaults could be closed at will by a heavy trap-door in the back hall, which we found open. The Baron himself led the way down the stairs. We remarked that it might be awkward if that trap-door fell down and closed the opening behind us. The Baron smiled at the idea. 'Don't be alarmed, gentlemen,' he said; 'the door is safe. I had an interest in seeing to it myself, when we first inhabited the palace. My favourite study is the study of experimental chemistry—and my workshop, since we have been in Venice, is down here.'

"These last words explained a curious smell in the vaults, which we noticed the moment we entered them. We can only describe the smell by saying that it was of a twofold sort—faintly aromatic, as it were, in its first effect, but with some after-odour very sickening in our nostrils. The Baron's furnaces and retorts, and other things, were all there to speak for themselves, together with some packages of chemicals, having the name and address of the person who had supplied them plainly visible on their labels. 'Not a pleasant place for study,' Baron Rivar observed, 'but my sister is timid. She has a horror of chemical smells and explosions—and she has banished me to these lower regions, so that my experiments may neither be smelt nor heard.' He held out his hands, on which we had noticed that he wore gloves in the house. 'Accidents will happen sometimes,' he said, 'no matter how careful a man may be. I burnt my hands severely in trying a new combination the other day, and they are only recovering now.'

"We mention these otherwise unimportant incidents, in order to show that our exploration of the palace was not impeded by any attempt at concealment. We were even admitted to her ladyship's own room—on a subsequent occasion, when she went out to take the air. Our instructions recommended us to examine his lordship's residence, because the extreme privacy of his life at Venice, and the remarkable departure of the only two servants in the house, might have some suspicious connection with the nature of his death. We found nothing to justify suspicion.

"As to his lordship's retired way of life, we have conversed on the subject with the consul and the banker—the only two strangers who held any communication with him. He called once at the bank to obtain money on his letter of credit, and excused himself from accepting an invitation to visit the banker at his private residence, on the ground of delicate health. His lordship wrote to the same effect on sending his card to the consul, to excuse himself from personally returning that gentleman's visit to the palace. We have seen the letter, and we beg to offer the following copy of it. 'Many years passed in India have injured my constitution. I have ceased to go into society; the one occupation of my life now is the study of Oriental literature. The air of Italy is better for me than the air of England, or I should never have left home. Pray accept the apologies of a student and an invalid. The active part of my life is at an end.' The self-seclusion of his lordship seems to us to be explained in these brief lines. We have not, however, on that account spared our inquiries in other directions. Nothing to excite a suspicion of anything wrong has come to our knowledge.

"As to the departure of the lady's maid, we have seen the woman's receipt for her wages, in which it is expressly stated that she left Lady Montbarry's service because she disliked the Continent, and wished to get back to her own country. This is not an uncommon result of taking English servants to foreign parts. Lady Montbarry has informed us that she abstained from engaging another maid in consequence of the extreme dislike which his lordship expressed to having strangers in the house, in the state of his health at that time.

"The disappearance of the courier Ferrari is, in itself, unquestionably a suspicious circumstance. Neither her ladyship nor the Baron can explain it; and no investigation that we could make has thrown the smallest light on this event, or has justified us in associating it, directly or indirectly, with the object of our inquiry. We have even gone the length of examining the portmanteau which Ferrari left behind him. It contains nothing but clothes and linen—no money, and not even a scrap of paper in the pockets of the clothes. The portmanteau remains in charge of the police.

"We have also found opportunities of speaking privately to the old woman who attends to the rooms occupied by her ladyship and the Baron. She was recommended to fill this situation by the keeper of the restaurant who has supplied the meals to the family throughout the period of their residence at the palace. Her character is most favourably spoken of. Unfortunately, her limited intelligence makes her of no value as a witness. We were patient and careful in questioning her, and we found her perfectly willing to answer us; but we could elicit nothing which is worth including in the present report.

"On the second day of our inquiries, we had the honour of an interview with Lady Montbarry. Her ladyship looked miserably worn and ill, and seemed to be quite at a loss to understand what we wanted with her. Baron Rivar, who introduced us, explained the nature of our errand in Venice, and took pains to assure her that it was a purely formal duty on which we were engaged. Having satisfied her ladyship on this point, he discreetly left the room.

"The questions which we addressed to Lady Montbarry related mainly, of course, to his lordship's illness. The answers, given with great nervousness of manner, but without the slightest appearance of reserve, informed us of the facts that follow:

"Lord Montbarry had been out of order for some time past— nervous and irritable. He first complained of having taken cold on November 13 last; he passed a wakeful and feverish night, and remained in bed the next day. Her ladyship proposed sending for medical advice. He refused to allow her to do this, saying that he could quite easily be his own doctor in such a trifling matter as a cold. Some hot lemonade was made at his request, with a view to producing perspiration. Lady Montbarry's maid having left her at that time, the courier Ferrari (then the only servant in the house) went out to buy the lemons. Her ladyship made the drink with her own hands. It was successful in producing perspiration—and Lord Montbarry had some hours of sleep afterwards. Later in the day, having need of Ferrari's services, Lady Montbarry rang for him. The bell was not answered. Baron Rivar searched for the man, in the palace and out of it, in vain. From that time forth not a trace of Ferrari could be discovered. This happened on November 14.

"On the night of the 14th, the feverish symptoms accompanying his lordship's cold returned. They were in part perhaps attributable to the annoyance and alarm caused by Ferrari's mysterious disappearance. It had been impossible to conceal the circumstance, as his lordship rang repeatedly for the courier; insisting that the man should relieve Lady Montbarry and the Baron by taking their places during the night at his bedside.

"On the 15th (the day on which the old woman first came to do the housework), his lordship complained of sore throat, and of a feeling of oppression on the chest. On this day, and again on the 16th, her ladyship and the Baron entreated him to see a doctor. He still refused. 'I don't want strange faces about me; my cold will run its course, in spite of the doctor,' that was his answer. On the 17th he was so much worse that it was decided to send for medical help whether he liked it or not. Baron Rivar, after inquiry at the consul's, secured the services of Doctor Bruno, well known as an eminent physician in Venice; with the additional recommendation of having resided in England, and having made himself acquainted with English forms of medical practice.

"Thus far our account of his lordship's illness has been derived from statements made by Lady Montbarry. The narrative will now be most fitly continued in the language of the doctor's own report, herewith subjoined.

" 'My medical diary informs me that I first saw the English Lord Montbarry, on November 17. He was suffering from a sharp attack of bronchitis. Some precious time had been lost, through his obstinate objection to the presence of a medical man at his bedside. Generally speaking, he appeared to be in a delicate state of health. His nervous system was out of order—he was at once timid and contradictory. When I spoke to him in English, he answered in Italian; and when I tried him in Italian, he went back to English. It mattered little—the malady had already made such progress that he could only speak a few words at a time, and those in a whisper.

" 'I at once applied the necessary remedies. Copies of my prescriptions (with translation into English) accompany the present statement, and are left to speak for themselves.

" 'For the next three days I was in constant attendance on my patient. He answered to the remedies employed—improving slowly, but decidedly. I could conscientiously assure Lady Montbarry that no danger was to be apprehended thus far. She was indeed a most devoted wife. I vainly endeavoured to induce her to accept the services of a competent nurse; she would allow nobody to attend on her husband but herself. Night and day this estimable woman was at his bedside. In her brief intervals of repose, her brother watched the sick man in her place. This brother was, I must say, very good company, in the intervals when we had time for a little talk. He dabbled in chemistry, down in the horrid under-water vaults of the palace; and he wanted to show me some of his experiments. I have enough of chemistry in writing prescriptions—and I declined. He took it quite good-humouredly.

" 'I am straying away from my subject. Let me return to the sick lord.

" 'Up to the 20th, then, things went well enough. I was quite unprepared for the disastrous change that showed itself, when I paid Lord Montbarry my morning visit on the 21st. He had relapsed, and seriously relapsed. Examining him to discover the cause, I found symptoms of pneumonia—that is to say, in un-medical language, inflammation of the substance of the lungs. He breathed with difficulty, and was only partially able to relieve himself by coughing. I made the strictest inquiries, and was assured that his medicine had been administered as carefully as usual, and that he had not been exposed to any changes of temperature. It was with great reluctance that I added to Lady Montbarry's distress; but I felt bound, when she suggested a consultation with another physician, to own that I too thought there was really need for it.

" 'Her ladyship instructed me to spare no expense, and to get the best medical opinion in Italy. The best opinion was happily within our reach. The first and foremost of Italian physicians is Torello of Padua. I sent a special messenger for the great man. He arrived on the evening of the 21st, and confirmed my opinion that pneumonia had set in, and that our patient's life was in danger. I told him what my treatment of the case had been, and he approved of it in every particular. He made some valuable suggestions, and (at Lady Montbarry's express request) he consented to defer his return to Padua until the following morning.

" 'We both saw the patient at intervals in the course of the night. The disease, steadily advancing, set our utmost resistance at defiance. In the morning Doctor Torello took his leave. 'I can be of no further use,' he said to me. 'The man is past all help —and he ought to know it.'

" 'Later in the day I warned my lord, as gently as I could, that his time had come. I am informed that there are serious reasons for my stating what passed between us on this occasion, in detail, and without any reserve. I comply with the request.

" 'Lord Montbarry received the intelligence of his approaching death with becoming composure, but with a certain doubt. He signed to me to put my ear to his mouth. He whispered faintly, 'Are you sure?' It was no time to deceive him; I said, 'Positively sure.' He waited a little, gasping for breath, and then he whispered again, 'Feel under my pillow.' I found under his pillow a letter, sealed and stamped, ready for the post. His next words were just audible and no more—'Post it yourself.' I answered, of course, that I would do so—and I did post the letter with my own hand. I looked at the address. It was directed to a lady in London. The street I cannot remember. The name I can perfectly recall: it was an Italian name—'Mrs. Ferrari.'

" 'That night my lord nearly died of asphyxia. I got him through it for the time; and his eyes showed that he understood me when I told him, the next morning, that I had posted the letter. This was his last effort of consciousness. When I saw him again he was sunk in apathy. He lingered in a state of insensibility, supported by stimulants, until the 25th, and died (unconscious to the last) on the evening of that day.

" 'As to the cause of his death, it seems (if I may be excused for saying so) simply absurd to ask the question. Bronchitis, terminating in pneumonia—there is no more doubt that this, and this only, was the malady of which he expired, than that two and two make four. Doctor Torello's own note of the case is added here to a duplicate of my certificate, in order (as I am informed) to satisfy some English offices in which his lordship's life was insured. The English offices must have been founded by that celebrated saint and doubter, mentioned in the New Testament, whose name was Thomas!"

"Doctor Bruno's evidence ends here.

"Reverting for a moment to our inquiries addressed to Lady Montbarry, we have to report that she can give us no information on the subject of the letter which the doctor posted at Lord Montbarry's request. When his lordship wrote it? what it contained? why he kept it a secret from Lady Montbarry (and from the Baron also); and why he should write at all to the wife of his courier? these are questions to which we find it simply impossible to obtain any replies. It seems even useless to say that the matter is open to suspicion. Suspicion implies conjecture of some kind— and the letter under my lord's pillow baffles all conjecture. Application to Mrs. Ferrari may perhaps clear up the mystery. Her residence in London will be easily discovered at the Italian Couriers' Office, Golden Square.

"Having arrived at the close of the present report, we have now to draw your attention to the conclusion which is justified by the results of our investigation.

"The plain question before our Directors and ourselves appears to be this: Has the inquiry revealed any extraordinary circumstances which render the death of Lord Montbarry open to suspicion? The inquiry has revealed extraordinary circumstances beyond all doubt—such as the disappearance of Ferrari, the remarkable absence of the customary establishment of servants in the house, and the mysterious letter which his lordship asked the doctor to post. But where is the proof that any one of these circumstances is associated—suspiciously and directly associated—with the only event which concerns us, the event of Lord Montbarry's death? In the absence of any such proof, and in the face of the evidence of two eminent physicians, it is impossible to dispute the statement on the certificate that his lordship died a natural death. We are bound, therefore, to report, that there are no valid grounds for refusing the payment of the sum for which the late Lord Montbarry's life was assured.

"We shall send these lines to you by the post of to-morrow, December 10; leaving time to receive your further instructions (if any), in reply to our telegram of this evening announcing the conclusion of the inquiry."

CHAPTER IX

"NOW, my good creature, whatever you have to say to me, out with it at once! I don't want to hurry you needlessly; but these are business hours, and I have other people's affairs to attend to besides yours."

Addressing Ferrari's wife, with his usual blunt good-humour, in these terms, Mr. Troy registered the lapse of time by a glance at the watch on his desk, and then waited to hear what his client had to say to him.

"It's something more, sir, about the letter with the thousand-pound note," Mrs. Ferrari began. "I have found out who sent it to me."

Mr. Troy started. "This is news indeed!" he said. "Who sent you the letter?"

"Lord Montbarry sent it, sir."

It was not easy to take Mr. Troy by surprise. But Mrs. Ferrari threw him completely off his balance. For awhile he could only look at her in silent surprise. "Nonsense!" he said, as soon as he had recovered himself. "There is some mistake—it can't be!"

"There is no mistake," Mrs. Ferrari rejoined, in her most positive manner. "Two gentlemen from the insurance offices called on me this morning, to see the letter. They were completely puzzled—especially when they heard of the bank-note inside. But they know who sent the letter. His lordship's doctor in Venice posted it at his lordship's request. Go to the gentlemen yourself, sir, if you don't believe me. They were polite enough to ask if I could account for Lord Montbarry writing to me and sending me the money. I gave them my opinion directly—I said it was like his lordship's kindness."

"Like his lordship's kindness?" Mr. Troy repeated, in blank amazement.

"Yes, sir! Lord Montbarry knew me, like all the other members of his family, when I was at school on the estate in Ireland. If he could have done it, he would have protected my poor dear husband. But he was helpless himself in the hands of my lady and the Baron—and the only kind thing he could do was to provide for me in my widowhood, like the true nobleman he was!"

"A very pretty explanation!" said Mr. Troy. "What did your visitors from the insurance offices think of it?"

"They asked if I had any proof of my husband's death."

"And what did you say?"

"I said, 'I give you better than proof, gentlemen; I give you my positive opinion.'"

"That satisfied them, of course?"

"They didn't say so in words, sir. They looked at each other — and wished me good-morning."

"Well, Mrs. Ferrari, unless you have some more extraordinary news for me, I think I shall wish you good-morning too. I can take a note of your information (very startling information, I own); and, in the absence of proof, I can do no more."

"I can provide you with proof, sir—if that is all you want," said Mrs. Ferrari, with great dignity. "I only wish to know, first, whether the law justifies me in doing it. You may have seen in the fashionable intelligence of the newspapers, that Lady Montbarry has arrived in London, at Newbury's Hotel. I propose to go and see her."

"The deuce you do! May I ask for what purpose?"

Mrs. Ferrari answered in a mysterious whisper. "For the purpose of catching her in a trap! I shan't send in my name—I shall announce myself as a person on business, and the first words I say to her will be these: 'I come, my lady, to acknowledge the receipt of the money sent to Ferrari's widow.' Ah! you may well start, Mr. Troy! It almost takes *you* off your guard, doesn't it? Make your mind easy, sir; I shall find the proof that everybody asks me for in her guilty face. Let her only change colour by the shadow of a shade—let her eyes only drop for half an instant— I shall discover her! The one thing I want to know is, does the law permit it?"

"The law permits it," Mr. Troy answered gravely; "but whether her ladyship will permit it, is quite another question. Have you really courage enough, Mrs. Ferrari, to carry out this notable scheme of yours? You have been described to me, by Miss Lockwood, as rather a nervous, timid sort of person—and, if I may trust my own observation, I should say you justify the description."

"If you had lived in the country, sir, instead of living in London," Mrs. Ferrari replied, "you would sometimes have seen even a sheep turn on a dog. I am far from saying that I am a bold woman—quite the reverse. But when I stand in that wretch's presence, and think of my murdered husband, the one of us two who is likely to be frightened is not *me*. I am going there now, sir. You shall hear how it ends. I wish you good-morning."

With those brave words the courier's wife gathered her mantle about her, and walked out of the room.

Mr. Troy smiled—not satirically, but compassionately. "The little simpleton!" he thought to himself. "If half of what they say of Lady Montbarry is true, Mrs. Ferrari and her trap have but a poor prospect before them. I wonder how it will end?"

All Mr. Troy's experience failed to forewarn him of how it *did* end.

CHAPTER X

IN the mean time, Mrs. Ferrari held to her resolution. She went straight from Mr. Troy's office to Newbury's Hotel.

Lady Montbarry was at home, and alone. But the authorities of the hotel hesitated to disturb her when they found that the visitor declined to mention her name. Her ladyship's new maid happened to cross the hall while the matter was still in debate. She was a Frenchwoman, and, on being appealed to, she settled the question in the swift, easy, rational French way. "Madame's appearance was perfectly respectable. Madame might have reasons for not mentioning her name which Miladi might approve. In any case, there being no orders forbidding the introduction of a strange lady, the matter clearly rested between Madame and Miladi. Would Madame, therefore, be good enough to follow Miladi's maid up the stairs?"

In spite of her resolution, Mrs. Ferrari's heart beat as if it would burst out of her bosom, when her conductress led her into an ante-room, and knocked at a door opening into a room beyond. But it is remarkable that persons of sensitively-nervous organisation are the very persons who are capable of forcing themselves (apparently by the exercise of a spasmodic effort of will) into the performance of acts of the most audacious courage. A low, grave voice from the inner room said, "Come in." The maid, opening the door, announced, "A person to see you, Miladi, on business," and immediately retired. In the one instant while these events passed, timid little Mrs. Ferrari mastered her own throbbing heart; stepped over the threshold, conscious of her clammy hands, dry lips, and burning head; and stood in the presence of Lord Montbarry's widow, to all outward appearance as supremely self-possessed as her ladyship herself.

It was still early in the afternoon, but the light in the room was dim. The blinds were drawn down. Lady Montbarry sat with her back to the windows, as if even the subdued daylight were disagreeable to her. She had altered sadly for the worse in her personal appearance, since the memorable day when Doctor Wybrow had seen her in his consulting-room. Her beauty was gone—her face had fallen away to mere skin and bone; the contrast between her ghastly complexion and her steely glittering black eyes was more startling than ever. Robed in dismal black, relieved only by the brilliant whiteness of her widow's cap —reclining in a panther-like suppleness of attitude on a little green sofa—she looked at the stranger who had intruded on her, with a moment's languid curiosity, then dropped her eyes again to the hand-screen which she held between her face and the fire. "I don't know you," she said. "What do you want with me?"

Mrs. Ferrari tried to answer. Her first burst of courage had already worn itself out. The bold words that she had determined to speak were living words still in her mind, but they died on her lips.

There was a moment of silence. Lady Montbarry looked round again at the speechless stranger. "Are you deaf?" she asked. There was another pause. Lady Montbarry quietly looked back again at the screen, and put another question. "Do you want money?"

"Money!" That one word roused the sinking spirit of the courier's wife. She recovered her courage; she found her voice. "Look at me, my lady, if you please," she said, with a sudden outbreak of audacity.

Lady Montbarry looked round for the third time. The fatal words passed Mrs. Ferrari's lips.

"I come, my lady, to acknowledge the receipt of the money sent to Ferrari's widow."

Lady Montbarry's glittering black eyes rested with steady attention on the woman who had addressed her in those terms. Not the faintest expression of confusion or alarm, not even a momentary flutter of interest stirred the deadly stillness of her face. She reposed as quietly, she held the screen as composedly, as ever. The test had been tried, and had utterly failed.

There was another silence. Lady Montbarry considered with herself. The smile that came slowly and went away suddenly—the smile at once so sad and so cruel—showed itself on her thin lips. She lifted her screen, and pointed with it to a seat at the farther end of the room. "Be so good as to take that chair," she said.

Helpless under her first bewildering sense of failure—not knowing what to say or what to do next—Mrs. Ferrari mechanically obeyed. Lady Montbarry, rising on the sofa for the first time, watched her with undisguised scrutiny as she crossed the room—then sank back into a reclining position once more. "No," she said to herself, "the woman walks steadily; she is not intoxicated—the only other possibility is that she may be mad."

She had spoken loud enough to be heard. Stung by the insult, Mrs. Ferrari instantly answered her: "I am no more drunk or mad than you are!"

"No?" said Lady Montbarry. "Then you are only insolent? The ignorant English mind (I have observed) is apt to be insolent in the exercise of unrestrained English liberty. This is very noticeable to us foreigners among you people in the streets. Of course I can't be insolent to you, in return. I hardly know what to say to you. My maid was imprudent in admitting you so easily to my room. I suppose your respectable appearance misled her. I wonder who you are? You mentioned the name of a courier who left us very strangely. Was he married by any chance? Are you his wife? And do you know where he is?"

Mrs. Ferrari's indignation burst its way through all restraints. She advanced to the sofa; she feared nothing, in the fervour and rage of her reply.

"I am his widow—and you know it, you wicked woman! Ah! it was an evil hour when Miss Lockwood recommended my husband to be his lordship's courier——!"

Before she could add another word, Lady Montbarry sprang from the sofa with the stealthy suddenness of a cat—seized her by both shoulders—and shook her with the strength and frenzy of a madwoman. "You lie! you lie! you lie!" She dropped her hold at the third repetition of the accusation, and threw up her hands wildly with a gesture of despair. "Oh, Jesu Maria! is it possible?" she cried. "*Can* the courier have come to me through that woman?" She turned like lightning on Mrs. Ferrari, and stopped her as she was escaping from the room. "Stay here, you fool—stay here, and answer me! If you cry out, as sure as the heavens are above you, I'll strangle you with my own hands. Sit down again—and fear nothing. Wretch! It is I who am frightened—frightened out of my senses. Confess that you lied, when you used Miss Lockwood's name just now! No! I don't believe you on your oath; I will believe nobody but Miss Lockwood herself. Where does she live? Tell me that, you noxious stinging little insect—and you may go." Terrified as she was, Mrs. Ferrari hesitated. Lady Montbarry lifted her hands threateningly, with the long, lean, yellow-white fingers outspread and crooked at the tips. Mrs. Ferrari shrank at the sight of them, and gave the address. Lady Montbarry pointed contemptuously to the door—then changed her mind. "No! not yet! you will tell Miss Lockwood what has happened, and she may refuse to see me. I will go there at once, and you shall go with me. As far as the house—not inside of it. Sit down again. I am going to ring for my maid. Turn your back to the door—your cowardly face is not fit to be seen!"

She rang the bell. The maid appeared.

"My cloak and bonnet—instantly!"

The maid produced the cloak and bonnet from the bedroom.

"A cab at the door—before I can count ten!"

The maid vanished. Lady Montbarry surveyed herself in the glass, and wheeled round again, with her cat-like suddenness, to Mrs. Ferrari.

"I look more than half dead already, don't I?" she said with a grim outburst of irony. "Give me your arm."

She took Mrs. Ferrari's arm, and left the room. "You have nothing to fear, so long as you obey," she whispered, on the way downstairs. "You leave me at Miss Lockwood's door, and never see me again."

In the hall they were met by the landlady of the hotel. Lady Montbarry graciously presented her companion. "My good friend Mrs. Ferrari; I am so glad to have seen her." The landlady accompanied them to the door. The cab was waiting. "Get in first, good Mrs. Ferrari," said her ladyship; "and tell the man where to go."

They were driven away. Lady Montbarry's variable humour changed again. With a low groan of misery, she threw herself back in the cab. Lost in her own dark thoughts, as careless of the woman whom she had bent to her iron will as if no such person sat by her side, she preserved a sinister silence, until they reached the house where Miss Lockwood lodged. In an instant, she roused herself to action. She opened the door of the cab, and closed it again on Mrs. Ferrari, before the driver could get off his box.

"Take that lady a mile farther on her way home!" she said, as she paid the man his fare. The next moment she had knocked at the house-door. "Is Miss Lockwood at home?" "Yes, ma'am." She stepped over the threshold—the door closed on her.

"Which way, ma'am?" asked the driver of the cab.

Mrs. Ferrari put her hand to her head, and tried to collect her thoughts. Could she leave her friend and benefactress helpless at

Lady Montbarry's mercy? She was still vainly endeavouring to decide on the course that she ought to follow—when a gentleman, stopping at Miss Lockwood's door, happened to look towards the cab-window, and saw her.

"Are you going to call on Miss Agnes too?" he asked.

It was Henry Westwick. Mrs. Ferrari clasped her hands in gratitude as she recognised him.

"Go in, sir!" she cried. "Go in, directly. That dreadful woman is with Miss Agnes. Go and protect her!"

"What woman?" Henry asked.

The answer literally struck him speechless. With amazement and indignation in his face, he looked at Mrs. Ferrari as she pronounced the hated name of "Lady Montbarry." "I'll see to it," was all he said. He knocked at the house-door; and he too, in his turn, was let in.

CHAPTER XI

∽∾∿∾∽

"LADY Montbarry, Miss."

Agnes was writing a letter, when the servant astonished her by announcing the visitor's name. Her first impulse was to refuse to see the woman who had intruded on her. But Lady Montbarry had taken care to follow close on the servant's heels. Before Agnes could speak, she had entered the room.

"I beg to apologise for my intrusion, Miss Lockwood. I have a question to ask you, in which I am very much interested. No one can answer me but yourself." In low hesitating tones, with her glittering black eyes bent modestly on the ground, Lady Montbarry opened the interview in those words.

Without answering, Agnes pointed to a chair. She could do this, and, for the time, she could do no more. All that she had read of the hidden and sinister life in the palace at Venice; all that she had heard of Montbarry's melancholy death and burial in a foreign land; all that she knew of the mystery of Ferrari's disappearance, rushed into her mind, when the black-robed figure confronted her, standing just inside the door. The strange conduct of Lady Montbarry added a new perplexity to the doubts and misgivings that troubled her. There stood the adventuress whose character had left its mark on society all over Europe—the Fury who had terrified Mrs. Ferrari at the hotel—inconceivably transformed into a timid, shrinking woman! Lady Montbarry had not once ventured to look at Agnes, since she had made her way into the room. Advancing to take the chair that had been pointed out to her, she hesitated, put her hand on the rail to support herself, and still remained standing. "Please give me a moment to compose myself," she said faintly. Her head sank on her bosom: she stood before Agnes like a conscious culprit before a merciless judge.

The silence that followed was, literally, the silence of fear on both sides. In the midst of it, the door was opened once more — and Henry Westwick appeared.

He looked at Lady Montbarry with a moment's steady attention—bowed to her with formal politeness—and passed on in silence. At the sight of her husband's brother, the sinking spirit of the woman sprang to life again. Her drooping figure became erect. Her eyes met Westwick's look, brightly defiant. She returned his bow with an icy smile of contempt.

Henry crossed the room to Agnes.

"Is Lady Montbarry here by your invitation?" he asked quietly.

"No."

"Do you wish to see her?"

"It is very painful to me to see her."

He turned and looked at his sister-in-law. "Do you hear that?" he asked coldly.

"I hear it," she answered, more coldly still.

"Your visit is, to say the least of it, ill-timed."

"Your interference is, to say the least of it, out of place."

With that retort, Lady Montbarry approached Agnes. The presence of Henry Westwick seemed at once to relieve and embolden her. "Permit me to ask my question, Miss Lockwood," she said, with graceful courtesy. "It is nothing to embarrass you. When the courier Ferrari applied to my late husband for employment, did you—" Her resolution failed her, before she could say more. She sank trembling into the nearest chair, and, after a moment's struggle, composed herself again. "Did you permit Ferrari," she resumed, "to make sure of being chosen for our courier by using your name?"

Agnes did not reply with her customary directness. Trifling as it was, the reference to Montbarry, proceeding from *that* woman of all others, confused and agitated her.

"I have known Ferrari's wife for many years," she began. "And I take an interest——"

Lady Montbarry abruptly lifted her hands with a gesture of entreaty. "Ah, Miss Lockwood, don't waste time by talking of his wife! Answer my plain question, plainly!"

"Let me answer her," Henry whispered. "I will undertake to speak plainly enough."

Agnes refused by a gesture. Lady Montbarry's interruption had roused her sense of what was due to herself. She resumed her reply in plainer terms.

"When Ferrari wrote to the late Lord Montbarry," she said, "he did certainly mention my name."

Even now, she had innocently failed to see the object which her visitor had in view. Lady Montbarry's impatience became ungovernable. She started to her feet, and advanced to Agnes.

"Was it with your knowledge and permission that Ferrari used your name?" she asked. "The whole soul of my question is in *that*. For God's sake answer me—Yes, or No!"

"Yes."

That one word struck Lady Montbarry as a blow might have struck her. The fierce life that had animated her face the instant before, faded out of it suddenly, and left her like a woman turned to stone. She stood, mechanically confronting Agnes, with a stillness so wrapt and perfect that not even the breath she drew was perceptible to the two persons who were looking at her.

Henry spoke to her roughly. "Rouse yourself," he said. "You have received your answer."

She looked round at him. "I have received my Sentence," she rejoined—and turned slowly to leave the room.

To Henry's astonishment, Agnes stopped her. "Wait a moment, Lady Montbarry. I have something to ask on my side. You have spoken of Ferrari. I wish to speak of him too."

Lady Montbarry bent her head in silence. Her hand trembled as she took out her handkerchief, and passed it over her forehead. Agnes detected the trembling, and shrank back a step. "Is the subject painful to you?" she asked timidly.

Still silent, Lady Montbarry invited her by a wave of the hand to go on. Henry approached, attentively watching his sister-in-law. Agnes went on.

"No trace of Ferrari has been discovered in England," she said. "Have you any news of him? And will you tell me (if you have heard anything), in mercy to his wife?"

Lady Montbarry's thin lips suddenly relaxed into their sad and cruel smile.

"Why do you ask *me* about the lost courier?" she said. "You will know what has become of him, Miss Lockwood, when the time is ripe for it."

Agnes started. "I don't understand you," she said. "How shall I know? Will some one tell me?"

"Some one will tell you."

Henry could keep silence no longer. "Perhaps, your ladyship may be the person?" he interrupted with ironical politeness.

She answered him with contemptuous ease. "You may be right, Mr. Westwick. One day or another, I may be the person who tells Miss Lockwood what has become of Ferrari, if——" She stopped; with her eyes fixed on Agnes.

"If what?" Henry asked.

"If Miss Lockwood forces me to it."

Agnes listened in astonishment. "Force you to it?" she repeated. "How can I do that? Do you mean to say my will is stronger than yours?"

"Do *you* mean to say that the candle doesn't burn the moth, when the moth flies into it?" Lady Montbarry rejoined. "Have you ever heard of such a thing as the fascination of terror? I am drawn to you by a fascination of terror. I have no right to visit you, I have no wish to visit you: you are my enemy. For the first time in my life, against my own will, I submit to my enemy. See! I am waiting because you told me to wait—and the fear of you (I swear it!) creeps through me while I stand here. Oh, don't let me excite your curiosity or your pity! Follow the example of Mr. Westwick. Be hard and brutal and unforgiving, like him. Grant me my release. Tell me to go."

The frank and simple nature of Agnes could discover but one intelligible meaning in this strange outbreak.

"You are mistaken in thinking me your enemy," she said. "The wrong you did me when you gave your hand to Lord Montbarry was not intentionally done. I forgave you my sufferings in his lifetime. I forgive you even more freely now that he has gone."

Henry heard her with mingled emotions of admiration and distress. "Say no more!" he exclaimed. "You are too good to her; she is not worthy of it."

The interruption passed unheeded by Lady Montbarry. The simple words in which Agnes had replied seemed to have absorbed the whole attention of this strangely-changeable woman. As she listened, her face settled slowly into an expression of hard and tearless sorrow. There was a marked change in her voice when she spoke next. It expressed that last worst resignation which has done with hope.

"You good innocent creature," she said, "what does your amiable forgiveness matter? What are your poor little wrongs, in the reckoning for greater wrongs which is demanded of me? I am not trying to frighten you, I am only miserable about myself. Do you know what it is to have a firm presentiment of calamity that is coming to you—and yet to hope that your own positive conviction will not prove true? When I first met you, before my marriage, and first felt your influence over me, I had that hope. It was a starveling sort of hope that lived a lingering life in me until to-day. *You* struck it dead, when you answered my question about Ferrari."

"How have I destroyed your hopes?" Agnes asked. "What connection is there between my permitting Ferrari to use my name to Lord Montbarry, and the strange and dreadful things you are saying to me now?"

"The time is near, Miss Lockwood, when you will discover that for yourself. In the mean while, you shall know what my fear of you is, in the plainest words I can find. On the day when I took your hero from you and blighted your life—I am firmly persuaded of it!—you were made the instrument of the retribution that my sins of many years had deserved. Oh, such things have happened before to-day! One person has, before now, been the means of innocently ripening the growth of evil in another. You have done that already—and you have more to do yet. You have still to bring me to the day of discovery, and to the punishment that is my doom. We shall meet again—here in England, or there in Venice where my husband died—and meet for the last time."

In spite of her better sense, in spite of her natural superiority to superstitions of all kinds, Agnes was impressed by the terrible earnestness with which those words were spoken. She turned pale as she looked at Henry. "Do *you* understand her?" she asked.

"Nothing is easier than to understand her," he replied contemptuously. "She knows what has become of Ferrari; and she is confusing you in a cloud of nonsense, because she daren't own the truth. Let her go!"

If a dog had been under one of the chairs, and had barked, Lady Montbarry could not have proceeded more impenetrably with the last words she had to say to Agnes.

"Advise your interesting Mrs. Ferrari to wait a little longer," she said. "*You* will know what has become of her husband, and you will tell her. There will be nothing to alarm you. Some trifling event will bring us together the next time—as trifling, I dare say, as the engagement of Ferrari. Sad nonsense, Mr. Westwick, is it not? But you make allowances for women; we all talk nonsense. Good morning, Miss Lockwood."

She opened the door—suddenly, as if she was afraid of being called back for the second time—and left them.

CHAPTER XII

❧❧❧❧❧

"Do you think she is mad?" Agnes asked.

"I think she is simply wicked. False, superstitious, inveterately cruel—but not mad. I believe her main motive in coming here was to enjoy the luxury of frightening you."

"She *has* frightened me. I am ashamed to own it—but so it is."

Henry looked at her, hesitated for a moment, and seated himself on the sofa by her side.

"I am very anxious about you, Agnes," he said. "But for the fortunate chance which led me to call here to-day—who knows what that vile woman might not have said or done, if she had found you alone? My dear, you are leading a sadly unprotected solitary life. I don't like to think of it; I want to see it changed—especially after what has happened to-day. No! no! it is useless to tell me that you have your old nurse. She is too old; she is not in your rank of life—there is no sufficient protection in the companionship of such a person for a lady in your position. Don't mistake me, Agnes! what I say, I say in the sincerity of my devotion to you." He paused, and took her hand. She made a feeble effort to withdraw it—and yielded. "Will the day never come," he pleaded, "when the privilege of protecting you may be mine? when you will be the pride and joy of my life, as long as my life lasts?" He pressed her hand gently. She made no reply. The colour came and went on her face; her eyes were turned away from him. "Have I been so unhappy as to offend you?" he asked.

She answered that—she said, almost in a whisper, "No."

"Have I distressed you?"

"You have made me think of the sad days that are gone." She said no more; she only tried to withdraw her hand from his for the second time. He still held it; he lifted it to his lips.

"Can I never make you think of other days than those—of the happier days to come? Or, if you must think of the time that is passed, can you not look back to the time when I first loved you?"

She sighed as he put the question. "Spare me Henry," she answered sadly. "Say no more!"

The colour again rose in her cheeks; her hand trembled in his. She looked lovely, with her eyes cast down and her bosom heaving gently. At that moment he would have given everything he had in the world to take her in his arms and kiss her. Some mysterious sympathy, passing from his hand to hers, seemed to tell her what was in his mind. She snatched her hand away, and suddenly looked up at him. The tears were in her eyes. She said nothing; she let her eyes speak for her. They warned him—without anger, without unkindness—but still they warned him to press her no further that day.

"Only tell me that I am forgiven," he said, as he rose from the sofa.

"Yes," she answered quietly, "you are forgiven."

"I have not lowered myself in your estimation, Agnes?"

"Oh, no!"

"Do you wish me to leave you?"

She rose, in her turn, from the sofa, and walked to her writing-table before she replied. The unfinished letter which she had been writing when Lady Montbarry interrupted her, lay open on the blotting-book. As she looked at the letter, and then looked at Henry, the smile that charmed everybody showed itself in her face.

"You must not go just yet," she said: "I have something to tell you. I hardly know how to express it. The shortest way perhaps will be to let you find it out for yourself. You have been speaking of my lonely unprotected life here. It is not a very happy life, Henry—I own that." She paused, observing the growing anxiety of his expression as he looked at her, with a shy satisfaction that perplexed him. "Do you know that I have anticipated your idea?" she went on. "I am going to make a great change in my life—if your brother Stephen and his wife will only consent to it." She opened the desk of the writing-table while she spoke, took a letter out, and handed it to Henry.

He received it from her mechanically. Vague doubts, which he hardly understood himself, kept him silent. It was impossible that the "change in her life" of which she had spoken could mean that she was about to be married—and yet he was conscious of a perfectly unreasonable reluctance to open the letter. Their eyes met; she smiled again. "Look at the address," she said. "You ought to know the handwriting—but I dare say you don't."

He looked at the address. It was in the large, irregular, uncertain writing of a child. He opened the letter instantly.

"Dear Aunt Agnes,——Our governess is going away. She has had money left to her, and a house of her own. We have had cake and wine to drink her health. You promised to be our governess if we wanted another. We want you. Mamma knows nothing about this. Please come before Mamma can get another governess. Your loving Lucy, who writes this. Clara and Blanche have tried to write too. But they are too young to do it. They blot the paper."

"Your eldest niece," Agnes explained, as Henry looked at her in amazement. "The children used to call me aunt when I was staying with their mother in Ireland, in the autumn. The three girls were my inseparable companions—they are the most charming children I know. It is quite true that I offered to be their governess, if they ever wanted one, on the day when I left them to return to London. I was writing to propose it to their mother, just before you came."

"Not seriously!" Henry exclaimed.

Agnes placed her unfinished letter in his hand. Enough of it had been written to show that she did seriously propose to enter the household of Mr. and Mrs. Stephen Westwick as governess to their children! Henry's bewilderment was not to be expressed in words.

"They won't believe you are in earnest," he said.

"Why not?" Agnes asked quietly.

"You are my brother Stephen's cousin; you are his wife's old friend."

"All the more reason, Henry, for trusting me with the charge of their children."

"But you are their equal; you are not obliged to get your living by teaching. There is something absurd in your entering their service as a governess!"

"What is there absurd in it? The children love me; the mother loves me; the father has shown me innumerable instances of his true friendship and regard. I am the very woman for the place—and, as to my education, I must have completely forgotten it indeed, if I am not fit to teach three children the eldest of whom is only eleven years old. You say I am their equal. Are there no other women who serve as governesses, and who are the equals of the persons whom they serve? Besides, I don't know that I *am* their equal. Have I not heard that your brother Stephen was the next heir to the title? Will he not be the new lord? Never mind answering me! We won't dispute whether I am right or wrong in turning governess—we will wait the event. I am weary of my lonely useless existence here, and eager to make my life more happy and more useful, in the household of all others in which I should like most to have a place. If you will look again, you will see that I have these personal considerations still to urge before I finish my letter. You don't know your brother and his wife as well as I do, if you doubt their answer. I believe they have courage enough and heart enough to say Yes."

Henry submitted without being convinced.

He was a man who disliked all eccentric departures from custom and routine; and he felt especially suspicious of the change proposed in the life of Agnes. With new interests to occupy her mind, she might be less favourably disposed to listen to him, on the next occasion when he urged his suit. The influence of the "lonely useless existence" of which she complained, was distinctly an influence in his favour. While her heart was empty, her heart was accessible. But with his nieces in full possession of it, the clouds of doubt overshadowed his prospects. He knew the sex well enough to keep these purely selfish perplexities to himself. The waiting policy was especially the policy to pursue with a woman as sensitive as Agnes. If he once offended her delicacy he was lost. For the moment he wisely controlled himself and changed the subject.

"My little niece's letter has had an effect," he said, "which the child never contemplated in writing it. She has just reminded me of one of the objects that I had in calling on you to-day."

Agnes looked at the child's letter. "How does Lucy do that?" she asked.

"Lucy's governess is not the only lucky person who has had money left her," Henry answered. "Is your old nurse in the house?"

"You don't mean to say that nurse has got a legacy?"

"She has got a hundred pounds. Send for her, Agnes, while I show you the letter."

He took a handful of letters from his pocket, and looked through them, while Agnes rang the bell. Returning to him, she noticed a printed letter among the rest, which lay open on the table. It was a "prospectus," and the title of it was "Palace Hotel Company of Venice (Limited)." The two words, "Palace" and "Venice," instantly recalled her mind to the unwelcome visit of Lady Montbarry. "What is that?" she asked, pointing to the title.

Henry suspended his search, and glanced at the prospectus. "A really promising speculation," he said. "Large hotels always pay well, if they are well managed. I know the man who is appointed to be manager of this hotel when it is opened to the public; and I have such entire confidence in him that I have become one of the shareholders of the Company."

The reply did not appear to satisfy Agnes. "Why is the hotel called the 'Palace Hotel'?" she inquired.

Henry looked at her, and at once penetrated her motive for asking the question. "Yes," he said, "it *is* the palace that Montbarry hired at Venice; and it has been purchased by the Company to be changed into an hotel."

Agnes turned away in silence, and took a chair at the farther end of the room. Henry had disappointed her. His income as a younger son stood in need, as she well knew, of all the additions that he could make to it by successful speculation. But she was unreasonable enough, nevertheless, to disapprove of his attempting to make money already out of the house in which his brother had died. Incapable of understanding this purely sentimental view of a plain matter of business, Henry returned to his papers, in some perplexity at the sudden change in the manner of Agnes towards him. Just as he found the letter of which he was in search, the nurse made her appearance. He glanced at Agnes, expecting that she would speak first. She never even looked up when the nurse came in. It was left to Henry to tell the old woman why the bell had summoned her to the drawing-room.

"Well, nurse," he said, "you have had a windfall of luck. You have had a legacy left you of a hundred pounds."

The nurse showed no outward signs of exultation. She waited a little to get the announcement of the legacy well settled in her mind—and then she said quietly, "Master Henry, who gives me that money, if you please?"

"My late brother, Lord Montbarry, gives it to you." (Agnes instantly looked up, interested in the matter for the first time. Henry went on.) "His will leaves legacies to the surviving old servants of the family. There is a letter from his lawyers, authorising you to apply to them for the money."

In every class of society, gratitude is the rarest of all human virtues. In the nurse's class it is extremely rare. Her opinion of the man who had deceived and deserted her mistress remained the same opinion still, perfectly undisturbed by the passing circumstance of the legacy.

"I wonder who reminded my lord of the old servants?" she said. "He would never have heart enough to remember them himself!"

Agnes suddenly interposed. Nature, always abhorring monotony, institutes reserves of temper as elements in the composition of the gentlest women living. Even Agnes could, on rare occasions, be angry. The nurse's view of Montbarry's character seemed to have provoked her beyond endurance.

"If you have any sense of shame in you," she broke out, "you ought to be ashamed of what you have just said! Your ingratitude disgusts me. I leave you to speak with her, Henry—*you* won't mind it!" With this significant intimation that he too had dropped out of his customary place in her good opinion, she left the room.

The nurse received the smart reproof administered to her with every appearance of feeling rather amused by it than not. When the door had closed, this female philosopher winked at Henry.

"There's a power of obstinacy in young women," she remarked. "Miss Agnes wouldn't give my lord up as a bad one, even when he jilted her. And now she's sweet on him after he's dead. Say a word against him, and she fires up as you see. All obstinacy! It will wear out with time. Stick to her, Master Henry—stick to her!"

"She doesn't seem to have offended you," said Henry.

"*She?*" the nurse repeated in amazement—"she offend me? I like her in her tantrums; it reminds me of her when she was a baby. Lord bless you! when I go to bid her good-night, she'll give me a big kiss, poor dear—and say, Nurse, I didn't mean it! About this money, Master Henry? If I was younger I should spend it in dress and jewellery. But I'm too old for that. What shall I do with my legacy when I have got it?"

"Put it out at interest," Henry suggested. "Get so much a year for it, you know."

"How much shall I get?" the nurse asked.

"If you put your hundred pounds into the Funds, you will get between three and four pounds a year."

The nurse shook her head. "Three or four pounds a year? That won't do! I want more than that. Look here, Master Henry. I don't care about this bit of money—I never did like the man who has left it to me, though he *was* your brother. If I lost it all to-morrow, I shouldn't break my heart; I'm well enough off, as it is, for the rest of my days. They say you're a speculator. Put me in for a good thing, there's a dear! Neck-or-nothing—and *that* for the Funds!" She snapped her fingers to express her contempt for security of investment at three per cent.

Henry produced the prospectus of the Venetian Hotel Company. "You're a funny old woman," he said. "There, you dashing speculator—there is neck-or-nothing for you! You must keep it a secret from Miss Agnes, mind. I'm not at all sure that she would approve of my helping you to this investment."

The nurse took out her spectacles. "Six per cent. guaranteed," she read; "and the Directors have every reason to believe that ten per cent., or more, will be ultimately realised to the shareholders by the hotel." "Put me into that, Master Henry! And, wherever you go, for Heaven's sake recommend the hotel to your friends!"

So the nurse, following Henry's mercenary example, had *her* pecuniary interest, too, in the house in which Lord Montbarry had died.

Three days passed before Henry was able to visit Agnes again. In that time, the little cloud between them had entirely passed away. Agnes received him with even more than her customary kindness. She was in better spirits than usual. Her letter to Mrs. Stephen Westwick had been answered by return of post; and her proposal had been joyfully accepted, with one modification. She was to visit the Westwicks for a month—and, if she really liked teaching the children, she was then to be governess, aunt, and cousin, all in one—and was only to go away in an event which her friends in Ireland persisted in contemplating, the event of her marriage.

"You see I was right," she said to Henry.

He was still incredulous. "Are you really going?" he asked.

"I am going next week."

"When shall I see you again?"

"You know you are always welcome at your brother's house. You can see me when you like." She held out her hand. "Pardon me for leaving you—I am beginning to pack up already."

Henry tried to kiss her at parting. She drew back directly.

"Why not? I am your cousin," he said.

"I don't like it," she answered.

Henry looked at her, and submitted. Her refusal to grant him his privilege as a cousin was a good sign—it was indirectly an act of encouragement to him in the character of her lover.

On the first day in the new week, Agnes left London on her way to Ireland. As the event proved, this was not destined to be the end of her journey. The way to Ireland was only the first stage on a roundabout road—the road that led to the palace at Venice.

THE THIRD PART

CHAPTER XIII

～～～～～～

In the spring of the year 1861, Agnes was established at the country-seat of her two friends—now promoted (on the death of the first lord, without offspring) to be the new Lord and Lady Montbarry. The old nurse was not separated from her mistress. A place, suited to her time of life, had been found for her in the pleasant Irish household. She was perfectly happy in her new sphere; and she spent her first half-year's dividend from the Venice Hotel Company, with characteristic prodigality, in presents for the children.

Early in the year, also, the Directors of the life insurance offices submitted to circumstances, and paid the ten thousand pounds. Immediately afterwards, the widow of the first Lord Montbarry (otherwise, the dowager Lady Montbarry) left England, with Baron Rivar, for the United States. The Baron's object was announced, in the scientific columns of the newspapers, to be investigation into the present state of experimental chemistry in the great American republic. His sister informed inquiring friends that she accompanied him, in the hope of finding consolation in change of scene after the bereavement that had fallen on her. Hearing this news from Henry Westwick (then paying a visit at his brother's house), Agnes was conscious of a certain sense of relief. "With the Atlantic between us," she said, "surely I have done with that terrible woman now!"

Barely a week passed after those words had been spoken, before an event happened which reminded Agnes of "the terrible woman" once more.

On that day, Henry's engagements had obliged him to return to London. He had ventured, on the morning of his departure, to press his suit once more on Agnes; and the children, as he had anticipated, proved to be innocent obstacles in the way of his success. On the other hand, he had privately secured a firm ally in his sister-in-law. "Have a little patience," the new Lady Montbarry had said, "and leave me to turn the influence of the children in the right direction. If they can persuade her to listen to you—they shall!"

The two ladies had accompanied Henry, and some other guests who went away at the same time, to the railway station, and had just driven back to the house, when the servant announced that "a person of the name of Rolland was waiting to see her ladyship."

"Is it a woman?"

"Yes, my lady."

Young Lady Montbarry turned to Agnes.

"This is the very person," she said, "whom your lawyer thought likely to help him, when he was trying to trace the lost courier."

"You don't mean the English maid who was with Lady Montbarry at Venice?"

"My dear! don't speak of Montbarry's horrid widow by the name which is *my* name now. Stephen and I have arranged to call her by her foreign title, before she was married. I am 'Lady Montbarry,' and she is 'the Countess.' In that way there will be no confusion.—Yes, Mrs. Rolland was in my service before she became the Countess's maid. She was a perfectly trustworthy person, with one defect that obliged me to send her away—a sullen temper which led to perpetual complaints of her in the servants' hall. Would you like to see her?"

Agnes accepted the proposal, in the faint hope of getting some information for the courier's wife. The complete defeat of every attempt to trace the lost man had been accepted as final by Mrs. Ferrari. She had deliberately arrayed herself in widow's mourning; and was earning her livelihood in an employment which the unwearied kindness of Agnes had procured for her in London. The last chance of penetrating the mystery of Ferrari's disappearance seemed to rest now on what Ferrari's former fellow-servant might be able to tell. With highly-wrought expectations, Agnes followed her friend into the room in which Mrs. Rolland was waiting.

A tall bony woman, in the autumn of life, with sunken eyes and iron-grey hair, rose stiffly from her chair, and saluted the ladies with stern submission as they opened the door. A person of unblemished character, evidently—but not without visible draw-backs. Big bushy eyebrows, an awfully deep and solemn voice, a harsh unbending manner, a complete absence in her figure of the undulating lines characteristic of the sex, presented Virtue in this excellent person under its least alluring aspect. Strangers, on a first introduction to her, were accustomed to wonder why she was not a man.

"Are you pretty well, Mrs. Rolland?"

"I am as well as I can expect to be, my lady, at my time of life."

"Is there anything I can do for you?"

"Your ladyship can do me a great favour, if you will please speak to my character while I was in your service. I am offered a place, to wait on an invalid lady who has lately come to live in this neighbourhood."

"Ah, yes—I have heard of her. A Mrs. Carbury, with a very pretty niece I am told. But, Mrs. Rolland, you left my service some time ago. Mrs. Carbury will surely expect you to refer to the last mistress by whom you were employed."

A flash of virtuous indignation irradiated Mrs. Rolland's sunken eyes. She coughed before she answered, as if her "last mistress" stuck in her throat.

"I have explained to Mrs. Carbury, my lady, that the person I last served—I really cannot give her her title in your ladyship's presence!—has left England for America. Mrs. Carbury knows that I quitted the person of my own free will, and knows why, and approves of my conduct so far. A word from your ladyship will be amply sufficient to get me the situation."

"Very well, Mrs. Rolland, I have no objection to be your reference, under the circumstances. Mrs. Carbury will find me at home to-morrow until two o'clock."

"Mrs. Carbury is not well enough to leave the house, my lady.

Her niece, Miss Haldane, will call and make the inquiries, if your ladyship has no objection."

"I have not the least objection. The pretty niece carries her own welcome with her. Wait a minute, Mrs. Rolland. This lady is Miss Lockwood—my husband's cousin, and my friend. She is anxious to speak to you about the courier who was in the late Lord Montbarry's service at Venice."

Mrs. Rolland's bushy eyebrows frowned in stern disapproval of the new topic of conversation. "I regret to hear it, my lady," was all she said.

"Perhaps you have not been informed of what happened after you left Venice?" Agnes ventured to add. "Ferrari left the palace secretly; and he has never been heard of since."

Mrs. Rolland mysteriously closed her eyes—as if to exclude some vision of the lost courier which was of a nature to disturb a respectable woman. "Nothing that Mr. Ferrari could do would surprise me," she replied in her deepest bass tones.

"You speak rather harshly of him," said Agnes.

Mrs. Rolland suddenly opened her eyes again. "I speak harshly of nobody without reason," she said. "Mr. Ferrari behaved to me, Miss Lockwood, as no man living has ever behaved—before or since."

"What did he do?"

Mrs. Rolland answered, with a stony stare of horror:—

"He took liberties with me."

Young Lady Montbarry suddenly turned aside, and put her handkerchief over her mouth in convulsions of suppressed laughter.

Mrs. Rolland went on, with a grim enjoyment of the bewilderment which her reply had produced in Agnes: "And when I insisted on an apology, Miss, he had the audacity to say that the life at the palace was dull, and he didn't know how else to amuse himself!"

"I am afraid I have hardly made myself understood," said Agnes. "I am not speaking to you out of any interest in Ferrari. Are you aware that he is married?"

"I pity his wife," said Mrs. Rolland.

"She is naturally in great grief about him," Agnes proceeded.

"She ought to thank God she is rid of him," Mrs. Rolland interposed.

Agnes still persisted. "I have known Mrs. Ferrari from her childhood, and I am sincerely anxious to help her in this matter. Did you notice anything, while you were at Venice, that would account for her husband's extraordinary disappearance? On what sort of terms, for instance, did he live with his master and mistress?"

"On terms of familiarity with his mistress," said Mrs. Rolland, "which were simply sickening to a respectable English servant. She used to encourage him to talk to her about all his affairs—how he got on with his wife, and how pressed he was for money, and such like—just as if they were equals. Contemptible—that's what I call it."

"And his master?" Agnes continued. "How did Ferrari get on with Lord Montbarry?"

"My lord used to live shut up with his studies and his sorrows," Mrs. Rolland answered, with a hard solemnity expressive of respect for his lordship's memory. Mr. Ferrari got his money when it was due; and he cared for nothing else. "If I could afford it, I would leave the place too; but I can't afford it." Those were the last words he said to me, on the morning when I left the palace. I made no reply. After what had happened (on that other occasion) I was naturally not on speaking terms with Mr. Ferrari."

"Can you really tell me nothing which will throw any light on this matter?"

"Nothing," said Mrs. Rolland, with an undisguised relish of the disappointment that she was inflicting.

"There was another member of the family at Venice," Agnes resumed, determined to sift the question to the bottom while she had the chance. "There was Baron Rivar."

Mrs. Rolland lifted her large hands, covered with rusty black gloves, in mute protest against the introduction of Baron Rivar as a subject of inquiry. "Are you aware, Miss," she began, "that I left my place in consequence of what I observed——?"

Agnes stopped her there. "I only wanted to ask," she explained, "if anything was said or done by Baron Rivar which might account for Ferrari's strange conduct."

"Nothing that I know of," said Mrs. Rolland. "The Baron and Mr. Ferrari (if I may use such an expression) were 'birds of a feather,' so far as I could see—I mean, one was as unprincipled as the other. I am a just woman; and I will give you an example. Only the day before I left, I heard the Baron say (through the open door of his room while I was passing along the corridor), 'Ferrari, I want a thousand pounds. What would you do for a thousand pounds?' And I heard Mr. Ferrari answer, 'Anything, sir, as long as I was not found out.' And then they both burst out laughing. I heard no more than that. Judge for yourself, Miss."

Agnes reflected for a moment. A thousand pounds was the sum that had been sent to Mrs. Ferrari in the anonymous letter. Was that enclosure in any way connected, as a result, with the conversation between the Baron and Ferrari? It was useless to press any more inquiries on Mrs. Rolland. She could give no further information which was of the slightest importance to the object in view. There was no alternative but to grant her her dismissal. One more effort had been made to find a trace of the lost man, and once again the effort had failed.

They were a family party at the dinner-table that day. The only guest left in the house was a nephew of the new Lord Montbarry —the eldest son of his sister, Lady Barville. Lady Montbarry could not resist telling the story of the first (and last) attack made on the virtue of Mrs. Rolland, with a comically-exact imitation of Mrs. Rolland's deep and dismal voice. Being asked by her husband what was the object which had brought that formidable person to the house, she naturally mentioned the expected visit of Miss Haldane. Arthur Barville, unusually silent and pre-occupied so far, suddenly struck into the conversation with a burst of enthusiasm. "Miss Haldane is the most charming girl in all Ireland!" he said. "I caught sight of her yesterday, over the wall of her garden, as I was riding by. What time is she coming to-morrow? Before two? I'll look into the drawing-room by accident—I am dying to be introduced to her!"

Agnes was amused by his enthusiasm. "Are you in love with

Miss Haldane already?" she asked.

Arthur answered gravely, "It's no joking matter. I have been all day at the garden wall, waiting to see her again! It depends on Miss Haldane to make me the happiest or the wretchedest man living."

"You foolish boy! How can you talk such nonsense?"

He was talking nonsense undoubtedly. But, if Agnes had only known it, he was doing something more than that. He was innocently leading her another stage nearer on the way to Venice.

CHAPTER XIV

As the summer months advanced, the transformation of the Venetian palace into the modern hotel proceeded rapidly towards completion.

The outside of the building, with its fine Palladian front looking on the canal, was wisely left unaltered. Inside, as a matter of necessity, the rooms were almost rebuilt—so far at least as the size and the arrangement of them were concerned. The vast saloons were partitioned off into "apartments" containing three or four rooms each. The broad corridors in the upper regions afforded spare space enough for rows of little bedchambers, devoted to servants and to travellers with limited means. Nothing was spared but the solid floors and the finely-carved ceilings. These last, in excellent preservation as to workmanship, merely required cleaning, and regilding here and there, to add greatly to the beauty and importance of the best rooms in the hotel. The only exception to the complete re-organisation of the interior was at one extremity of the edifice, on the first and second floors. Here there happened, in each case, to be rooms of such comparatively moderate size, and so attractively decorated, that the architect suggested leaving them as they were. It was afterwards discovered that these were no other than the apartments formerly occupied by Lord Montbarry (on the first floor), and by Baron Rivar (on the second). The room in which Montbarry had died was still fitted up as a bedroom, and was now distinguished as Number Fourteen. The room above it, in which the Baron had slept, took its place on the hotel-register as Number Thirty-Eight. With the ornaments on the walls and ceilings cleaned and brightened up, and with the heavy old-fashioned beds, chairs, and tables replaced by bright, pretty, and luxurious modern furniture, these two promised to be at once the most attractive and the most comfortable bed-chambers in the hotel. As for the once-desolate and disused ground floor of the building, it was now transformed, by means of splendid dining-rooms, reception-rooms, billiard-rooms, and smoking-rooms, into a palace by itself. Even the dungeon-like vaults beneath, now lighted and ventilated on the most approved modern plan, had been turned as if by magic into kitchens, servants' offices, ice-rooms, and wine cellars, worthy of the splendour of the grandest hotel in Italy, in the now bygone period of seventeen years since.

Passing from the lapse of the summer months at Venice, to the lapse of the summer months in Ireland, it is next to be recorded that Mrs. Rolland obtained the situation of attendant on the invalid Mrs. Carbury; and that the fair Miss Haldane, like a female Caesar, came, saw, and conquered, on her first day's visit to the new Lord Montbarry's house.

The ladies were as loud in her praises as Arthur Barville himself. Lord Montbarry declared that she was the only perfectly pretty woman he had ever seen, who was really unconscious of her own attractions. The old nurse said she looked as if she had just stepped out of a picture, and wanted nothing but a gilt frame round her to make her complete. Miss Haldane, on her side, returned from her first visit to the Montbarrys charmed with her new acquaintances. Later on the same day, Arthur called with an offering of fruit and flowers for Mrs. Carbury, and with instructions to ask if she was well enough to receive Lord and Lady Montbarry and Miss Lockwood on the morrow. In a week's time, the two households were on the friendliest terms. Mrs. Carbury, confined to the sofa by a spinal malady, had been hitherto dependent on her niece for one of the few pleasures she could enjoy, the pleasure of having the best new novels read to her as they came out. Discovering this, Arthur volunteered to relieve Miss Haldane, at intervals, in the office of reader. He was clever at mechanical contrivances of all sorts, and he introduced improvements in Mrs. Carbury's couch, and in the means of conveying her from the bedchamber to the drawing-room, which alleviated the poor lady's sufferings and brightened her gloomy life. With these claims on the gratitude of the aunt, aided by the personal advantages which he unquestionably possessed, Arthur advanced rapidly in the favour of the charming niece. She was, it is needless to say, perfectly well aware that he was in love with her, while he was himself modestly reticent on the subject—so far as words went. But she was not equally quick in penetrating the nature of her own feelings towards Arthur. Watching the two young people with keen powers of observation, necessarily concentrated on them by the complete seclusion of her life, the invalid lady discovered signs of roused sensibility in Miss Haldane, when Arthur was present, which had never yet shown themselves in her social relations with other admirers eager to pay their addresses to her. Having drawn her own conclusions in private, Mrs. Carbury took the first favourable opportunity (in Arthur's interests) of putting them to the test.

"I don't know what I shall do," she said one day, "when Arthur goes away."

Miss Haldane looked up quickly from her work. "Surely he is not going to leave us!" she exclaimed.

"My dear! he has already stayed at his uncle's house a month longer than he intended. His father and mother naturally expect to see him at home again."

Miss Haldane met this difficulty with a suggestion, which could only have proceeded from a judgment already disturbed by the ravages of the tender passion. "Why can't his father and mother go and see him at Lord Montbarry's?" she asked. "Sir Theodore's place is only thirty miles away, and Lady Barville is Lord Montbarry's sister. They needn't stand on ceremony."

"They may have other engagements," Mrs. Carbury remarked.

"My dear aunt, we don't know that! Suppose you ask Arthur?"

"Suppose *you* ask him?"

Miss Haldane bent her head again over her work. Suddenly as it was done, her aunt had seen her face—and her face betrayed her.

When Arthur came the next day, Mrs. Carbury said a word to him in private, while her niece was in the garden. The last new novel lay neglected on the table. Arthur followed Miss Haldane into the garden. The next day he wrote home, enclosing in his letter a photograph of Miss Haldane. Before the end of the week, Sir Theodore and Lady Barville arrived at Lord Montbarry's, and formed their own judgment of the fidelity of the portrait. They had themselves married early in life—and, strange to say, they did not object on principle to the early marriages of other people. The question of age being thus disposed of, the course of true love had no other obstacles to encounter. Miss Haldane was an only child, and was possessed of an ample fortune. Arthur's career at the university had been creditable, but certainly not brilliant enough to present his withdrawal in the light of a disaster. As Sir Theodore's eldest son, his position was already made for him. He was two-and-twenty years of age; and the young lady was eighteen. There was really no producible reason for keeping the lovers waiting, and no excuse for deferring the wedding-day beyond the first week in September. In the interval, while the bride and bridegroom would be necessarily absent on the inevitable tour abroad, a sister of Mrs. Carbury volunteered to stay with her during the temporary separation from her niece. On the conclusion of the honeymoon, the young couple were to return to Ireland, and were to establish themselves in Mrs. Carbury's spacious and comfortable house.

These arrangements were decided upon early in the month of August. About the same date, the last alterations in the old palace at Venice were completed. The rooms were dried by steam; the cellars were stocked; the manager collected round him his army of skilled servants; and the new hotel was advertised all over Europe to open in October.

CHAPTER XV

~~~~~~~~~~

(MISS AGNES LOCKWOOD TO MRS. FERRARI)

"I promised to give you some account, dear Emily, of the marriage of Mr. Arthur Barville and Miss Haldane. It took place ten days since. But I have had so many things to look after in the absence of the master and mistress of this house, that I am only able to write to you to-day.

"The invitations to the wedding were limited to members of the families on either side, in consideration of the ill health of Miss Haldane's aunt. On the side of the Montbarry family, there were present, besides Lord and Lady Montbarry, Sir Theodore and Lady Barville; Mrs. Norbury (whom you may remember as his lordship's second sister); and Mr. Francis Westwick, and Mr Henry Westwick. The three children and I attended the ceremony as bridesmaids. We were joined by two young ladies, cousins of the bride and very agreeable girls. Our dresses were white, trimmed with green in honour of Ireland; and we each had a handsome gold bracelet given to us as a present from the bridegroom. If you add to the persons whom I have already mentioned, the elder members of Mrs. Carbury's family, and the old servants in both houses—privileged to drink the healths of the married pair at the lower end of the room—you will have the list of the company at the wedding-breakfast complete.

"The weather was perfect, and the ceremony (with music) was beautifully performed. As for the bride, no words can describe how lovely she looked, or how well she went through it all. We were very merry at the breakfast, and the speeches went off on the whole quite well enough. The last speech, before the party broke up, was made by Mr. Henry Westwick, and was the best of all. He offered a happy suggestion, at the end, which has produced a very unexpected change in my life here.

"As well as I remember, he concluded in these words:—'On one point, we are all agreed—we are sorry that the parting hour is near, and we should be glad to meet again. Why should we not meet again? This is the autumn time of the year; we are most of us leaving home for the holidays. What do you say (if you have no engagements that will prevent it) to joining our young married friends before the close of their tour, and renewing the social success of this delightful breakfast by another festival in honour of the honeymoon? The bride and bridegroom are going to Germany and the Tyrol, on their way to Italy. I propose that we allow them a month to themselves, and that we arrange to meet them afterwards in the North of Italy—say at Venice.'

"This proposal was received with great applause, which was changed into shouts of laughter by no less a person than my dear old nurse. The moment Mr. Westwick pronounced the word "Venice," she started up among the servants at the lower end of the room, and called out at the top of her voice, 'Go to our hotel, ladies and gentlemen! We get six per cent. on our money already; and if you will only crowd the place and call for the best of everything, it will be ten per cent in our pockets in no time. Ask Master Henry!'

"Appealed to in this irresistible manner, Mr. Westwick had no choice but to explain that he was concerned as a shareholder in a new Hotel Company at Venice, and that he had invested a small sum of money for the nurse (not very considerately, as I think) in the speculation. Hearing this, the company, by way of humouring the joke, drank a new toast:—Success to the nurse's hotel, and a speedy rise in the dividend!

"When the conversation returned in due time to the more serious question of the proposed meeting at Venice, difficulties began to present themselves, caused of course by invitations for the autumn which many of the guests had already accepted. Only two members of Mrs. Carbury's family were at liberty to keep the proposed appointment. On our side we were more at leisure to do as we pleased. Mr. Henry Westwick decided to go to Venice in advance of the rest, to test the accommodation of the new hotel on the opening day. Mrs. Norbury and Mr. Francis Westwick volunteered to follow him; and, after some persuasion, Lord and Lady Montbarry consented to a species of compromise. His lordship could not conveniently spare time enough for the journey to Venice, but he and Lady Montbarry arranged to accompany Mrs. Norbury and Mr. Francis Westwick as far on their way to Italy as Paris. Five days since, they took their departure to meet their travelling companions in London; leaving me here in charge of the three dear children. They begged hard, of course, to be taken with papa and mamma. But it was thought better not to interrupt the progress of their education, and not to expose them (especially the two younger girls) to the fatigues of travelling.

"I have had a charming letter from the bride, this morning, dated Cologne. You cannot think how artlessly and prettily she assures me of her happiness. Some people, as they say in Ireland, are born to good luck—and I think Arthur Barville is one of them.

"When you next write, I hope to hear that you are in better health and spirits, and that you continue to like your employment. Believe me, sincerely your friend,——A. L."

Agnes had just closed and directed her letter, when the eldest of her three pupils entered the room with the startling announcement that Lord Montbarry's travelling-servant had arrived from Paris! Alarmed by the idea that some misfortune had happened, she ran out to meet the man in the hall. Her face told him how seriously he had frightened her, before she could speak. "There's nothing wrong, Miss," he hastened to say. "My lord and my lady are enjoying themselves at Paris. They only want you and the young ladies to be with them." Saying these amazing words, he handed to Agnes a letter from Lady Montbarry.

"Dearest Agnes," (she read), "I am so charmed with the delightful change in my life—it is six years, remember, since I last travelled on the Continent—that I have exerted all my fascinations to persuade Lord Montbarry to go on to Venice. And, what is more to the purpose, I have actually succeeded! He has just gone to his room to write the necessary letters of excuse in time for the post to England. May you have as good a husband, my dear, when your time comes! In the mean while, the one thing wanting now to make my happiness complete, is to have you and the darling children with us. Montbarry is just as miserable without them as I am—though he doesn't confess it so freely. You will have no difficulties to trouble you. Louis will deliver these hurried lines, and will take care of you on the journey to Paris. Kiss the children for me a thousand times—and never mind their education for the present! Pack up instantly, my dear, and I will be fonder of you than ever. Your affectionate friend, Adela Montbarry."

Agnes folded up the letter; and, feeling the need of composing herself, took refuge for a few minutes in her own room.

Her first natural sensations of surprise and excitement at the prospect of going to Venice were succeeded by impressions of a less agreeable kind. With the recovery of her customary composure came the unwelcome remembrance of the parting words spoken to her by Montbarry's widow:—'We shall meet again—here in England, or there in Venice where my husband died—and meet for the last time."

It was an odd coincidence, to say the least of it, that the march of events should be unexpectedly taking Agnes to Venice, after those words had been spoken! Was the woman of the mysterious warnings and the wild black eyes still thousands of miles away in America? Or was the march of events taking *her* unexpectedly, too, on the journey to Venice? Agnes started out of her chair, ashamed of even the momentary concession to superstition which was implied by the mere presence of such questions as these in her mind.

She rang the bell, and sent for her little pupils, and announced their approaching departure to the household. The noisy delight of the children, the inspiriting effort of packing up in a hurry, roused all her energies. She dismissed her own absurd misgivings from consideration, with the contempt that they deserved. She worked as only women *can* work, when their hearts are in what they do. The travellers reached Dublin that day, in time for the boat to England. Two days later, they were with Lord and Lady Montbarry at Paris.

THE FOURTH PART

CHAPTER XVI

∽∾∽∾∽

It was only the twentieth of September, when Agnes and the children reached Paris. Mrs. Norbury and her brother Francis had then already started on their journey to Italy—at least three weeks before the date at which the new hotel was to open for the reception of travellers.

The person answerable for this premature departure was Francis Westwick.

Like his younger brother Henry, he had increased his pecuniary resources by his own enterprise and ingenuity; with this difference, that his speculations were connected with the Arts. He had made money, in the first instance, by a weekly newspaper; and he had then invested his profits in a London theatre. This latter enterprise, admirably conducted, had been rewarded by the public with steady and liberal encouragement. Pondering over a new form of theatrical attraction for the coming winter season, Francis had determined to revive the languid public taste for the ballet by means of an entertainment of his own invention, combining dramatic interest with dancing. He was now, accordingly, in search of the best dancer (possessed of the indispensable personal attractions) who was to be found in the theatres of the Continent. Hearing from his foreign correspondents of two women who had made successful first appearances, one at Milan and one at Florence, he had arranged to visit those cities, and to judge of the merits of the dancers for himself, before he joined the bride and bridegroom. His widowed sister, having friends at Florence whom she was anxious to see, readily accompanied him. The Montbarrys remained at Paris, until it was time to present themselves at the family meeting in Venice. Henry found them still in the French capital, when he arrived from London on his way to the opening of the new hotel.

Against Lady Montbarry's advice, he took the opportunity of renewing his addresses to Agnes. He could hardly have chosen a more unpropitious time for pleading his cause with her. The gaieties of Paris (quite incomprehensibly to herself as well as to everyone about her) had a depressing effect on her spirits. She had no illness to complain of; she shared willingly in the ever-varying succession of amusements offered to strangers by the ingenuity of the liveliest people in the world—but nothing roused her: she remained persistently dull and weary through it all. In this frame of mind and body, she was in no humour to receive Henry's ill-timed addresses with favour, or even with patience: she plainly and positively refused to listen to him. "Why do you remind me of what I have suffered?" she asked petulantly. "Don't you see that it has left its mark on me for life?"

"I thought I knew something of women by this time," Henry said, appealing privately to Lady Montbarry for consolation. "But Agnes completely puzzles me. It is a year since Montbarry's death; and she remains as devoted to his memory as if he had died faithful to her—she still feels the loss of him, as none of *us* feel it!"

"She is the truest woman that ever breathed the breath of life," Lady Montbarry answered. "Remember that, and you will understand her. Can such a woman as Agnes give her love or refuse it, according to circumstances? Because the man was unworthy of her, was he less the man of her choice? The truest and best friend to him (little as he deserved it) in his lifetime, she naturally remains the truest and best friend to his memory now. If you really love her, wait; and trust to your two best friends—to time and to me. There is my advice; let your own experience decide whether it is not the best advice that I can offer. Resume your journey to Venice to-morrow; and when you take leave of Agnes, speak to her as cordially as if nothing had happened."

Henry wisely followed this advice. Thoroughly understanding him, Agnes made the leave-taking friendly and pleasant on her side. When he stopped at the door for a last look at her, she hurriedly turned her head so that her face was hidden from him. Was that a good sign? Lady Montbarry, accompanying Henry down the stairs, said, "Yes, decidedly! Write when you get to Venice. We shall wait here to receive letters from Arthur and his wife, and we shall time our departure for Italy accordingly."

A week passed, and no letter came from Henry. Some days later, a telegram was received from him. It was despatched from Milan, instead of from Venice; and it brought this strange message: —"I have left the hotel. Will return on the arrival of Arthur and his wife. Address, meanwhile, Albergo Reale, Milan."

Preferring Venice before all other cities of Europe, and having arranged to remain there until the family meeting took place, what unexpected event had led Henry to alter his plans? and why did he state the bare fact, without adding a word of explanation? Let the narrative follow him—and find the answer to those questions at Venice.

CHAPTER XVII

∽∾∾∽∾∾∾

THE Palace Hotel, appealing for encouragement mainly to English and American travellers, celebrated the opening of its doors, as a matter of course, by the giving of a grand banquet, and the delivery of a long succession of speeches.

Delayed on his journey, Henry Westwick only reached Venice in time to join the guests over their coffee and cigars. Observing the splendour of the reception rooms, and taking note especially of the artful mixture of comfort and luxury in the bedchambers, he began to share the old nurse's view of the future, and to contemplate seriously the coming dividend of ten per cent. The hotel was beginning well, at all events. So much interest in the enterprise had been aroused, at home and abroad, by profuse advertising, that the whole accommodation of the building had been secured by travellers of all nations for the opening night. Henry only obtained one of the small rooms on the upper floor, by a lucky accident—the absence of the gentleman who had written to engage it. He was quite satisfied, and was on his way to bed, when another accident altered his prospects for the night, and moved him into another and a better room.

Ascending on his way to the higher regions as far as the first floor of the hotel, Henry's attention was attracted by an angry voice protesting, in a strong New England accent, against one of the greatest hardships that can be inflicted on a citizen of the United States—the hardship of sending him to bed without gas in his room.

The Americans are not only the most hospitable people to be found on the face of the earth—they are (under certain conditions) the most patient and good-tempered people as well. But they are human; and the limit of American endurance is found in the obsolete institution of a bedroom candle. The American traveller, in the present case, declined to believe that his bedroom was in a completely finished state without a gas-burner. The manager pointed to the fine antique decorations (renewed and regilt) on the walls and the ceiling, and explained that the emanations of burning gas-light would certainly spoil them in the course of a few months. To this the traveller replied that it was possible, but that he did not understand decorations. A bedroom with gas in it was what he was used to, was what he wanted, and was what he was determined to have. The compliant manager volunteered to ask some other gentleman, housed on the inferior upper storey (which was lit throughout with gas), to change rooms. Hearing this, and being quite willing to exchange a small bedchamber for a large one, Henry volunteered to be the other gentleman. The excellent American shook hands with him on the spot. "You are a cultured person, sir," he said; "and *you* will no doubt understand the decorations."

Henry looked at the number of the room on the door as he opened it. The number was Fourteen.

Tired and sleepy, he naturally anticipated a good night's rest. In the thoroughly healthy state of his nervous system, he slept as well in a bed abroad as in a bed at home. Without the slightest assign-able reason, however, his just expectations were disappointed. The luxurious bed, the well-ventilated room, the delicious tranquillity of Venice by night, all were in favour of his sleeping well. He never slept at all. An indescribable sense of depression and discomfort kept him waking through darkness and daylight alike. He went down to the coffee-room as soon as the hotel was astir, and ordered some breakfast. Another unaccountable change in himself appeared with the appearance of the meal. He was absolutely without appetite. An excellent omelette, and cutlets cooked to perfection, he sent away untasted—he, whose appetite never failed him, whose digestion was still equal to any demands on it!

The day was bright and fine. He sent for a gondola, and was rowed to the Lido.

Out on the airy Lagoon, he felt like a new man. He had not left the hotel ten minutes before he was fast asleep in the gondola. Waking, on reaching the landing-place, he crossed the Lido, and enjoyed a morning's swim in the Adriatic. There was only a poor restaurant on the island, in those days; but his appetite was now ready for anything; he ate whatever was offered to him, like a famished man. He could hardly believe, when he reflected on it, that he had sent away untasted his excellent breakfast at the hotel.

Returning to Venice, he spent the rest of the day in the picture-galleries and the churches. Towards six o'clock his gondola took him back, with another fine appetite, to meet some travelling acquaintances with whom he had engaged to dine at the table d'hôte.

The dinner was deservedly rewarded with the highest approval by every guest in the hotel but one. To Henry's astonishment, the appetite with which he had entered the house mysteriously and completely left him when he sat down to table. He could drink some wine, but he could literally eat nothing. "What in the world is the matter with you?" his travelling acquaintances asked. He could honestly answer, "I know no more than you do."

When night came, he gave his comfortable and beautiful bedroom another trial. The result of the second experiment was a repetition of the result of the first. Again he felt the all-pervading sense of depression and discomfort. Again he passed a sleepless night. And once more, when he tried to eat his breakfast, his appetite completely failed him!

This personal experience of the new hotel was too extraordinary to be passed over in silence. Henry mentioned it to his friends in the public room, in the hearing of the manager. The manager, naturally zealous in defence of the hotel, was a little hurt at the implied reflection cast on Number Fourteen. He invited the travellers present to judge for themselves whether Mr. Westwick's bedroom was to blame for Mr. Westwick's sleepless nights; and he especially appealed to a grey-headed gentleman, a guest at the breakfast-table of an English traveller, to take the lead in the investigation. "This is Doctor Bruno, our first physician in Venice," he explained. "I appeal to him to say if there are any unhealthy influences in Mr. Westwick's room."

Introduced to Number Fourteen, the doctor looked round him with a certain appearance of interest which was noticed by everyone present. "The last time I was in this room," he said, "was on a melancholy occasion. It was before the palace was changed into an hotel. I was in professional attendance on an English nobleman who died here." One of the persons present inquired the name of the nobleman. Doctor Bruno answered (without the slightest suspicion that he was speaking before a brother of the dead man), "Lord Montbarry."

Henry quietly left the room, without saying a word to anybody.

He was not, in any sense of the term, a superstitious man. But he felt, nevertheless, an insurmountable reluctance to remaining in the hotel. He decided on leaving Venice. To ask for another room would be, as he could plainly see, an offence in the eyes of the manager. To remove to another hotel, would be to openly abandon an establishment in the success of which he had a pecuniary interest. Leaving a note for Arthur Barville, on his arrival in Venice, in which he merely mentioned that he had gone to look at the Italian lakes, and that a line addressed to his hotel at Milan would bring him back again, he took the afternoon train to Padua—and dined with his usual appetite, and slept as well as ever that night.

The next day, a gentleman and his wife (perfect strangers to the Montbarry family), returning to England by way of Venice, arrived at the hotel and occupied Number Fourteen.

Still mindful of the slur that had been cast on one of his best bedchambers, the manager took occasion to ask the travellers the next morning how they liked their room. They left him to judge for himself how well they were satisfied, by remaining a day longer in Venice than they had originally planned to do, solely for the purpose of enjoying the excellent accommodation offered to them by the new hotel. "We have met with nothing like it in Italy," they said; "you may rely on our recommending you to all our friends."

On the day when Number Fourteen was again vacant, an English lady travelling alone with her maid arrived at the hotel, saw the room, and at once engaged it.

The lady was Mrs. Norbury. She had left Francis Westwick at Milan, occupied in negotiating for the appearance at his theatre of the new dancer at the Scala. Not having heard to the contrary, Mrs. Norbury supposed that Arthur Barville and his wife had already arrived at Venice. She was more interested in meeting the young married couple than in awaiting the result of the hard bargaining which delayed the engagement of the new dancer; and she volunteered to make her brother's apologies, if his theatrical business caused him to be late in keeping his appointment at the honeymoon festival.

Mrs. Norbury's experience of Number Fourteen differed entirely from her brother Henry's experience of the room.

Failing asleep as readily as usual, her repose was disturbed by a succession of frightful dreams; the central figure in every one of them being the figure of her dead brother, the first Lord Montbarry. She saw him starving in a loathsome prison; she saw him pursued by assassins, and dying under their knives; she saw him drowning in immeasurable depths of dark water; she saw him in a bed on fire, burning to death in the flames; she saw him tempted by a shadowy creature to drink, and dying of the poisonous draught. The reiterated horror of these dreams had such an effect on her that she rose with the dawn of day, afraid to trust herself again in bed. In the old times, she had been noted in the family as the one member of it who lived on affectionate terms with Montbarry. His other sister and his brothers were constantly quarrelling with him. Even his mother owned that her eldest son was of all her children the child whom she least liked. Sensible and resolute woman as she was, Mrs. Norbury shuddered with terror as she sat at the window of her room, watching the sunrise, and thinking of her dreams.

She made the first excuse that occurred to her, when her maid came in at the usual hour, and noticed how ill she looked. The woman was of so superstitious a temperament that it would have been in the last degree indiscreet to trust her with the truth. Mrs. Norbury merely remarked that she had not found the bed quite to her liking, on account of the large size of it. She was accustomed at home, as her maid knew, to sleep in a small bed. Informed of this objection later in the day, the manager regretted that he could only offer to the lady the choice of one other bedchamber, numbered Thirty-eight, and situated immediately over the bedchamber which she desired to leave. Mrs. Norbury accepted the proposed change of quarters. She was now about to pass her second night in the room occupied in the old days of the palace by Baron Rivar.

Once more, she fell asleep as usual. And, once more, the frightful dreams of the first night terrified her, following each other in the same succession. This time her nerves, already shaken, were not equal to the renewed torture of terror inflicted on them. She threw on her dressing-gown, and rushed out of her room in the middle of the night. The porter, alarmed by the banging of the door, met her hurrying headlong down the stairs, in search of the first human being she could find to keep her company. Considerably surprised at this last new manifestation of the famous "English eccentricity," the man looked at the hotel register, and led the lady upstairs again to the room occupied by her maid. The maid was not asleep, and, more wonderful still, was not even undressed. She received her mistress quietly. When they were alone, and when Mrs. Norbury had, as a matter of necessity, taken her attendant into her confidence, the woman made a very strange reply.

"I have been asking about the hotel, at the servants' supper to-night," she said. "The valet of one of the gentlemen staying here has heard that the late Lord Montbarry was the last person who lived in the palace, before it was made into an hotel. The room he died in, ma'am, was the room you slept in last night. Your room tonight is the room just above it. I said nothing for fear of frightening you. For my own part, I have passed the night as you see, keeping my light in, and reading my Bible. In my opinion, no member of your family can hope to be happy or comfortable in this house."

"What do you mean?"

"Please to let me explain myself, ma'am. When Mr. Henry Westwick was here (I have this from the valet, too) he occupied the room his brother died in (without knowing it), like you. For two nights he never closed his eyes. Without any reason for it (the valet heard him tell the gentlemen in the coffee-room) he could *not* sleep; he felt so low and so wretched in himself. And what is more, when daytime came, he couldn't even eat while he was under this roof. You may laugh at me, ma'am—but even a servant may draw her own conclusions. It's my conclusion that something happened to my lord, which we none of us know about, when he died in this house. His ghost walks in torment until he can tell it—and the living persons related to him are the persons who feel he is near them. Those persons may yet see him in the time to come. Don't, pray don't stay any longer in this dreadful place! I wouldn't stay another night here myself—no, not for anything that could be offered me!"

Mrs. Norbury at once set her servant's mind at ease on this last point.

"I don't think about it as you do," she said gravely. "But I should like to speak to my brother of what has happened. We will go back to Milan."

Some hours necessarily elapsed before they could leave the hotel, by the first train in the forenoon.

In that interval, Mrs. Norbury's maid found an opportunity of confidentially informing the valet of what had passed between her mistress and herself. The valet had other friends to whom he related the circumstances in his turn. In due course of time, the narrative, passing from mouth to mouth, reached the ears of the manager. He instantly saw that the credit of the hotel was in danger, unless something was done to retrieve the character of the room numbered Fourteen. English travellers, well acquainted with the peerage of their native country, informed him that Henry Westwick and Mrs. Norbury were by no means the only members of the Montbarry family. Curiosity might bring more of them to the hotel, after hearing what had happened. The manager's ingenuity easily hit on the obvious means of misleading them, in this case. The numbers of all the rooms were enamelled in blue, on white china plates, screwed to the doors. He ordered a new plate to be prepared, bearing the number, "13 A'; and he kept the room empty, after its tenant for the time being had gone away, until the plate was ready. He then re-numbered the room; placing the removed Number Fourteen on the door of his own room (on the second floor), which, not being to let, had not previously been numbered at all. By this device, Number Fourteen disappeared at once and for ever from the books of the hotel, as the number of a bedroom to let.

Having warned the servants to beware of gossiping with travellers, on the subject of the changed numbers, under penalty of being dismissed, the manager composed his mind with the reflection that he had done his duty to his employers. "Now," he thought to himself, with an excusable sense of triumph, "let the whole family come here if they like! The hotel is a match for them."

CHAPTER XVIII

BEFORE the end of the week, the manager found himself in relations with "the family" once more. A telegram from Milan announced that Mr. Francis Westwick would arrive in Venice on the next day; and would be obliged if Number Fourteen, on the first floor, could be reserved for him, in the event of its being vacant at the time.

The manager paused to consider, before he issued his directions.

The re-numbered room had been last let to a French gentleman. It would be occupied on the day of Mr. Francis Westwick's arrival, but it would be empty again on the day after. Would it be well to reserve the room for the special occupation of Mr. Francis? and when he had passed the night unsuspiciously and comfortably in "No. 13 A," to ask him in the presence of witnesses how he liked his bedchamber? In this case, if the reputation of the room happened to be called in question again, the answer would vindicate it, on the evidence of a member of the very family which had first given Number Fourteen a bad name. After a little reflection, the manager decided on trying the experiment, and directed that "13 A" should be reserved accordingly.

On the next day, Francis Westwick arrived in excellent spirits.

He had signed agreements with the most popular dancer in Italy; he had transferred the charge of Mrs. Norbury to his brother Henry, who had joined him in Milan; and he was now at full liberty to amuse himself by testing in every possible way the extraordinary influence exercised over his relatives by the new hotel. When his brother and sister first told him what their experience had been, he instantly declared that he would go to Venice in the interest of his theatre. The circumstances related to him contained invaluable hints for a ghost-drama. The title occurred to him in the railway: "The Haunted Hotel." Post that in red letters six feet high, on a black ground, all over London—and trust the excitable public to crowd into the theatre!

Received with the politest attention by the manager, Francis met with a disappointment on entering the hotel. "Some mistake, sir. No such room on the first floor as Number Fourteen. The room bearing that number is on the second floor, and has been occupied by me, from the day when the hotel opened. Perhaps you meant number 13 A, on the first floor? It will be at your service to-morrow—a charming room. In the mean time, we will do the best we can for you, to-night."

A man who is the successful manager of a theatre is probably the last man in the civilised universe who is capable of being impressed with favourable opinions of his fellow-creatures. Francis privately set the manager down as a humbug, and the story about the numbering of the rooms as a lie.

On the day of his arrival, he dined by himself in the restaurant, before the hour of the table d'hôte, for the express purpose of questioning the waiter, without being overheard by anybody. The answer led him to the conclusion that "13 A" occupied the situation in the hotel which had been described by his brother and sister as the situation of "14." He asked next for the Visitors' List; and found that the French gentleman who then occupied "13 A," was the proprietor of a theatre in Paris, personally well known to him. Was the gentleman then in the hotel? He had gone out, but would certainly return for the table d'hôte. When the public dinner was over, Francis entered the room, and was welcomed by his Parisian colleague, literally, with open arms. "Come and have a cigar in my room," said the friendly Frenchman. "I want to hear whether you have really engaged that woman at Milan or not." In this easy way, Francis found his opportunity of comparing the interior of the room with the description which he had heard of it at Milan.

Arriving at the door, the Frenchman bethought himself of his travelling companion. "My scene-painter is here with me," he said, "on the look-out for materials. An excellent fellow, who will take it as a kindness if we ask him to join us. I'll tell the porter to send him up when he comes in." He handed the key of his room to Francis. "I will be back in a minute. It's at the end of the corridor—13 A."

Francis entered the room alone. There were the decorations on the walls and the ceiling, exactly as they had been described to him! He had just time to perceive this at a glance, before his attention was diverted to himself and his own sensations, by a grotesquely disagreeable occurrence which took him completely by surprise.

He became conscious of a mysteriously offensive odour in the room, entirely new in his experience of revolting smells. It was composed (if such a thing could be) of two mingling exhalations, which were separately-discoverable exhalations nevertheless. This strange blending of odours consisted of something faintly and unpleasantly aromatic, mixed with another underlying smell, so unutterably sickening that he threw open the window, and put his head out into the fresh air, unable to endure the horribly infected atmosphere for a moment longer.

The French proprietor joined his English friend, with his cigar already lit. He started back in dismay at a sight terrible to his countrymen in general—the sight of an open window. "You English people are perfectly mad on the subject of fresh air!" he exclaimed. "We shall catch our deaths of cold."

Francis turned, and looked at him in astonishment. "Are you really not aware of the smell there is in the room?" he asked.

"Smell!" repeated his brother-manager. "I smell my own good cigar. Try one yourself. And for Heaven's sake shut the window!"

Francis declined the cigar by a sign. "Forgive me," he said. "I will leave you to close the window. I feel faint and giddy—I had better go out." He put his handkerchief over his nose and mouth, and crossed the room to the door.

The Frenchman followed the movements of Francis, in such a state of bewilderment that he actually forgot to seize the opportunity of shutting out the fresh air. "Is it so nasty as that?" he asked, with a broad stare of amazement.

"Horrible!" Francis muttered behind his handkerchief. "I never smelt anything like it in my life!"

There was a knock at the door. The scene-painter appeared. His employer instantly asked him if he smelt anything.

"I smell your cigar. Delicious! Give me one directly!"

"Wait a minute. Besides my cigar, do you smell anything else— vile, abominable, overpowering, indescribable, never-never-never-smelt before?"

The scene-painter appeared to be puzzled by the vehement energy of the language addressed to him. "The room is as fresh and sweet as a room can be," he answered. As he spoke, he looked back with astonishment at Francis Westwick, standing outside in the corridor, and eyeing the interior of the bedchamber with an expression of undisguised disgust.

The Parisian director approached his English colleague, and looked at him with grave and anxious scrutiny.

"You see, my friend, here are two of us, with as good noses as yours, who smell nothing. If you want evidence from more noses, look there!" He pointed to two little English girls, at play in the corridor. "The door of my room is wide open—and you know how fast a smell can travel. Now listen, while I appeal to these innocent noses, in the language of their own dismal island. My little loves, do you sniff a nasty smell here—ha?" The children burst out laughing, and answered emphatically, "No." "My good Westwick," the Frenchman resumed, in his own language, "the conclusion is surely plain? There is something wrong, very wrong, with your own nose. I recommend you to see a medical man."

Having given that advice, he returned to his room, and shut out the horrid fresh air with a loud exclamation of relief. Francis left the hotel, by the lanes that led to the Square of St. Mark. The night-breeze soon revived him. He was able to light a cigar, and to think quietly over what had happened.

CHAPTER XIX

∽∾∽∾∽∾

AVOIDING the crowd under the colonnades, Francis walked slowly up and down the noble open space of the square, bathed in the light of the rising moon.

Without being aware of it himself, he was a thorough materialist. The strange effect produced on him by the room—following on the other strange effects produced on the other relatives of his dead brother—exercised no perplexing influence over the mind of this sensible man. "Perhaps," he reflected, "my temperament is more imaginative than I supposed it to be—and this is a trick played on me by my own fancy? Or, perhaps, my friend is right; something is physically amiss with me? I don't feel ill, certainly. But that is no safe criterion sometimes. I am not going to sleep in that abominable room to-night—I can well wait till to-morrow to decide whether I shall speak to a doctor or not. In the mean time, the hotel doesn't seem likely to supply me with the subject of a piece. A terrible smell from an invisible ghost is a perfectly new idea. But it has one drawback. If I realise it on the stage, I shall drive the audience out of the theatre."

As his strong common sense arrived at this facetious conclusion, he became aware of a lady, dressed entirely in black, who was observing him with marked attention. "Am I right in supposing you to be Mr. Francis Westwick?" the lady asked, at the moment when he looked at her.

"That is my name, madam. May I inquire to whom I have the honour of speaking?"

"We have only met once," she answered a little evasively, "when your late brother introduced me to the members of his family. I wonder if you have quite forgotten my big black eyes and my hideous complexion?" She lifted her veil as she spoke, and turned so that the moonlight rested on her face.

Francis recognised at a glance the woman of all others whom he most cordially disliked—the widow of his dead brother, the first Lord Montbarry. He frowned as he looked at her. His experience on the stage, gathered at innumerable rehearsals with actresses who had sorely tried his temper, had accustomed him to speak roughly to women who were distasteful to him. "I remember you," he said. "I thought you were in America!"

She took no notice of his ungracious tone and manner; she simply stopped him when he lifted his hat, and turned to leave her.

"Let me walk with you for a few minutes," she quietly replied. "I have something to say to you."

He showed her his cigar. "I am smoking," he said.

"I don't mind smoking."

After that, there was nothing to be done (short of downright brutality) but to yield. He did it with the worst possible grace. "Well?" he resumed. "What do you want of me?"

"You shall hear directly, Mr. Westwick. Let me first tell you what my position is. I am alone in the world. To the loss of my husband has now been added another bereavement, the loss of my companion in America, my brother—Baron Rivar."

The reputation of the Baron, and the doubt which scandal had thrown on his assumed relationship to the Countess, were well known to Francis. "Shot in a gambling-saloon?" he asked brutally.

"The question is a perfectly natural one on your part," she said, with the impenetrably ironical manner which she could assume on certain occasions. "As a native of horse-racing England, you belong to a nation of gamblers. My brother died no extraordinary death, Mr. Westwick. He sank, with many other unfortunate people, under a fever prevalent in a Western city which we happened to visit. The calamity of his loss made the United States unendurable to me. I left by the first steamer that sailed from New York—a French vessel which brought me to Havre. I continued my lonely journey to the South of France. And then I went on to Venice."

"What does all this matter to me?" Francis thought to himself. She paused, evidently expecting him to say something. "So you have come to Venice?" he said carelessly. "Why?"

"Because I couldn't help it," she answered.

Francis looked at her with cynical curiosity. "That sounds odd," he remarked. "Why couldn't you help it?"

"Women are accustomed to act on impulse," she explained. "Suppose we say that an impulse has directed my journey? And yet, this is the last place in the world that I wish to find myself in. Associations that I detest are connected with it in my mind. If I had a will of my own, I would never see it again. I hate Venice. As you see, however, I am here. When did you meet with such an unreasonable woman before? Never, I am sure!" She stopped, eyed him for a moment, and suddenly altered her tone. "When is Miss Agnes Lockwood expected to be in Venice?" she asked.

It was not easy to throw Francis off his balance, but that extraordinary question did it. "How the devil did you know that Miss Lockwood was coming to Venice?" he exclaimed.

She laughed—a bitter mocking laugh. "Say, I guessed it!"

Something in her tone, or perhaps something in the audacious defiance of her eyes as they rested on him, roused the quick temper that was in Francis Warwick. "Lady Montbarry——!" he began.

"Stop there!" she interposed. "Your brother Stephen's wife calls herself Lady Montbarry now. I share my title with no woman. Call me by my name before I committed the fatal mistake of marrying your brother. Address me, if you please, as Countess Narona."

"Countess Narona," Francis resumed, "if your object in claiming my acquaintance is to mystify me, you have come to the wrong man. Speak plainly, or permit me to wish you good evening."

"If your object is to keep Miss Lockwood's arrival in Venice a secret," she retorted, "speak plainly, Mr. Westwick, on *your* side, and say so."

Her intention was evidently to irritate him; and she succeeded. "Nonsense!" he broke out petulantly. "My brother's travelling arrangements are secrets to nobody. He brings Miss Lockwood here, with Lady Montbarry and the children. As you seem so well informed, perhaps you know why she is coming to Venice?"

The Countess had suddenly become grave and thoughtful. She made no reply. The two strangely associated companions, having reached one extremity of the square, were now standing before the church of St. Mark. The moonlight was bright enough to show the architecture of the grand cathedral in its wonderful variety of detail. Even the pigeons of St. Mark were visible, in dark closely packed rows, roosting in the archways of the great entrance doors.

"I never saw the old church look so beautiful by moonlight," the Countess said quietly; speaking, not to Francis, but to herself. "Good-bye, St. Mark's by moonlight! I shall not see you again."

She turned away from the church, and saw Francis listening to her with wondering looks. "No," she resumed, placidly picking up the lost thread of the conversation, "I don't know why Miss Lockwood is coming here, I only know that we are to meet in Venice."

"By previous appointment?"

"By Destiny," she answered, with her head on her breast, and her eyes on the ground. Francis burst out laughing. "Or, if you like it better," she instantly resumed, "by what fools call Chance." Francis answered easily, out of the depths of his strong common sense. "Chance seems to be taking a queer way of bringing the meeting about," he said. "We have all arranged to meet at the Palace Hotel. How is it that your name is not on the Visitors" List? Destiny ought to have brought you to the Palace Hotel too."

She abruptly pulled down her veil. "Destiny may do that yet!"

she said. "The Palace Hotel?" she repeated, speaking once more to herself. "The old hell, transformed into the new purgatory. The place itself! Jesu Maria! the place itself!" She paused and laid her hand on her companion's arm. "Perhaps Miss Lockwood is not going there with the rest of you?" she burst out with sudden eagerness. "Are you positively sure she will be at the hotel?"

"Positively! Haven't I told you that Miss Lockwood travels with Lord and Lady Montbarry? and don't you know that she is a member of the family? You will have to move, Countess, to our hotel."

She was perfectly impenetrable to the bantering tone in which he spoke. "Yes," she said faintly, "I shall have to move to your hotel." Her hand was still on his arm—he could feel her shivering from head to foot while she spoke. Heartily as he disliked and distrusted her, the common instinct of humanity obliged him to ask if she felt cold.

"Yes," she said. "Cold and faint."

"Cold and faint, Countess, on such a night as this?"

"The night has nothing to do with it, Mr. Westwick. How do you suppose the criminal feels on the scaffold, while the hangman is putting the rope around his neck? Cold and faint, too, I should think. Excuse my grim fancy. You see, Destiny has got the rope round *my* neck—and *I* feel it."

She looked about her. They were at that moment close to the famous café known as "Florian's." "Take me in there," she said; "I must have something to revive me. You had better not hesitate. You are interested in reviving me. I have not said what I wanted to say to you yet. It's business, and it's connected with your theatre."

Wondering inwardly what she could possibly want with his theatre, Francis reluctantly yielded to the necessities of the situation, and took her into the café. He found a quiet corner in which they could take their places without attracting notice. "What will you have?" he inquired resignedly. She gave her own orders to the waiter, without troubling him to speak for her.

"Maraschino. And a pot of tea."

The waiter stared; Francis stared. The tea was a novelty (in connection with maraschino) to both of them. Careless whether she surprised them or not, she instructed the waiter, when her directions had been complied with, to pour a large wine-glass-full of the liqueur into a tumbler, and to fill it up from the teapot. "I can't do it for myself," she remarked, "my hand trembles so." She drank the strange mixture eagerly, hot as it was. "Maraschino punch—will you taste some of it?" she said. "I inherit the discovery of this drink. When your English Queen Caroline was on the Continent, my mother was attached to her Court. That much injured Royal Person invented, in her happier hours, maraschino punch. Fondly attached to her gracious mistress, my mother shared her tastes. And I, in my turn, learnt from my mother. Now, Mr. Westwick, suppose I tell you what my business is. You are manager of a theatre. Do you want a new play?"

"I always want a new play—provided it's a good one."

"And you pay, if it's a good one?"

"I pay liberally—in my own interests."

"If *I* write the play, will you read it?"

Francis hesitated. "What has put writing a play into your head?" he asked.

"Mere accident," she answered. "I had once occasion to tell my late brother of a visit which I paid to Miss Lockwood, when I was last in England. He took no interest in what happened at the interview, but something struck him in my way of relating it. He said, "You describe what passed between you and the lady with the point and contrast of good stage dialogue. You have the dramatic instinct—try if you can write a play. You might make money." *That* put it into my head."

Those last words seemed to startle Francis. "Surely you don't want money!" he exclaimed.

"I always want money. My tastes are expensive. I have nothing but my poor little four hundred a year—and the wreck that is left of the other money: about two hundred pounds in circular notes —no more."

Francis knew that she was referring to the ten thousand pounds paid by the insurance offices. "All those thousands gone already!" he exclaimed.

She blew a little puff of air over her fingers. "Gone like that!"

she answered coolly.

"Baron Rivar?"

She looked at him with a flash of anger in her hard black eyes.

"My affairs are my own secret, Mr. Westwick. I have made you a proposal—and you have not answered me yet. Don't say No, without thinking first. Remember what a life mine has been. I have seen more of the world than most people, playwrights included. I have had strange adventures; I have heard remarkable stories; I have observed; I have remembered. Are there no materials, here in my head, for writing a play—if the opportunity is granted to me?" She waited a moment, and suddenly repeated her strange question about Agnes.

"When is Miss Lockwood expected to be in Venice?"

"What has that to do with your new play, Countess?"

The Countess appeared to feel some difficulty in giving that question its fit reply. She mixed another tumbler full of maraschino punch, and drank one good half of it before she spoke again.

"It has everything to do with my new play," was all she said. "Answer me." Francis answered her.

"Miss Lockwood may be here in a week. Or, for all I know to the contrary, sooner than that."

"Very well. If I am a living woman and a free woman in a week's time—or if I am in possession of my senses in a week's time (don't interrupt me; I know what I am talking about)—I shall have a sketch or outline of my play ready, as a specimen of what I can do. Once again, will you read it?"

"I will certainly read it. But, Countess, I don't understand—"

She held up her hand for silence, and finished the second tumbler of maraschino punch.

"I am a living enigma—and you want to know the right reading of me," she said. "Here is the reading, as your English phrase goes, in a nutshell. There is a foolish idea in the minds of many persons that the natives of the warm climates are imaginative people. There never was a greater mistake. You will find no such unimaginative people anywhere as you find in Italy, Spain, Greece, and the other Southern countries. To anything fanciful, to anything spiritual, their minds are deaf and blind by nature. Now and then, in the course of centuries, a great genius springs up among them; and he is the exception which proves the rule. Now see! I, though I am no genius—I am, in my little way (as I suppose), an exception too. To my sorrow, I have some of that imagination which is so common among the English and the Germans—so rare among the Italians, the Spaniards, and the rest of them! And what is the result? I think it has become a disease in me. I am filled with presentiments which make this wicked life of mine one long terror to me. It doesn't matter, just now, what they are. Enough that they absolutely govern me—they drive me over land and sea at their own horrible will; they are in me, and torturing me, at this moment! Why don't I resist them? Ha! but I do resist them. I am trying (with the help of the good punch) to resist them now. At intervals I cultivate the difficult virtue of sound sense. Sometimes, sound sense makes a hopeful woman of me. At one time, I had the hope that what seemed reality to me was only mad delusion, after all—I even asked the question of an English doctor! At other times, other sensible doubts of myself beset me. Never mind dwelling on them now—it always ends in the old terrors and superstitions taking possession of me again. In a week's time, I shall know whether Destiny does indeed decide my future for me, or whether I decide it for myself. In the last case, my resolution is to absorb this self-tormenting fancy of mine in the occupation that I have told you of already. Do you understand me a little better now? And, our business being settled, dear Mr. Westwick, shall we get out of this hot room into the nice cool air again?"

They rose to leave the café. Francis privately concluded that the maraschino punch offered the only discoverable explanation of what the Countess had said to him.

CHAPTER XX

"SHALL I see you again?" she asked, as she held out her hand to take leave. "It is quite understood between us, I suppose, about the play?"

Francis recalled his extraordinary experience of that evening in the re-numbered room. "My stay in Venice is uncertain," he replied. "If you have anything more to say about this dramatic venture of yours, it may be as well to say it now. Have you decided on a subject already? I know the public taste in England better than you do—I might save you some waste of time and trouble, if you have not chosen your subject wisely."

"I don't care what subject I write about, so long as I write," she answered carelessly. "If *you* have got a subject in your head, give it to me. I answer for the characters and the dialogue."

"You answer for the characters and the dialogue," Francis repeated. "That's a bold way of speaking for a beginner! I wonder if I should shake your sublime confidence in yourself, if I suggested the most ticklish subject to handle which is known to the stage? What do you say, Countess, to entering the lists with Shakespeare, and trying a drama with a ghost in it? A true story, mind! founded on events in this very city in which you and I are interested."

She caught him by the arm, and drew him away from the crowded colonnade into the solitary middle space of the square. "Now tell me!" she said eagerly. "Here, where nobody is near us. How am I interested in it? How? how?"

Still holding his arm, she shook him in her impatience to hear the coming disclosure. For a moment he hesitated. Thus far, amused by her ignorant belief in herself, he had merely spoken in jest. Now, for the first time, impressed by her irresistible earnestness, he began to consider what he was about from a more serious point of view. With her knowledge of all that had passed in the old palace, before its transformation into an hotel, it was surely possible that she might suggest some explanation of what had happened to his brother, and sister, and himself. Or, failing to do this, she might accidentally reveal some event in her own experience which, acting as a hint to a competent dramatist, might prove to be the making of a play. The prosperity of his theatre was his one serious object in life. "I may be on the trace of another 'Corsican Brothers,'" he thought. "A new piece of that sort would be ten thousand pounds in my pocket, at least."

With these motives (worthy of the single-hearted devotion to dramatic business which made Francis a successful manager) he related, without further hesitation, what his own experience had been, and what the experience of his relatives had been, in the haunted hotel. He even described the outbreak of superstitious terror which had escaped Mrs. Norbury's ignorant maid. "Sad stuff, if you look at it reasonably," he remarked. "But there is something dramatic in the notion of the ghostly influence making itself felt by the relations in succession, as they one after another enter the fatal room—until the one chosen relative comes who will see the Unearthly Creature, and know the terrible truth. Material for a play, Countess—first-rate material for a play!"

There he paused. She neither moved nor spoke. He stooped and looked closer at her.

What impression had he produced? It was an impression which his utmost ingenuity had failed to anticipate. She stood by his side—just as she had stood before Agnes when her question about Ferrari was plainly answered at last—like a woman turned to stone. Her eyes were vacant and rigid; all the life in her face had faded out of it. Francis took her by the hand. Her hand was as cold as the pavement that they were standing on. He asked her if she was ill.

Not a muscle in her moved. He might as well have spoken to the dead.

"Surely," he said, "you are not foolish enough to take what I have been telling you seriously?"

Her lips moved slowly. As it seemed, she was making an effort to speak to him.

"Louder," he said. "I can't hear you."

She struggled to recover possession of herself. A faint light began to soften the dull cold stare of her eyes. In a moment more she spoke so that he could hear her.

"I never thought of the other world," she murmured, in low dull tones, like a woman talking in her sleep.

Her mind had gone back to the day of her last memorable interview with Agnes; she was slowly recalling the confession that had escaped her, the warning words which she had spoken at that past time. Necessarily incapable of understanding this, Francis looked at her in perplexity. She went on in the same dull vacant tone, steadily following out her own train of thought, with her heedless eyes on his face, and her wandering mind far away from him.

"I said some trifling event would bring us together the next time. I was wrong. No trifling event will bring us together. I said I might be the person who told her what had become of Ferrari, if she forced me to it. Shall I feel some other influence than hers? Will *he* force me to it? When *she* sees him, shall *I* see him too?"

Her head sank a little; her heavy eyelids dropped slowly; she heaved a long low weary sigh. Francis put her arm in his, and made an attempt to rouse her.

"Come, Countess, you are weary and over-wrought. We have had enough talking to-night. Let me see you safe back to your hotel. Is it far from here?"

She started when he moved, and obliged her to move with him, as if he had suddenly awakened her out of a deep sleep.

"Not far," she said faintly. "The old hotel on the quay. My mind's in a strange state; I have forgotten the name."

"Danieli's?"

"Yes!"

He led her on slowly. She accompanied him in silence as far as the end of the Piazzetta. There, when the full view of the moonlit Lagoon revealed itself, she stopped him as he turned towards the Riva degli Schiavoni. "I have something to ask you. I want to wait and think."

She recovered her lost idea, after a long pause.

"Are you going to sleep in the room to-night?" she asked.

He told her that another traveller was in possession of the room that night. "But the manager has reserved it for me to-morrow," he added, "if I wish to have it."

"No," she said. "You must give it up."

"To whom?"

"To me!"

He started. "After what I have told you, do you really wish to sleep in that room to-morrow night?"

"I *must* sleep in it."

"Are you not afraid?"

"I am horribly afraid."

"So I should have thought, after what I have observed in you to-night. Why should you take the room? you are not obliged to occupy it, unless you like."

"I was not obliged to go to Venice, when I left America," she answered. "And yet I came here. I must take the room, and keep the room, until——" She broke off at those words. "Never mind the rest," she said. "It doesn't interest you."

It was useless to dispute with her. Francis changed the subject. "We can do nothing to-night," he said. "I will call on you to-morrow morning, and hear what you think of it then."

They moved on again to the hotel. As they approached the door, Francis asked if she was staying in Venice under her own name.

She shook her head. "As your brother's widow, I am known here. As Countess Narona, I am known here. I want to be un-known, this time, to strangers in Venice; I am travelling under a common English name." She hesitated, and stood still. "What has come to me?" she muttered to herself. "Some things I remember; and some I forget. I forgot Danieli's—and now I forget my English name." She drew him hurriedly into the hall of the hotel, on the wall of which hung a list of visitors' names. Running her finger slowly down the list, she pointed to the English name that she had assumed:—'Mrs. James."

"Remember that when you call to-morrow," she said. "My head is heavy. Good night."

Francis went back to his own hotel, wondering what the events of the next day would bring forth. A new turn in his affairs had taken place in his absence. As he crossed the hall, he was requested by one of the servants to walk into the private office. The manager was waiting there with a gravely pre-occupied manner, as if he had something serious to say. He regretted to hear that Mr. Francis Westwick had, like other members of the family, discovered mysterious sources of discomfort in the new hotel. He had been informed in strict confidence of Mr. Westwick's extraordinary objection to the atmosphere of the bedroom upstairs. Without presuming to discuss the matter, he must beg to be excused from reserving the room for Mr. Westwick after what had happened.

Francis answered sharply, a little ruffled by the tone in which the manager had spoken to him. "I might, very possibly, have declined to sleep in the room, if you *had* reserved it," he said. "Do you wish me to leave the hotel?"

The manager saw the error that he had committed, and hastened to repair it. "Certainly not, sir! We will do our best to make you comfortable while you stay with us. I beg your pardon, if I have said anything to offend you. The reputation of an establishment like this is a matter of very serious importance. May I hope that you will do us the great favour to say nothing about what has happened upstairs? The two French gentlemen have kindly promised to keep it a secret."

This apology left Francis no polite alternative but to grant the manager's request. "There is an end to the Countess's wild scheme," he thought to himself, as he retired for the night. "So much the better for the Countess!"

He rose late the next morning. Inquiring for his Parisian friends, he was informed that both the French gentlemen had left for Milan. As he crossed the hall, on his way to the restaurant, he noticed the head porter chalking the numbers of the rooms on some articles of luggage which were waiting to go upstairs. One trunk attracted his attention by the extraordinary number of old travelling labels left on it. The porter was marking it at the moment—and the number was, "13 A." Francis instantly looked at the card fastened on the lid. It bore the common English name,

"Mrs. James!" He at once inquired about the lady. She had arrived early that morning, and she was then in the Reading Room. Looking into the room, he discovered a lady in it alone. Advancing a little nearer, he found himself face to face with the Countess.

She was seated in a dark corner, with her head down and her arms crossed over her bosom. "Yes," she said, in a tone of weary impatience, before Francis could speak to her. "I thought it best not to wait for you—I determined to get here before anybody else could take the room."

"Have you taken it for long?" Francis asked.

"You told me Miss Lockwood would be here in a week's time. I have taken it for a week."

"What has Miss Lockwood to do with it?"

"She has everything to do with it—she must sleep in the room. I shall give the room up to her when she comes here."

Francis began to understand the superstitious purpose that she had in view. "Are you (an educated woman) really of the same opinion as my sister's maid!" he exclaimed. "Assuming your absurd superstition to be a serious thing, you are taking the wrong means to prove it true. If I and my brother and sister have seen nothing, how should Agnes Lockwood discover what was not revealed to *us*? She is only distantly related to the Montbarrys—she is only our cousin."

"She was nearer to the heart of the Montbarry who is dead than any of you," the Countess answered sternly. "To the last day of his life, my miserable husband repented his desertion of her. She will see what none of you have seen—she shall have the room."

Francis listened, utterly at a loss to account for the motives that animated her. "I don't see what interest *you* have in trying this extraordinary experiment," he said.

"It is my interest *not* to try it! It is my interest to fly from Venice, and never set eyes on Agnes Lockwood or any of your family again!"

"What prevents you from doing that?"

She started to her feet and looked at him wildly. "I know no more what prevents me than you do!" she burst out. "Some will that is stronger than mine drives me on to my destruction, in spite of my own self!" She suddenly sat down again, and waved her hand for him to go. "Leave me," she said. "Leave me to my thoughts."

Francis left her, firmly persuaded by this time that she was out of her senses. For the rest of the day, he saw nothing of her. The night, so far as he knew, passed quietly. The next morning he breakfasted early, determining to wait in the restaurant for the appearance of the Countess. She came in and ordered her breakfast quietly, looking dull and worn and self-absorbed, as she had looked when he last saw her. He hastened to her table, and asked if anything had happened in the night.

"Nothing," she answered.

"You have rested as well as usual?"

"Quite as well as usual. Have you had any letters this morning? Have you heard when she is coming?"

"I have had no letters. Are you really going to stay here? Has your experience of last night not altered the opinion which you expressed to me yesterday?"

"Not in the least."

The momentary gleam of animation which had crossed her face when she questioned him about Agnes, died out of it again when he answered her. She looked, she spoke, she eat her breakfast, with a vacant resignation, like a woman who had done with hopes, done with interests, done with everything but the mechanical movements and instincts of life.

Francis went out, on the customary travellers' pilgrimage to the shrines of Titian and Tintoret. After some hours of absence, he found a letter waiting for him when he got back to the hotel. It was written by his brother Henry, and it recommended him to return to Milan immediately. The proprietor of a French theatre, recently arrived from Venice, was trying to induce the famous dancer whom Francis had engaged to break faith with him and accept a higher salary.

Having made this startling announcement, Henry proceeded to inform his brother that Lord and Lady Montbarry, with Agnes and the children, would arrive in Venice in three days more. "They know nothing of our adventures at the hotel," Henry wrote; "and they have telegraphed to the manager for the accommodation that they want. There would be something absurdly superstitious in our giving them a warning which would frighten the ladies and children out of the best hotel in Venice. We shall be a strong party this time—too strong a party for ghosts! I shall meet the travellers on their arrival, of course, and try my luck again at what you call the Haunted Hotel. Arthur Barville and his wife have already got as far on their way as Trent; and two of the lady's relations have arranged to accompany them on the journey to Venice."

Naturally indignant at the conduct of his Parisian colleague, Francis made his preparations for returning to Milan by the train of that day.

On his way out, he asked the manager if his brother's telegram had been received. The telegram had arrived, and, to the surprise of Francis, the rooms were already reserved. "I thought you would refuse to let any more of the family into the house," he said satirically. The manager answered (with the due dash of respect) in the same tone. "Number 13 A is safe, sir, in the occupation of a stranger. I am the servant of the Company; and I dare not turn money out of the hotel."

Hearing this, Francis said good-bye—and said nothing more. He was ashamed to acknowledge it to himself, but he felt an irresistible curiosity to know what would happen when Agnes arrived at the hotel. Besides, "Mrs. James" had reposed a confidence in him. He got into his gondola, respecting the confidence of "Mrs. James."

Towards evening on the third day, Lord Montbarry and his travelling companions arrived, punctual to their appointment.

"Mrs. James," sitting at the window of her room watching for them, saw the new Lord land from the gondola first. He handed his wife to the steps. The three children were next committed to his care. Last of all, Agnes appeared in the little black doorway of the gondola cabin, and, taking Lord Montbarry's hand, passed in her turn to the steps. She wore no veil. As she ascended to the door of the hotel, the Countess (eyeing her through an opera-glass) noticed that she paused to look at the outside of the building, and that her face was very pale.

CHAPTER XXI

∽∾∽∾∽∾

LORD and Lady Montbarry were received by the housekeeper; the manager being absent for a day or two on business connected with the affairs of the hotel.

The rooms reserved for the travellers on the first floor were three in number; consisting of two bedrooms opening into each other, and communicating on the left with a drawing-room. Complete so far, the arrangements proved to be less satisfactory in reference to the third bedroom required for Agnes and for the eldest daughter of Lord Montbarry, who usually slept with her on their travels. The bedchamber on the right of the drawing-room was already occupied by an English widow lady. Other bedchambers at the other end of the corridor were also let in every case. There was accordingly no alternative but to place at the disposal of Agnes a comfortable room on the second floor. Lady Montbarry vainly complained of this separation of one of the members of her travelling party from the rest. The housekeeper politely hinted that it was impossible for her to ask other travellers to give up their rooms. She could only express her regret, and assure Miss Lockwood that her bedchamber on the second floor was one of the best rooms in that part of the hotel.

On the retirement of the housekeeper, Lady Montbarry noticed that Agnes had seated herself apart, feeling apparently no interest in the question of the bedrooms. Was she ill? No; she felt a little unnerved by the railway journey, and that was all. Hearing this, Lord Montbarry proposed that she should go out with him, and try the experiment of half an hour's walk in the cool evening air. Agnes gladly accepted the suggestion. They directed their steps towards the square of St. Mark, so as to enjoy the breeze blowing over the lagoon. It was the first visit of Agnes to Venice. The fascination of the wonderful city of the waters exerted its full influence over her sensitive nature. The proposed half-hour of the walk had passed away, and was fast expanding to half an hour more, before Lord Montbarry could persuade his companion to remember that dinner was waiting for them. As they returned, passing under the colonnade, neither of them noticed a lady in deep mourning, loitering in the open space of the square. She started as she recognised Agnes walking with the new Lord Montbarry—hesitated for a moment—and then followed them, at a discreet distance, back to the hotel.

Lady Montbarry received Agnes in high spirits—with news of an event which had happened in her absence.

She had not left the hotel more than ten minutes, before a little note in pencil was brought to Lady Montbarry by the housekeeper. The writer proved to be no less a person than the widow lady who occupied the room on the other side of the drawing-room, which her ladyship had vainly hoped to secure for Agnes. Writing under the name of Mrs. James, the polite widow explained that she had heard from the housekeeper of the disappointment experienced by Lady Montbarry in the matter of the rooms. Mrs. James was quite alone; and as long as her bedchamber was airy and comfortable, it mattered nothing to her whether she slept on the first or the second floor of the house. She had accordingly much pleasure in proposing to change rooms with Miss Lockwood. Her luggage had already been removed, and Miss Lockwood had only to take possession of the room (Number 13 A), which was now entirely at her disposal.

"I immediately proposed to see Mrs. James," Lady Montbarry continued, "and to thank her personally for her extreme kindness. But I was informed that she had gone out, without leaving word at what hour she might be expected to return. I have written a little note of thanks, saying that we hope to have the pleasure of personally expressing our sense of Mrs. James's courtesy to-morrow. In the mean time, Agnes, I have ordered your boxes to be removed downstairs. Go!—and judge for yourself, my dear, if that good lady has not given up to you the prettiest room in the house!"

With those words, Lady Montbarry left Miss Lockwood to

make a hasty toilet for dinner.

The new room at once produced a favourable impression on Agnes. The large window, opening into a balcony, commanded an admirable view of the canal. The decorations on the walls and ceiling were skilfully copied from the exquisitely graceful designs of Raphael in the Vatican. The massive wardrobe possessed compartments of unusual size, in which double the number of dresses that Agnes possessed might have been conveniently hung at full length. In the inner corner of the room, near the head of the bedstead, there was a recess which had been turned into a little dressing-room, and which opened by a second door on the inferior staircase of the hotel, commonly used by the servants. Noticing these aspects of the room at a glance, Agnes made the necessary change in her dress, as quickly as possible. On her way back to the drawing-room she was addressed by a chambermaid in the corridor who asked for her key. "I will put your room tidy for the night, Miss," the woman said, "and I will then bring the key back to you in the drawing-room."

While the chambermaid was at her work, a solitary lady, loitering about the corridor of the second storey, was watching her over the bannisters. After awhile, the maid appeared, with her pail in her hand, leaving the room by way of the dressing-room and the back stairs. As she passed out of sight, the lady on the second floor (no other, it is needless to add, than the Countess herself) ran swiftly down the stairs, entered the bedchamber by the principal door, and hid herself in the empty side compartment of the wardrobe. The chambermaid returned, completed her work, locked the door of the dressing-room on the inner side, locked the principal entrance-door on leaving the room, and returned the key to Agnes in the drawing-room.

The travellers were just sitting down to their late dinner, when one of the children noticed that Agnes was not wearing her watch. Had she left it in her bedchamber in the hurry of changing her dress? She rose from the table at once in search of her watch; Lady Montbarry advising her, as she went out, to see to the security of her bedchamber, in the event of there being thieves in the house. Agnes found her watch, forgotten on the toilet table, as she had anticipated. Before leaving the room again she acted on Lady Montbarry's advice, and tried the key in the lock of the dressing-room door. It was properly secured. She left the bedchamber, locking the main door behind her.

Immediately on her departure, the Countess, oppressed by the confined air in the wardrobe, ventured on stepping out of her hiding place into the empty room.

Entering the dressing-room, she listened at the door, until the silence outside informed her that the corridor was empty. Upon this, she unlocked the door, and, passing out, closed it again softly; leaving it to all appearance (when viewed on the inner side) as carefully secured as Agnes had seen it when she tried the key in the lock with her own hand.

While the Montbarrys were still at dinner, Henry Westwick joined them, arriving from Milan.

When he entered the room, and again when he advanced to shake hands with her, Agnes was conscious of a latent feeling which secretly reciprocated Henry's unconcealed pleasure on meeting her again. For a moment only, she returned his look; and in that moment her own observation told her that she had silently encouraged him to hope. She saw it in the sudden glow of happiness which overspread his face; and she confusedly took refuge in the usual conventional inquiries relating to the relatives whom he had left at Milan.

Taking his place at the table, Henry gave a most amusing account of the position of his brother Francis between the mercenary opera-dancer on one side, and the unscrupulous manager of the French theatre on the other. Matters had proceeded to such extremities, that the law had been called on to interfere, and had decided the dispute in favour of Francis. On winning the victory the English manager had at once left Milan, recalled to London by the affairs of his theatre. He was accompanied on the journey back, as he had been accompanied on the journey out, by his sister. Resolved, after passing two nights of terror in the Venetian hotel, never to enter it again, Mrs. Norbury asked to be excused from appearing at the family festival, on the ground of ill-health. At her age, travelling fatigued her, and she was glad to take advantage of her brother's escort to return to England.

While the talk at the dinner-table flowed easily onward, the evening-time advanced to night—and it became necessary to think of sending the children to bed.

As Agnes rose to leave the room, accompanied by the eldest girl, she observed with surprise that Henry's manner suddenly changed. He looked serious and pre-occupied; and when his niece wished him good night, he abruptly said to her, "Marian, I want to know what part of the hotel you sleep in?" Marian, puzzled by the question, answered that she was going to sleep, as usual, with "Aunt Agnes." Not satisfied with that reply, Henry next inquired whether the bedroom was near the rooms occupied by the other members of the travelling party. Answering for the child, and wondering what Henry's object could possibly be, Agnes mentioned the polite sacrifice made to her convenience by Mrs. James. "Thanks to that lady's kindness," she said, "Marian and I are only on the other side of the drawing-room." Henry made no remark; he looked incomprehensibly discontented as he opened the door for Agnes and her companion to pass out. After wishing them good night, he waited in the corridor until he saw them enter the fatal corner-room—and then he called abruptly to his brother, "Come out, Stephen, and let us smoke!"

As soon as the two brothers were at liberty to speak together privately, Henry explained the motive which had led to his strange inquiries about the bedrooms. Francis had informed him of the meeting with the Countess at Venice, and of all that had followed it; and Henry now carefully repeated the narrative to his brother in all its details. "I am not satisfied," he added, "about that woman's purpose in giving up her room. Without alarming the ladies by telling them what I have just told you, can you not warn Agnes to be careful in securing her door?"

Lord Montbarry replied, that the warning had been already given by his wife, and that Agnes might be trusted to take good care of herself and her little bedfellow. For the rest, he looked upon the story of the Countess and her superstitions as a piece of theatrical exaggeration, amusing enough in itself, but unworthy of a moment's serious attention.

While the gentlemen were absent from the hotel, the room which had been already associated with so many startling circumstances, became the scene of another strange event in which Lady Montbarry's eldest child was concerned.

Little Marian had been got ready for bed as usual, and had (so far) taken hardly any notice of the new room. As she knelt down to say her prayers, she happened to look up at that part of the ceiling above her which was just over the head of the bed. The next instant she alarmed Agnes, by starting to her feet with a cry of terror, and pointing to a small brown spot on one of the white panelled spaces of the carved ceiling. "It's a spot of blood!" the child exclaimed. "Take me away! I won't sleep here!"

Seeing plainly that it would be useless to reason with her while she was in the room, Agnes hurriedly wrapped Marian in a dressing-gown, and carried her back to her mother in the drawing-room. Here, the ladies did their best to soothe and reassure the trembling girl. The effort proved to be useless; the impression that had been produced on the young and sensitive mind was not to be removed by persuasion. Marian could give no explanation of the panic of terror that had seized her. She was quite unable to say why the spot on the ceiling looked like the colour of a spot of blood. She only knew that she should die of terror if she saw it again. Under these circumstances, but one alternative was left. It was arranged that the child should pass the night in the room occupied by her two younger sisters and the nurse.

In half an hour more, Marian was peacefully asleep with her arm around her sister's neck. Lady Montbarry went back with Agnes to her room to see the spot on the ceiling which had so strangely frightened the child. It was so small as to be only just perceptible, and it had in all probability been caused by the carelessness of a workman, or by a dripping from water accidentally spilt on the floor of the room above.

"I really cannot understand why Marian should place such a shocking interpretation on such a trifling thing," Lady Montbarry remarked.

"I suspect the nurse is in some way answerable for what has

happened," Agnes suggested. "She may quite possibly have been telling Marian some tragic nursery story which has left its mischievous impression behind it. Persons in her position are sadly ignorant of the danger of exciting a child's imagination. You had better caution the nurse to-morrow."

Lady Montbarry looked round the room with admiration. "Is it not prettily decorated?" she said. "I suppose, Agnes, you don't mind sleeping here by yourself?"

Agnes laughed. "I feel so tired," she replied, "that I was thinking of bidding you good-night, instead of going back to the drawing-room."

Lady Montbarry turned towards the door. "I see your jewel-case on the table," she resumed. "Don't forget to lock the other door there, in the dressing-room."

"I have already seen to it, and tried the key myself," said Agnes. "Can I be of any use to you before I go to bed?"

"No, my dear, thank you; I feel sleepy enough to follow your example. Good night, Agnes—and pleasant dreams on your first night in Venice."

CHAPTER XXII

HAVING closed and secured the door on Lady Montbarry's departure, Agnes put on her dressing-gown, and, turning to her open boxes, began the business of unpacking. In the hurry of making her toilet for dinner, she had taken the first dress that lay uppermost in the trunk, and had thrown her travelling costume on the bed. She now opened the doors of the wardrobe for the first time, and began to hang her dresses on the hooks in the large compartment on one side.

After a few minutes only of this occupation, she grew weary of it, and decided on leaving the trunks as they were, until the next morning. The oppressive south wind, which had blown throughout the day, still prevailed at night. The atmosphere of the room felt close; Agnes threw a shawl over her head and shoulders, and, opening the window, stepped into the balcony to look at the view.

The night was heavy and overcast: nothing could be distinctly seen. The canal beneath the window looked like a black gulf; the opposite houses were barely visible as a row of shadows, dimly relieved against the starless and moonless sky. At long intervals, the warning cry of a belated gondolier was just audible, as he turned the corner of a distant canal, and called to invisible boats which might be approaching him in the darkness. Now and then, the nearer dip of an oar in the water told of the viewless passage of other gondolas bringing guests back to the hotel. Excepting these rare sounds, the mysterious night-silence of Venice was literally the silence of the grave.

Leaning on the parapet of the balcony, Agnes looked vacantly into the black void beneath. Her thoughts reverted to the miserable man who had broken his pledged faith to her, and who had died in that house. Some change seemed to have come over her since her arrival in Venice; some new influence appeared to be at work. For the first time in her experience of herself, compassion and regret were not the only emotions aroused in her by the remembrance of the dead Montbarry. A keen sense of the wrong that she had suffered, never yet felt by that gentle and forgiving nature, was felt by it now. She found herself thinking of the bygone days of her humiliation almost as harshly as Henry Westwick had thought of them—she who had rebuked him the last time he had spoken slightingly of his brother in her presence! A sudden fear and doubt of herself, startled her physically as well as morally. She turned from the shadowy abyss of the dark water as if the mystery and the gloom of it had been answerable for the emotions which had taken her by surprise. Abruptly closing the window, she threw aside her shawl, and lit the candles on the mantelpiece, impelled by a sudden craving for light in the solitude of her room.

The cheering brightness round her, contrasting with the black gloom outside, restored her spirits. She felt herself enjoying the light like a child!

Would it be well (she asked herself) to get ready for bed? No! The sense of drowsy fatigue that she had felt half an hour since was gone. She returned to the dull employment of unpacking her boxes. After a few minutes only, the occupation became irksome to her once more. She sat down by the table, and took up a guide-book. "Suppose I inform myself," she thought, "on the subject of Venice?"

Her attention wandered from the book, before she had turned the first page of it.

The image of Henry Westwick was the presiding image in her memory now. Recalling the minutest incidents and details of the evening, she could think of nothing which presented him under other than a favourable and interesting aspect. She smiled to herself softly, her colour rose by fine gradations, as she felt the full luxury of dwelling on the perfect truth and modesty of his devotion to her. Was the depression of spirits from which she had suffered so persistently on her travels attributable, by any chance, to their long separation from each other—embittered perhaps by her own vain regret when she remembered her harsh reception of him in Paris? Suddenly conscious of this bold question, and of the self-abandonment which it implied, she returned mechanically to her book, distrusting the unrestrained liberty of her own thoughts. What lurking temptations to forbidden tenderness find their hiding-places in a woman's dressing-gown, when she is alone in her room at night! With her heart in the tomb of the dead Montbarry, could Agnes even think of another man, and think of love? How shameful! how unworthy of her! For the second time, she tried to interest herself in the guide-book—and once more she tried in vain. Throwing the book aside, she turned desperately to the one resource that was left, to her luggage—resolved to fatigue herself without mercy, until she was weary enough and sleepy enough to find a safe refuge in bed.

For some little time, she persisted in the monotonous occupation of transferring her clothes from her trunk to the wardrobe. The large clock in the hall, striking midnight, reminded her that it was getting late. She sat down for a moment in an arm-chair by the bedside, to rest.

The silence in the house now caught her attention, and held it—held it disagreeably. Was everybody in bed and asleep but herself? Surely it was time for her to follow the general example? With a certain irritable nervous haste, she rose again and undressed herself. "I have lost two hours of rest," she thought, frowning at the reflection of herself in the glass, as she arranged her hair for the night. "I shall be good for nothing to-morrow!"

She lit the night-light, and extinguished the candles—with one exception, which she removed to a little table, placed on the side of the bed opposite to the side occupied by the arm-chair. Having put her travelling-box of matches and the guide-book near the candle, in case she might be sleepless and might want to read, she blew out the light, and laid her head on the pillow.

The curtains of the bed were looped back to let the air pass freely over her. Lying on her left side, with her face turned away from the table, she could see the arm-chair by the dim night-light. It had a chintz covering—representing large bunches of roses scattered over a pale green ground. She tried to weary herself into drowsiness by counting over and over again the bunches of roses that were visible from her point of view. Twice her attention was distracted from the counting, by sounds outside—by the clock chiming the half-hour past twelve; and then again, by the fall of a pair of boots on the upper floor, thrown out to be cleaned, with that barbarous disregard of the comfort of others which is observable in humanity when it inhabits an hotel. In the silence that followed these passing disturbances, Agnes went on counting the roses on the arm-chair, more and more slowly. Before long, she confused herself in the figures—tried to begin counting again—thought she would wait a little first—felt her eyelids drooping, and her head reclining lower and lower on the pillow—sighed faintly—and sank into sleep.

How long that first sleep lasted, she never knew. She could only remember, in the after-time, that she woke instantly.

Every faculty and perception in her passed the boundary line between insensibility and consciousness, so to speak, at a leap. Without knowing why, she sat up suddenly in the bed, listening for she knew not what. Her head was in a whirl; her heart beat furiously, without any assignable cause. But one trivial event had happened during the interval while she had been asleep. The night-light had gone out; and the room, as a matter of course, was in total darkness.

She felt for the match-box, and paused after finding it. A vague sense of confusion was still in her mind. She was in no hurry to light the match. The pause in the darkness was, for the moment, agreeable to her.

In the quieter flow of her thoughts during this interval, she could ask herself the natural question:—What cause had awakened her so suddenly, and had so strangely shaken her nerves? Had it been the influence of a dream? She had not dreamed at all— or, to speak more correctly, she had no waking remembrance of having dreamed. The mystery was beyond her fathoming: the darkness began to oppress her. She struck the match on the box, and lit her candle.

As the welcome light diffused itself over the room, she turned from the table and looked towards the other side of the bed.

In the moment when she turned, the chill of a sudden terror gripped her round the heart, as with the clasp of an icy hand.

She was not alone in her room!

There—in the chair at the bedside—there, suddenly revealed under the flow of light from the candle, was the figure of a woman, reclining. Her head lay back over the chair. Her face, turned up to the ceiling, had the eyes closed, as if she was wrapped in a deep sleep.

The shock of the discovery held Agnes speechless and helpless. Her first conscious action, when she was in some degree mistress of herself again, was to lean over the bed, and to look closer at the woman who had so incomprehensibly stolen into her room in the dead of night. One glance was enough: she started back with a cry of amazement. The person in the chair was no other than the widow of the dead Montbarry—the woman who had warned her that they were to meet again, and that the place might be Venice!

Her courage returned to her, stung into action by the natural sense of indignation which the presence of the Countess provoked.

"Wake up!" she called out. "How dare you come here? How did you get in? Leave the room—or I will call for help!"

She raised her voice at the last words. It produced no effect. Leaning farther over the bed, she boldly took the Countess by the shoulder and shook her. Not even this effort succeeded in rousing the sleeping woman. She still lay back in the chair, possessed by a torpor like the torpor of death—insensible to sound, insensible to touch. Was she really sleeping? Or had she fainted?

Agnes looked closer at her. She had not fainted. Her breathing was audible, rising and falling in deep heavy gasps. At intervals she ground her teeth savagely. Beads of perspiration stood thickly on her forehead. Her clenched hands rose and fell slowly from time to time on her lap. Was she in the agony of a dream? or was she spiritually conscious of something hidden in the room?

The doubt involved in that last question was unendurable. Agnes determined to rouse the servants who kept watch in the hotel at night.

The bell-handle was fixed to the wall, on the side of the bed by which the table stood.

She raised herself from the crouching position which she had assumed in looking close at the Countess; and, turning towards the other side of the bed, stretched out her hand to the bell. At the same instant, she stopped and looked upward. Her hand fell helplessly at her side. She shuddered, and sank back on the pillow.

What had she seen?

She had seen another intruder in her room.

Midway between her face and the ceiling, there hovered a human head—severed at the neck, like a head struck from the body by the guillotine.

Nothing visible, nothing audible, had given her any intelligible warning of its appearance. Silently and suddenly, the head had taken its place above her. No supernatural change had passed over the room, or was perceptible in it now. The dumbly-tortured figure in the chair; the broad window opposite the foot of the bed, with the black night beyond it; the candle burning on the table— these, and all other objects in the room, remained unaltered. One object more, unutterably horrid, had been added to the rest. That was the only change—no more, no less.

By the yellow candlelight she saw the head distinctly, hovering in mid-air above her. She looked at it steadfastly, spell-bound by the terror that held her.

The flesh of the face was gone. The shrivelled skin was darkened in hue, like the skin of an Egyptian mummy—except at the neck. There it was of a lighter colour; there it showed spots and splashes of the hue of that brown spot on the ceiling, which the child's fanciful terror had distorted into the likeness of a spot of blood. Thin remains of a discoloured moustache and whiskers, hanging over the upper lip, and over the hollows where the cheeks had once been, made the head just recognisable as the head of a man. Over all the features death and time had done their obliterating work. The eyelids were closed. The hair on the skull, discoloured like the hair on the face, had been burnt away in places. The bluish lips, parted in a fixed grin, showed the double row of teeth. By slow degrees, the hovering head (perfectly still when she first saw it) began to descend towards Agnes as she lay beneath. By slow degrees, that strange doubly-blended odour, which the Commissioners had discovered in the vaults of the old palace—which had sickened Francis Westwick in the bedchamber of the new hotel—spread its fetid exhalations over the room. Downward and downward the hideous apparition made its slow progress, until it stopped close over Agnes—stopped, and turned slowly, so that the face of it confronted the upturned face of the woman in the chair.

There was a pause. Then, a supernatural movement disturbed the rigid repose of the dead face.

The closed eyelids opened slowly. The eyes revealed themselves, bright with the glassy film of death—and fixed their dreadful look on the woman in the chair.

Agnes saw that look; saw the eyelids of the living woman open slowly like the eyelids of the dead; saw her rise, as if in obedience to some silent command—and saw no more.

Her next conscious impression was of the sunlight pouring in at the window; of the friendly presence of Lady Montbarry at the bedside; and of the children's wondering faces peeping in at the door.

CHAPTER XXIII

∽∾∽∾∽∾

"… You have some influence over Agnes. Try what you can do, Henry, to make her take a sensible view of the matter. There is really nothing to make a fuss about. My wife's maid knocked at her door early in the morning, with the customary cup of tea. Getting no answer, she went round to the dressing-room—found the door on that side unlocked—and discovered Agnes on the bed in a fainting fit. With my wife's help, they brought her to herself again; and she told the extraordinary story which I have just repeated to you. You must have seen for yourself that she has been over-fatigued, poor thing, by our long railway journeys: her nerves are out of order—and she is just the person to be easily terrified by a dream. She obstinately refuses, however, to accept this rational view. Don't suppose that I have been severe with her! All that a man can do to humour her I have done. I have written to the Countess (in her assumed name) offering to restore the room to her. She writes back, positively declining to return to it. I have accordingly arranged (so as not to have the thing known in the hotel) to occupy the room for one or two nights, and to leave Agnes to recover her spirits under my wife's care. Is there anything more that I can do? Whatever questions Agnes has asked of me I have answered to the best of my ability; she knows all that you told me about Francis and the Countess last night. But try as I may I can't quiet her mind. I have given up the attempt in despair, and left her in the drawing-room. Go, like a good fellow, and try what you can do to compose her."

In those words, Lord Montbarry stated the case to his brother from the rational point of view. Henry made no remark, he went straight to the drawing-room.

He found Agnes walking rapidly backwards and forwards, flushed and excited. "If you come here to say what your brother has been saying to me," she broke out, before he could speak, "spare yourself the trouble. I don't want common sense—I want a true friend who will believe in me."

"I am that friend, Agnes," Henry answered quietly, "and you know it."

"You really believe that I am not deluded by a dream?"

"I know that you are not deluded—in one particular, at least."

"In what particular?"

"In what you have said of the Countess. It is perfectly true——"

Agnes stopped him there. "Why do I only hear this morning that the Countess and Mrs. James are one and the same person?" she asked distrustfully. "Why was I not told of it last night?"

"You forget that you had accepted the exchange of rooms before I reached Venice," Henry replied. "I felt strongly tempted to tell you, even then—but your sleeping arrangements for the night were all made; I should only have inconvenienced and alarmed you. I waited till the morning, after hearing from my brother that you had yourself seen to your security from any intrusion. How that intrusion was accomplished it is impossible to say. I can only declare that the Countess's presence by your bedside last night was no dream of yours. On her own authority I can testify that it was a reality."

"On her own authority?" Agnes repeated eagerly. "Have you seen her this morning?"

"I have seen her not ten minutes since."

"What was she doing?"

"She was busily engaged in writing. I could not even get her to look at me until I thought of mentioning your name."

"She remembered me, of course?"

"She remembered you with some difficulty. Finding that she wouldn't answer me on any other terms, I questioned her as if I had come direct from you. Then she spoke. She not only admitted that she had the same superstitious motive for placing you in that room which she had acknowledged to Francis—she even owned that she had been by your bedside, watching through the night, "to see what you saw," as she expressed it. Hearing this, I tried to persuade her to tell me how she got into the room. Unluckily, her manuscript on the table caught her eye; she returned to her writing. 'The Baron wants money,' she said; 'I must get on with my play.' What she saw or dreamed while she was in your room last night, it is at present impossible to discover. But judging by my brother's account of her, as well as by what I remember of her myself, some recent influence has been at work which has produced a marked change in this wretched woman for the worse. Her mind (since last night, perhaps) is partially deranged. One proof of it is that she spoke to me of the Baron as if he were still a living man. When Francis saw her, she declared that the Baron was dead, which is the truth. The United States Consul at Milan showed us the announcement of the death in an American newspaper. So far as I can see, such sense as she still possesses seems to be entirely absorbed in one absurd idea—the idea of writing a play for Francis to bring out at his theatre. He admits that he encouraged her to hope she might get money in this way. I think he did wrong. Don't you agree with me?"

Without heeding the question, Agnes rose abruptly from her chair.

"Do me one more kindness, Henry," she said. "Take me to the Countess at once."

Henry hesitated. "Are you composed enough to see her, after the shock that you have suffered?" he asked.

She trembled, the flush on her face died away, and left it deadly pale. But she held to her resolution. "You have heard of what I saw last night?" she said faintly.

"Don't speak of it!" Henry interposed. "Don't uselessly agitate yourself."

"I must speak! My mind is full of horrid questions about it. I know I can't identify it—and yet I ask myself over and over again, in whose likeness did it appear? Was it in the likeness of Ferrari? or was it——?" she stopped, shuddering. "The Countess knows, I must see the Countess!" she resumed vehemently. "Whether my courage fails me or not, I must make the attempt. Take me to her before I have time to feel afraid of it!"

Henry looked at her anxiously. "If you are really sure of your own resolution," he said, "I agree with you—the sooner you see her the better. You remember how strangely she talked of your influence over her, when she forced her way into your room in London?"

"I remember it perfectly. Why do you ask?"

"For this reason. In the present state of her mind, I doubt if she will be much longer capable of realising her wild idea of you as £the avenging angel who is to bring her to a reckoning for her evil deeds. It may be well to try what your influence can do while she is still capable of feeling it."

He waited to hear what Agnes would say. She took his arm and led him in silence to the door.

They ascended to the second floor, and, after knocking, entered the Countess's room.

She was still busily engaged in writing. When she looked up from the paper, and saw Agnes, a vacant expression of doubt was the only expression in her wild black eyes. After a few moments, the lost remembrances and associations appeared to return slowly to her mind. The pen dropped from her hand. Haggard and trembling, she looked closer at Agnes, and recognised her at last. "Has the time come already?" she said in low awe-struck tones. "Give me a little longer respite, I haven't done my writing yet!"

She dropped on her knees, and held out her clasped hands entreatingly. Agnes was far from having recovered, after the shock that she had suffered in the night: her nerves were far from being equal to the strain that was now laid on them. She was so startled by the change in the Countess, that she was at a loss what to say or to do next. Henry was obliged to speak to her. "Put your questions while you have the chance," he said, lowering his voice. "See! the vacant look is coming over her face again."

Agnes tried to rally her courage. "You were in my room last night——" she began. Before she could add a word more, the Countess lifted her hands, and wrung them above her head with a low moan of horror. Agnes shrank back, and turned as if to leave the room. Henry stopped her, and whispered to her to try again. She obeyed him after an effort. "I slept last night in the room that you gave up to me," she resumed. "I saw——"

The Countess suddenly rose to her feet. "No more of that," she cried. "Oh, Jesu Maria! do you think I want to be told what you saw? Do you think I don't know what it means for you and for me? Decide for yourself, Miss. Examine your own mind. Are you well assured that the day of reckoning has come at last? Are you ready to follow me back, through the crimes of the past, to the secrets of the dead?"

She turned again to the writing-table, without waiting to be answered. Her eyes flashed; she looked like her old self once more as she spoke. It was only for a moment. The old ardour and impetuosity were nearly worn out. Her head sank; she sighed heavily as she unlocked a desk which stood on the table. Opening a drawer in the desk, she took out a leaf of vellum, covered with faded writing. Some ragged ends of silken thread were still attached to the leaf, as if it had been torn out of a book.

"Can you read Italian?" she asked, handing the leaf to Agnes.

Agnes answered silently by an inclination of her head.

"The leaf," the Countess proceeded, "once belonged to a book in the old library of the palace, while this building was still a palace. By whom it was torn out you have no need to know. For what purpose it was torn out you may discover for yourself, if you will. Read it first—at the fifth line from the top of the page."

Agnes felt the serious necessity of composing herself. "Give me a chair," she said to Henry; "and I will do my best." He placed himself behind her chair so that he could look over her shoulder and help her to understand the writing on the leaf. Rendered into English, it ran as follows:——

"I have now completed my literary survey of the first floor of the palace. At the desire of my noble and gracious patron, the lord of this glorious edifice, I next ascend to the second floor, and continue my catalogue or description of the pictures, decorations, and other treasures of art therein contained. Let me begin with the corner room at the western extremity of the palace, called the Room of the Caryatides, from the statues which support the mantel-piece. This work is of comparatively recent execution: it dates from the eighteenth century only, and reveals the corrupt taste of the period in every part of it. Still, there is a certain interest which attaches to the mantel-piece: it conceals a cleverly constructed hiding-place, between the floor of the room and the ceiling of the room beneath, which was made during the last evil days of the Inquisition in Venice, and which is reported to have saved an ancestor of my gracious lord pursued by that terrible tribunal. The machinery of this curious place of concealment has been kept in good order by the present lord, as a species of curiosity. He condescended to show me the method of working it. Approaching the two Caryatides, rest your hand on the forehead (midway between the eyebrows) of the figure which is on your left as you stand opposite to the fireplace, then press the head inwards as if you were pushing it against the wall behind. By doing this, you set in motion the hidden machinery in the wall which turns the hearthstone on a pivot, and discloses the hollow place below. There is room enough in it for a man to lie easily at full length. The method of closing the cavity again is equally simple. Place both your hands on the temples of the figures pull as if you were pulling it towards you—and the hearthstone will revolve into its proper position again."

"You need read no farther," said the Countess. "Be careful to remember what you have read."

She put back the page of vellum in her writing-desk, locked it, and led the way to the door.

"Come!" she said; "and see what the mocking Frenchman called 'The beginning of the end.' "

Agnes was barely able to rise from her chair; she trembled from head to foot. Henry gave her his arm to support her. "Fear nothing," he whispered; "I shall be with you."

The Countess proceeded along the westward corridor, and stopped at the door numbered Thirty-eight. This was the room which had been inhabited by Baron Rivar in the old days of the palace: it was situated immediately over the bedchamber in which Agnes had passed the night. For the last two days the room had been empty. The absence of luggage in it, when they opened the door, showed that it had not yet been let.

"You see?" said the Countess, pointing to the carved figure at the fire-place; "and you know what to do. Have I deserved that you should temper justice with mercy?" she went on in lower tones. "Give me a few hours more to myself. The Baron wants money—I must get on with my play."

She smiled vacantly, and imitated the action of writing with her right hand as she pronounced the last words. The effort of concentrating her weakened mind on other and less familiar topics than the constant want of money in the Baron's lifetime, and the vague prospect of gain from the still unfinished play, had evidently exhausted her poor reserves of strength. When her request had been granted, she addressed no expressions of gratitude to Agnes; she only said, "Feel no fear, miss, of my attempting to escape you. Where you are, there I must be till the end comes."

Her eyes wandered round the room with a last weary and stupefied look. She returned to her writing with slow and feeble steps, like the steps of an old woman.

CHAPTER XXIV

HENRY and Agnes were left alone in the Room of the Caryatides.

The person who had written the description of the palace— probably a poor author or artist—had correctly pointed out the defects of the mantel-piece. Bad taste, exhibiting itself on the most costly and splendid scale, was visible in every part of the work. It was nevertheless greatly admired by ignorant travellers of all classes; partly on account of its imposing size, and partly on account of the number of variously-coloured marbles which the sculptor had contrived to introduce into his design. Photographs of the mantel-piece were exhibited in the public rooms, and found a ready sale among English and American visitors to the hotel.

Henry led Agnes to the figure on the left, as they stood facing the empty fire-place. "Shall I try the experiment," he asked, "or will you?" She abruptly drew her arm away from him, and turned back to the door. "I can't even look at it," she said. "That merciless marble face frightens me!"

Henry put his hand on the forehead of the figure. "What is there to alarm you, my dear, in this conventionally classical face?" he asked jestingly. Before he could press the head inwards, Agnes hurriedly opened the door. "Wait till I am out of the room!" she cried. "The bare idea of what you may find there horrifies me!" She looked back into the room as she crossed the threshold. "I won't leave you altogether," she said, "I will wait outside."

She closed the door. Left by himself, Henry lifted his hand once more to the marble forehead of the figure.

For the second time, he was checked on the point of setting the machinery of the hiding-place in motion. On this occasion, the interruption came from an outbreak of friendly voices in the corridor. A woman's voice exclaimed, "Dearest Agnes, how glad I am to see you again!" A man's voice followed, offering to introduce some friend to "Miss Lockwood." A third voice (which Henry recognised as the voice of the manager of the hotel) became audible next, directing the housekeeper to show the ladies and gentlemen the vacant apartments at the other end of the corridor. "If more accommodation is wanted," the manager went on, "I have a charming room to let here." He opened the door as he spoke, and found himself face to face with Henry Westwick.

"This is indeed an agreeable surprise, sir!" said the manager cheerfully. "You are admiring our famous chimney-piece, I see. May I ask, Mr. Westwick, how you find yourself in the hotel, this time? Have the supernatural influences affected your appetite again?"

"The supernatural influences have spared me, this time," Henry answered. "Perhaps you may yet find that they have affected some other member of the family." He spoke gravely, resenting the familiar tone in which the manager had referred to his previous visit to the hotel. "Have you just returned?" he asked, by way of changing the topic.

"Just this minute, sir. I had the honour of travelling in the same train with friends of yours who have arrived at the hotel—Mr. and Mrs. Arthur Barville, and their travelling companions. Miss Lockwood is with them, looking at the rooms. They will be here before long, if they find it convenient to have an extra room at their disposal."

This announcement decided Henry on exploring the hiding-place, before the interruption occurred. It had crossed his mind, when Agnes left him, that he ought perhaps to have a witness, in the not very probable event of some alarming discovery taking place. The too-familiar manager, suspecting nothing, was there at his disposal. He turned again to the Caryan figure, maliciously resolving to make the manager his witness.

"I am delighted to hear that our friends have arrived at last," he said. "Before I shake hands with them, let me ask you a question about this queer work of art here. I see photographs of it down-stairs. Are they for sale?"

"Certainly, Mr. Westwick!"

"Do you think the chimney-piece is as solid as it looks?" Henry proceeded. "When you came in, I was just wondering whether this figure here had not accidentally got loosened from the wall behind it." He laid his hand on the marble forehead, for the third time. "To my eye, it looks a little out of the perpendicular. I almost fancied I could jog the head just now, when I touched it." He pressed the head inwards as he said those words.

A sound of jarring iron was instantly audible behind the wall. The solid hearthstone in front of the fire-place turned slowly at the feet of the two men, and disclosed a dark cavity below. At the same moment, the strange and sickening combination of odours, hitherto associated with the vaults of the old palace and with the bedchamber beneath, now floated up from the open recess, and filled the room.

The manager started back. "Good God, Mr. Westwick!" he exclaimed, "what does this mean?"

Remembering, not only what his brother Francis had felt in the room beneath, but what the experience of Agnes had been on the previous night, Henry was determined to be on his guard. "I am as much surprised as you are," was his only reply.

"Wait for me one moment, sir," said the manager. "I must stop the ladies and gentlemen outside from coming in."

He hurried away—not forgetting to close the door after him. Henry opened the window, and waited there breathing the purer air. Vague apprehensions of the next discovery to come, filled his mind for the first time. He was doubly resolved, now, not to stir a step in the investigation without a witness.

The manager returned with a wax taper in his hand, which he lighted as soon as he entered the room.

"We need fear no interruption now," he said. "Be so kind, Mr. Westwick, as to hold the light. It is *my* business to find out what this extraordinary discovery means."

Henry held the taper. Looking into the cavity, by the dim and flickering light, they both detected a dark object at the bottom of it. "I think I can reach the thing," the manager remarked, "if I lie down, and put my hand into the hole."

He knelt on the floor—and hesitated. "Might I ask you, sir, to give me my gloves?" he said. "They are in my hat, on the chair behind you."

Henry gave him the gloves. "I don't know what I may be going to take hold of," the manager explained, smiling rather uneasily as he put on his right glove.

He stretched himself at full length on the floor, and passed his right arm into the cavity. "I can't say exactly what I have got hold of," he said. "But I have got it."

Half raising himself, he drew his hand out.

The next instant, he started to his feet with a shriek of terror. A human head dropped from his nerveless grasp on the floor, and rolled to Henry's feet. It was the hideous head that Agnes had seen hovering above her, in the vision of the night!

The two men looked at each other, both struck speechless by the same emotion of horror. The manager was the first to control himself. "See to the door, for God's sake!" he said. "Some of the people outside may have heard me."

Henry moved mechanically to the door.

Even when he had his hand on the key, ready to turn it in the lock in case of necessity, he still looked back at the appalling object on the floor. There was no possibility of identifying those decayed and distorted features with any living creature whom he had seen—and, yet, he was conscious of feeling a vague and awful doubt which shook him to the soul. The questions which had tortured the mind of Agnes, were now *his* questions too. *He* asked himself, "In whose likeness might I have recognised it before the decay set in? The likeness of Ferrari? or the likeness of——?" He paused trembling, as Agnes had paused trembling before him. Agnes! The name, of all women's names the dearest to him, was a terror to him now! What was he to say to her? What might be the consequence if he trusted her with the terrible truth?

No footsteps approached the door; no voices were audible outside. The travellers were still occupied in the rooms at the eastern end of the corridor.

In the brief interval that had passed, the manager had sufficiently recovered himself to be able to think once more of the first and foremost interests of his life—the interests of the hotel. He approached Henry anxiously.

"If this frightful discovery becomes known," he said, "the closing of the hotel and the ruin of the Company will be the inevitable results. I feel sure that I can trust your discretion, sir, so far?"

"You can certainly trust me," Henry answered. "But surely discretion has its limits," he added, "after such a discovery as we have made?"

The manager understood that the duty which they owed to the community, as honest and law-abiding men, was the duty to which Henry now referred. "I will at once find the means," he said, "of conveying the remains privately out of the house, and I will myself place them in the care of the police authorities. Will you leave the room with me? or do you not object to keep watch here, and help me when I return?"

While he was speaking, the voices of the travellers made themselves heard again at the end of the corridor. Henry instantly consented to wait in the room. He shrank from facing the inevitable meeting with Agnes if he showed himself in the corridor at that moment.

The manager hastened his departure, in the hope of escaping notice. He was discovered by his guests before he could reach the head of the stairs. Henry heard the voices plainly as he turned the key. While the terrible drama of discovery was in progress on one side of the door, trivial questions about the amusements of Venice, and facetious discussions on the relative merits of French and Italian cookery, were proceeding on the other. Little by little, the sound of the talking grew fainter. The visitors, having arranged their plans of amusement for the day, were on their way out of the hotel. In a minute or two, there was silence once more.

Henry turned to the window, thinking to relieve his mind by looking at the bright view over the canal. He soon grew wearied of the familiar scene. The morbid fascination which seems to be exercised by all horrible sights, drew him back again to the ghastly object on the floor.

Dream or reality, how had Agnes survived the sight of it? As the question passed through his mind, he noticed for the first time something lying on the floor near the head. Looking closer, he perceived a thin little plate of gold, with three false teeth attached to it, which had apparently dropped out (loosened by the shock) when the manager let the head fall on the floor.

The importance of this discovery, and the necessity of not too readily communicating it to others, instantly struck Henry. Here surely was a chance—if any chance remained—of identifying the shocking relic of humanity which lay before him, the dumb witness of a crime! Acting on this idea, he took possession of the teeth, purposing to use them as a last means of inquiry when other attempts at investigation had been tried and had failed.

He went back again to the window: the solitude of the room began to weigh on his spirits. As he looked out again at the view, there was a soft knock at the door. He hastened to open it—and checked himself in the act. A doubt occurred to him. Was it the manager who had knocked? He called out, "Who is there?"

The voice of Agnes answered him. "Have you anything to tell me, Henry?"

He was hardly able to reply. "Not just now," he said, confusedly. "Forgive me if I don't open the door. I will speak to you a little later."

The sweet voice made itself heard again, pleading with him piteously. "Don't leave me alone, Henry! I can't go back to the happy people downstairs."

How could he resist that appeal? He heard her sigh—he heard the rustling of her dress as she moved away in despair. The very thing that he had shrunk from doing but a few minutes since was the thing that he did now! He joined Agnes in the corridor. She turned as she heard him, and pointed, trembling, in the direction of the closed room. "Is it so terrible as that?" she asked faintly.

He put his arm round her to support her. A thought came to him as he looked at her, waiting in doubt and fear for his reply. "You shall know what I have discovered," he said, "if you will first put on your hat and cloak, and come out with me."

She was naturally surprised. "Can you tell me your object in going out?" she asked.

He owned what his object was unreservedly. "I want, before all things," he said, "to satisfy your mind and mine, on the subject of Montbarry's death. I am going to take you to the doctor who attended him in his illness, and to the consul who followed him to the grave."

Her eyes rested on Henry gratefully. "Oh, how well you understand me!" she said. The manager joined them at the same moment, on his way up the stairs. Henry gave him the key of the room, and then called to the servants in the hall to have a gondola ready at the steps. "Are you leaving the hotel?" the manager asked. "In search of evidence," Henry whispered, pointing to the key. "If the authorities want me, I shall be back in an hour."

CHAPTER XXV

༄༅༄༅

THE day had advanced to evening. Lord Montbarry and the bridal party had gone to the Opera. Agnes alone, pleading the excuse of fatigue, remained at the hotel. Having kept up appearances by accompanying his friends to the theatre, Henry Westwick slipped away after the first act, and joined Agnes in the drawing-room.

"Have you thought of what I said to you earlier in the day?" he asked, taking a chair at her side. "Do you agree with me that the one dreadful doubt which oppressed us both is at least set at rest?"

Agnes shook her head sadly. "I wish I could agree with you, Henry—I wish I could honestly say that my mind is at ease."

The answer would have discouraged most men. Henry's patience (where Agnes was concerned) was equal to any demands on it.

"If you will only look back at the events of the day," he said, "you must surely admit that we have not been completely baffled. Remember how Doctor Bruno disposed of our doubts:—'After thirty years of medical practice, do you think I am likely to mistake the symptoms of death by bronchitis?' If ever there was an unanswerable question, there it is! Was the consul's testimony doubtful in any part of it? He called at the palace to offer his services, after hearing of Lord Montbarry's death; he arrived at the time when the coffin was in the house; he himself saw the corpse placed in it, and the lid screwed down. The evidence of the priest is equally beyond dispute. He remained in the room with the coffin, reciting the prayers for the dead, until the funeral left the palace. Bear all these statements in mind, Agnes; and how can you deny that the question of Montbarry's death and burial is a question set at rest? We have really but one doubt left: we have still to ask ourselves whether the remains which I discovered are the remains of the lost courier, or not. There is the case, as I understand it. Have

I stated it fairly?"

Agnes could not deny that he had stated it fairly.

"Then what prevents you from experiencing the same sense of relief that I feel?" Henry asked.

"What I saw last night prevents me," Agnes answered. "When we spoke of this subject, after our inquiries were over, you reproached me with taking what you called the superstitious view. I don't quite admit that—but I do acknowledge that I should find the superstitious view intelligible if I heard it expressed by some other person. Remembering what your brother and I once were to each other in the bygone time, I can understand the apparition making itself visible to *me*, to claim the mercy of Christian burial, and the vengeance due to a crime. I can even perceive some faint possibility of truth in the explanation which you described as the mesmeric theory—that what I saw might be the result of magnetic influence communicated to me, as I lay between the remains of the murdered husband above me and the guilty wife suffering the tortures of remorse at my bedside. But what I do *not* understand is, that I should have passed through that dreadful ordeal; having no previous knowledge of the murdered man in his lifetime, or only knowing him (if you suppose that I saw the apparition of Ferrari) through the interest which I took in his wife. I can't dispute your reasoning, Henry. But I feel in my heart of hearts that you are deceived. Nothing will shake my belief that we are still as far from having discovered the dreadful truth as ever."

Henry made no further attempt to dispute with her. She had impressed him with a certain reluctant respect for her own opinion, in spite of himself.

"Have you thought of any better way of arriving at the truth?" he asked. "Who is to help us? No doubt there is the Countess, who has the clue to the mystery in her own hands. But, in the present state of her mind, is her testimony to be trusted—even if she were willing to speak? Judging by my own experience, I should say decidedly not."

"You don't mean that you have seen her again?" Agnes eagerly interposed.

"Yes. I disturbed her once more over her endless writing; and I insisted on her speaking out plainly."

"Then you told her what you found when you opened the hiding-place?"

"Of course I did!" Henry replied. "I said that I held her responsible for the discovery, though I had not mentioned her connection with it to the authorities as yet. She went on with her writing as if I had spoken in an unknown tongue! I was equally obstinate, on my side. I told her plainly that the head had been placed under the care of the police, and that the manager and I had signed our declarations and given our evidence. She paid not the slightest heed to me. By way of tempting her to speak, I added that the whole investigation was to be kept a secret, and that she might depend on my discretion. For the moment I thought I had succeeded. She looked up from her writing with a passing flash of curiosity, and said, 'What are they going to do with it?'— meaning, I suppose, the head. I answered that it was to be privately buried, after photographs of it had first been taken. I even went the length of communicating the opinion of the surgeon consulted, that some chemical means of arresting decomposition had been used and had only partially succeeded—and I asked her point-blank if the surgeon was right? The trap was not a bad one—but it completely failed. She said in the coolest manner, 'Now you are here, I should like to consult you about my play; I am at a loss for some new incidents.' Mind! there was nothing satirical in this. She was really eager to read her wonderful work to me—evidently supposing that I took a special interest in such things, because my brother is the manager of a theatre! I left her, making the first excuse that occurred to me. So far as I am concerned, I can do nothing with her. But it is possible that *your* influence may succeed with her again, as it has succeeded already. Will you make the attempt, to satisfy your own mind? She is still upstairs; and I am quite ready to accompany you."

Agnes shuddered at the bare suggestion of another interview with the Countess.

"I can't! I daren't!" she exclaimed. "After what has happened in that horrible room, she is more repellent to me than ever. Don't ask me to do it, Henry! Feel my hand—you have turned me as cold as death only with talking of it!"

She was not exaggerating the terror that possessed her. Henry hastened to change the subject.

"Let us talk of something more interesting," he said. "I have a question to ask you about yourself. Am I right in believing that the sooner you get away from Venice the happier you will be?"

"Right?" she repeated excitedly. "You are more than right! No words can say how I long to be away from this horrible place. But you know how I am situated—you heard what Lord Montbarry said at dinner-time?"

"Suppose he has altered his plans, since dinner-time?" Henry suggested.

Agnes looked surprised. "I thought he had received letters from England which obliged him to leave Venice to-morrow," she said.

"Quite true," Henry admitted. "He had arranged to start for England to-morrow, and to leave you and Lady Montbarry and the children to enjoy your holiday in Venice, under my care. Circumstances have occurred, however, which have forced him to alter his plans. He must take you all back with him to-morrow because I am not able to assume the charge of you. I am obliged to give up my holiday in Italy, and return to England too."

Agnes looked at him in some little perplexity: she was not quite sure whether she understood him or not.

"Are you really obliged to go back?" she asked.

Henry smiled as he answered her. "Keep the secret," he said, "or Montbarry will never forgive me!"

She read the rest in his face. "Oh!" she exclaimed, blushing brightly, "you have not given up your pleasant holiday in Italy on my account?"

"I shall go back with you to England, Agnes. That will be holiday enough for *me*."

She took his hand in an irrepressible outburst of gratitude. "How good you are to me!" she murmured tenderly. "What should I have done in the troubles that have come to me, without your sympathy? I can't tell you, Henry, how I feel your kindness."

She tried impulsively to lift his hand to her lips. He gently stopped her. "Agnes," he said, "are you beginning to understand how truly I love you?"

That simple question found its own way to her heart. She owned the whole truth, without saying a word. She looked at him—and then looked away again.

He drew her nearer to him. "My own darling!" he whispered— and kissed her. Softly and tremulously, the sweet lips lingered, and touched his lips in return. Then her head drooped. She put her arms round his neck, and hid her face on his bosom. They spoke no more.

The charmed silence had lasted but a little while, when it was mercilessly broken by a knock at the door.

Agnes started to her feet. She placed herself at the piano; the instrument being opposite to the door, it was impossible, when she seated herself on the music-stool, for any person entering the room to see her face. Henry called out irritably, "Come in."

The door was not opened. The person on the other side of it asked a strange question.

"Is Mr. Henry Westwick alone?"

Agnes instantly recognised the voice of the Countess. She hurried to a second door, which communicated with one of the bedrooms. "Don't let her come near me!" she whispered nervously. "Good night, Henry! good night!"

If Henry could, by an effort of will, have transported the Countess to the uttermost ends of the earth, he would have made the effort without remorse. As it was, he only repeated, more irritably than ever, "Come in!"

She entered the room slowly with her everlasting manuscript in her hand. Her step was unsteady; a dark flush appeared on her face, in place of its customary pallor; her eyes were bloodshot and widely dilated. In approaching Henry, she showed a strange incapability of calculating her distances—she struck against the table near which he happened to be sitting. When she spoke, her articulation was confused, and her pronunciation of some of the longer words was hardly intelligible. Most men would have suspected her of being under the influence of some intoxicating liquor. Henry took a truer view—he said, as he placed a chair for her, "Countess, I am afraid you have been working too hard: you look as if you wanted rest."

She put her hand to her head. "My invention has gone," she said. "I can't write my fourth act. It's all a blank—all a blank!"

Henry advised her to wait till the next day. "Go to bed," he suggested; "and try to sleep."

She waved her hand impatiently. "I must finish the play," she answered. "I only want a hint from you. You must know something about plays. Your brother has got a theatre. You must often have heard him talk about fourth and fifth acts—you must have seen rehearsals, and all the rest of it." She abruptly thrust the manuscript into Henry's hand. "I can't read it to you," she said; "I feel giddy when I look at my own writing. Just run your eye over it, there's a good fellow—"and give me a hint."

Henry glanced at the manuscript. He happened to look at the list of the persons of the drama. As he read the list he started and turned abruptly to the Countess, intending to ask her for some explanation. The words were suspended on his lips. It was but too plainly useless to speak to her. Her head lay back on the rail of the chair. She seemed to be half asleep already. The flush on her face had deepened: she looked like a woman who was in danger of having a fit.

He rang the bell, and directed the man who answered it to send one of the chambermaids upstairs. His voice seemed to partially rouse the Countess; she opened her eyes in a slow drowsy way. "Have you read it?" she asked.

It was necessary as a mere act of humanity to humour her. "I will read it willingly," said Henry, "if you will go upstairs to bed. You shall hear what I think of it to-morrow morning. Our heads will be clearer, we shall be better able to make the fourth act in the morning."

The chambermaid came in while he was speaking. "I am afraid the lady is ill," Henry whispered. "Take her up to her room." The woman looked at the Countess and whispered back, "Shall we send for a doctor, sir?"

Henry advised taking her upstairs first, and then asking the manager's opinion. There was great difficulty in persuading her to rise, and accept the support of the chambermaid's arm. It was only by reiterated promises to read the play that night, and to make the fourth act in the morning, that Henry prevailed on the Countess to return to her room.

Left to himself, he began to feel a certain languid curiosity in relation to the manuscript. He looked over the pages, reading a line here and a line there. Suddenly he changed colour as he read—and looked up from the manuscript like a man bewildered. "Good God! what does this mean?" he said to himself.

His eyes turned nervously to the door by which Agnes had left him. She might return to the drawing-room, she might want to see what the Countess had written. He looked back again at the passage which had startled him—considered with himself for a moment—and, snatching up the unfinished play, suddenly and softly left the room.

CHAPTER XXVI

ENTERING his own room on the upper floor, Henry placed the manuscript on his table, open at the first leaf. His nerves were unquestionably shaken; his hand trembled as he turned the pages, he started at chance noises on the staircase of the hotel.

The scenario, or outline, of the Countess's play began with no formal prefatory phrases. She presented herself and her work with the easy familiarity of an old friend.

"Allow me, dear Mr. Francis Westwick, to introduce to you the persons in my proposed Play. Behold them, arranged sym-metrically in a line.

"My Lord. The Baron. The Courier. The Doctor. The Countess.

"I don't trouble myself, you see, to invest fictitious family names. My characters are sufficiently distinguished by their social titles, and by the striking contrast which they present one with another.

"The First Act opens——

"No! Before I open the First Act, I must announce, in justice to myself, that this Play is entirely the work of my own invention. I scorn to borrow from actual events; and, what is more extra-ordinary still, I have not stolen one of my ideas from the Modern French drama. As the manager of an English theatre, you will naturally refuse to believe this. It doesn't matter. Nothing matters —except the opening of my first act.

"We are at Homburg, in the famous Salon d'Or, at the height of the season. The Countess (exquisitely dressed) is seated at the green table. Strangers of all nations are standing behind the players, venturing their money or only looking on. My Lord is among the strangers. He is struck by the Countess's personal appearance, in which beauties and defects are fantastically mingled in the most attractive manner. He watches the Countess's game, and places his money where he sees her deposit her own little stake. She looks round at him, and says, "Don't trust to my colour; I have been unlucky the whole evening. Place your stake on the other colour, and you may have a chance of winning." My Lord (a true Englishman) blushes, bows, and obeys. The Countess proves to be a prophet. She loses again. My Lord wins twice the sum that he has risked.

"The Countess rises from the table. She has no more money, and she offers my Lord her chair.

"Instead of taking it, he politely places his winnings in her hand, and begs her to accept the loan as a favour to himself. The Countess stakes again, and loses again. My Lord smiles superbly, and presses a second loan on her. From that moment her luck turns. She wins, and wins largely. Her brother, the Baron, trying his fortune in another room, hears of what is going on, and joins my Lord and the Countess.

"Pay attention, if you please, to the Baron. He is delineated as a remarkable and interesting character.

"This noble person has begun life with a single-minded devotion to the science of experimental chemistry, very surprising in a young and handsome man with a brilliant future before him. A profound knowledge of the occult sciences has persuaded the

Baron that it is possible to solve the famous problem called the 'Philosopher's Stone.' His own pecuniary resources have long since been exhausted by his costly experiments. His sister has next supplied him with the small fortune at her disposal: reserving only the family jewels, placed in the charge of her banker and friend at Frankfort. The Countess's fortune also being swallowed up, the Baron has in a fatal moment sought for new supplies at the gaming table. He proves, at starting on his perilous career, to be a favourite of fortune; wins largely, and, alas! profanes his noble enthusiasm for science by yielding his soul to the all-debasing passion of the gamester.

"At the period of the Play, the Baron's good fortune has deserted him. He sees his way to a crowning experiment in the fatal search after the secret of transmuting the baser metals into gold. But how is he to pay the preliminary expenses? Destiny, like a mocking echo, answers, How?

"Will his sister's winnings (with my Lord's money) prove large enough to help him? Eager for this result, he gives the Countess his advice how to play. From that disastrous moment the infection of his own adverse fortune spreads to his sister. She loses again, and again—loses to the last farthing.

"The amiable and wealthy Lord offers a third loan; but the scrupulous Countess positively refuses to take it. On leaving the table, she presents her brother to my Lord. The gentlemen fall into pleasant talk. My Lord asks leave to pay his respects to the Countess, the next morning, at her hotel. The Baron hospitably invites him to breakfast. My Lord accepts, with a last admiring glance at the Countess which does not escape her brother's observation, and takes his leave for the night.

"Alone with his sister, the Baron speaks out plainly. 'Our affairs,' he says, 'are in a desperate condition, and must find a desperate remedy. Wait for me here, while I make inquiries about my Lord. You have evidently produced a strong impression on him. If we can turn that impression into money, no matter at what sacrifice, the thing must be done.'

"The Countess now occupies the stage alone, and indulges in a soliloquy which develops her character.

"It is at once a dangerous and attractive character. Immense capacities for good are implanted in her nature, side by side with equally remarkable capacities for evil. It rests with circumstances to develop either the one or the other. Being a person who produces a sensation wherever she goes, this noble lady is naturally made the subject of all sorts of scandalous reports. To one of these reports (which falsely and abominably points to the Baron as her lover instead of her brother) she now refers with just indignation. She has just expressed her desire to leave Homburg, as the place in which the vile calumny first took its rise, when the Baron returns, overhears her last words, and says to her, 'Yes, leave Homburg by all means; provided you leave it in the character of my Lord's betrothed wife!'

"The Countess is startled and shocked. She protests that she does not reciprocate my Lord's admiration for her. She even goes the length of refusing to see him again. The Baron answers, 'I must positively have command of money. Take your choice, between marrying my Lord's income, in the interest of my grand discovery—or leave me to sell myself and my title to the first rich woman of low degree who is ready to buy me.'

"The Countess listens in surprise and dismay. Is it possible that the Baron is in earnest? He is horribly in earnest. 'The woman who will buy me,' he says, 'is in the next room to us at this moment. She is the wealthy widow of a Jewish usurer. She has the money I want to reach the solution of the great problem. I have only to be that woman's husband, and to make myself master of untold millions of gold. Take five minutes to consider what I have said to you, and tell me on my return which of us is to marry for the money I want, you or I.'

"As he turns away, the Countess stops him.

"All the noblest sentiments in her nature are exalted to the highest pitch. 'Where is the true woman,' she exclaims, 'who wants time to consummate the sacrifice of herself, when the man to whom she is devoted demands it? She does not want five minutes—she does not want five seconds—she holds out her hand to him, and she says, Sacrifice me on the altar of your glory! Take as stepping-stones on the way to your triumph, my love, my liberty, and my life!'

"On this grand situation the curtain falls. Judging by my first act, Mr. Westwick, tell me truly, and don't be afraid of turning my head:—Am I not capable of writing a good play?"

Henry paused between the First and Second Acts; reflecting, not on the merits of the play, but on the strange resemblance which the incidents so far presented to the incidents that had attended the disastrous marriage of the first Lord Montbarry.

Was it possible that the Countess, in the present condition of her mind, supposed herself to be exercising her invention when she was only exercising her memory?

The question involved considerations too serious to be made the subject of a hasty decision. Reserving his opinion, Henry turned the page, and devoted himself to the reading of the next act. The manuscript proceeded as follows:——

"The Second Act opens at Venice. An interval of four months has elapsed since the date of the scene at the gambling table. The action now takes place in the reception-room of one of the Venetian palaces.

"The Baron is discovered, alone, on the stage. He reverts to the events which have happened since the close of the First Act. The Countess has sacrificed herself; the mercenary marriage has taken place—but not without obstacles, caused by difference of opinion on the question of marriage settlements.

"Private inquiries, instituted in England, have informed the Baron that my Lord's income is derived chiefly from what is called entailed property. In case of accidents, he is surely bound to do something for his bride? Let him, for example, insure his life, for a sum proposed by the Baron, and let him so settle the money that his widow shall have it, if he dies first.

"My Lord hesitates. The Baron wastes no time in useless discussion. 'Let us by all means' (he says) 'consider the marriage as broken off.' My Lord shifts his ground, and pleads for a smaller sum than the sum proposed. The Baron briefly replies, 'I never bargain.' My lord is in love; the natural result follows—he gives way.

"So far, the Baron has no cause to complain. But my Lord's turn comes, when the marriage has been celebrated, and when the honeymoon is over. The Baron has joined the married pair at a palace which they have hired in Venice. He is still bent on solving the problem of the 'Philosopher's Stone.' His laboratory is set up in the vaults beneath the palace—so that smells from chemical experiments may not incommode the Countess, in the higher regions of the house. The one obstacle in the way of his grand discovery is, as usual, the want of money. His position at the present time has become truly critical. He owes debts of honour to gentlemen in his own rank of life, which must positively be paid; and he proposes, in his own friendly manner, to borrow the money of my Lord. My Lord positively refuses, in the rudest terms. The Baron applies to his sister to exercise her conjugal influence. She can only answer that her noble husband (being no longer distractedly in love with her) now appears in his true character, as one of the meanest men living. The sacrifice of the marriage has been made, and has already proved useless.

"Such is the state of affairs at the opening of the Second Act.

"The entrance of the Countess suddenly disturbs the Baron's reflections. She is in a state bordering on frenzy. Incoherent expressions of rage burst from her lips: it is some time before she can sufficiently control herself to speak plainly. She has been doubly insulted—first, by a menial person in her employment; secondly, by her husband. Her maid, an Englishwoman, has declared that she will serve the Countess no longer. She will give up her wages, and return at once to England. Being asked her reason for this strange proceeding, she insolently hints that the Countess's service is no service for an honest woman, since the Baron has entered the house. The Countess does, what any lady in her position would do; she indignantly dismisses the wretch on the spot.

"My Lord, hearing his wife's voice raised in anger, leaves the study in which he is accustomed to shut himself up over his books, and asks what this disturbance means. The Countess informs him of the outrageous language and conduct of her maid. My Lord not only declares his entire approval of the woman's conduct, but expresses his own abominable doubts of his wife's fidelity in language of such horrible brutality that no lady could pollute her lips by repeating it. 'If I had been a man,' the Countess says, 'and if I had had a weapon in my hand, I would have struck him dead at my feet!'

"The Baron, listening silently so far, now speaks. 'Permit me to finish the sentence for you,' he says. 'You would have struck your husband dead at your feet; and by that rash act, you would have deprived yourself of the insurance money settled on the widow— the very money which is wanted to relieve your brother from the unendurable pecuniary position which he now occupies!'

"The Countess gravely reminds the Baron that this is no joking matter. After what my Lord has said to her, she has little doubt that he will communicate his infamous suspicions to his lawyers in England. If nothing is done to prevent it, she may be divorced and disgraced, and thrown on the world, with no resource but the sale of her jewels to keep her from starving.

"At this moment, the Courier who has been engaged to travel with my Lord from England crosses the stage with a letter to take to the post. The Countess stops him, and asks to look at the address on the letter. She takes it from him for a moment, and shows it to her brother. The handwriting is my Lord's; and the letter is directed to his lawyers in London.

"The Courier proceeds to the post-office. The Baron and the Countess look at each other in silence. No words are needed. They thoroughly understand the position in which they are placed; they clearly see the terrible remedy for it. What is the plain alternative before them? Disgrace and ruin—or, my Lord's death and the insurance money!

"The Baron walks backwards and forwards in great agitation, talking to himself. The Countess hears fragments of what he is saying. He speaks of my Lord's constitution, probably weakened in India—of a cold which my Lord has caught two or three days since—of the remarkable manner in which such slight things as colds sometimes end in serious illness and death.

"He observes that the Countess is listening to him, and asks if she has anything to propose. She is a woman who, with many defects, has the great merit of speaking out. 'Is there no such thing as a serious illness,' she asks, 'corked up in one of those bottles of yours in the vaults downstairs?'

"The Baron answers by gravely shaking his head. What is he afraid of?—a possible examination of the body after death? No: he can set any post-mortem examination at defiance. It is the process of administering the poison that he dreads. A man so distinguished as my Lord cannot be taken seriously ill without medical attendance. Where there is a Doctor, there is always danger of discovery. Then, again, there is the Courier, faithful to my Lord as long as my Lord pays him. Even if the Doctor sees nothing suspicious, the Courier may discover something. The poison, to do its work with the necessary secrecy, must be repeatedly administered in graduated doses. One trifling miscalculation or mistake may rouse suspicion. The insurance offices may hear of it, and may refuse to pay the money. As things are, the Baron will not risk it, and will not allow his sister to risk it in his place.

"My Lord himself is the next character who appears. He has repeatedly rung for the Courier, and the bell has not been answered. 'What does this insolence mean?'

"The Countess (speaking with quiet dignity—for why should her infamous husband have the satisfaction of knowing how deeply he has wounded her?) reminds my Lord that the Courier has gone to the post. My Lord asks suspiciously if she has looked at the letter. The Countess informs him coldly that she has no curiosity about his letters. Referring to the cold from which he is suffering, she inquires if he thinks of consulting a medical man. My Lord answers roughly that he is quite old enough to be capable of doctoring himself.

"As he makes this reply, the Courier appears, returning from the post. My Lord gives him orders to go out again and buy some lemons. He proposes to try hot lemonade as a means of inducing perspiration in bed. In that way he has formerly cured colds, and in that way he will cure the cold from which he is suffering now.

"The Courier obeys in silence. Judging by appearances, he goes very reluctantly on this second errand.

"My Lord turns to the Baron (who has thus far taken no part in the conversation) and asks him, in a sneering tone, how much longer he proposes to prolong his stay in Venice. The Baron answers quietly, 'Let us speak plainly to one another, my Lord. If you wish me to leave your house, you have only to say the word, and I go.' My Lord turns to his wife, and asks if she can support the calamity of her brother's absence—laying a grossly insulting emphasis on the word 'brother.' The Countess preserves her impenetrable composure; nothing in her betrays the deadly hatred with which she regards the titled ruffian who has insulted her. 'You are master in this house, my Lord,' is all she says. 'Do as you please.'

"My Lord looks at his wife; looks at the Baron—and suddenly alters his tone. Does he perceive in the composure of the Countess and her brother something lurking under the surface that threatens him? This is at least certain, he makes a clumsy apology for the language that he has used. (Abject wretch!)

"My Lord's excuses are interrupted by the return of the Courier with the lemons and hot water.

"The Countess observes for the first time that the man looks ill. His hands tremble as he places the tray on the table. My Lord orders his Courier to follow him, and make the lemonade in the bedroom. The Countess remarks that the Courier seems hardly capable of obeying his orders. Hearing this, the man admits that he is ill. He, too, is suffering from a cold; he has been kept waiting in a draught at the shop where he bought the lemons; he feels alternately hot and cold, and he begs permission to lie down for a little while on his bed.

"Feeling her humanity appealed to, the Countess volunteers to make the lemonade herself. My Lord takes the Courier by the arm, leads him aside, and whispers these words to him: 'Watch her, and see that she puts nothing into the lemonade; then bring it to me with your own hands; and, then, go to bed, if you like.'

"Without a word more to his wife, or to the Baron, my Lord leaves the room.

"The Countess makes the lemonade, and the Courier takes it to his master.

"Returning, on the way to his own room, he is so weak, and feels, he says, so giddy, that he is obliged to support himself by the backs of the chairs as he passes them. The Baron, always considerate to persons of low degree, offers his arm. 'I am afraid, my poor fellow,' he says, 'that you are really ill.' The Courier makes this extraordinary answer: 'It's all over with me, Sir: I have caught my death.'

"The Countess is naturally startled. 'You are not an old man,' she says, trying to rouse the Courier's spirits. 'At your age, catching cold doesn't surely mean catching your death?' The Courier fixes his eyes despairingly on the Countess.

" 'My lungs are weak, my Lady,' he says; 'I have already had two attacks of bronchitis. The second time, a great physician joined my own doctor in attendance on me. He considered my recovery almost in the light of a miracle. "Take care of yourself," he said. "If you have a third attack of bronchitis, as certainly as two and two make four, you will be a dead man." I feel the same inward shivering, my Lady, that I felt on those two former occasions—and I tell you again, I have caught my death in Venice.'

"Speaking some comforting words, the Baron leads him to his room. The Countess is left alone on the stage.

"She seats herself, and looks towards the door by which the Courier has been led out. 'Ah! my poor fellow,' she says, 'if you could only change constitutions with my Lord, what a happy result would follow for the Baron and for me! If *you* could only get cured of a trumpery cold with a little hot lemonade, and if *he* could only catch his death in your place——!'

"She suddenly pauses—considers for awhile—and springs to her feet, with a cry of triumphant surprise: the wonderful, the unparalleled idea has crossed her mind like a flash of lightning. Make the two men change names and places—and the deed is done! Where are the obstacles? Remove my Lord (by fair means or foul) from his room; and keep him secretly prisoner in the palace, to live or die as future necessity may determine. Place the Courier in the vacant bed, and call in the doctor to see him—ill, in my Lord's character, and (if he dies) dying under my Lord's name!"

The manuscript dropped from Henry's hands. A sickening sense of horror overpowered him. The question which had occurred to his mind at the close of the First Act of the Play assumed a new and terrible interest now. As far as the scene of the Countess's soliloquy, the incidents of the Second Act had reflected the events of his late brother's life as faithfully as the incidents of the First Act. Was the monstrous plot, revealed in the lines which he had just read, the offspring of the Countess's morbid imagination? or had she, in this case also, deluded herself with the idea that she was inventing when she was really writing under the influence of her own guilty remembrances of the past? If the latter interpretation were the true one, he had just read the narrative of the contemplated murder of his brother, planned in cold blood by a woman who was at that moment inhabiting the same house with him. While, to make the fatality complete, Agnes herself had innocently provided the conspirators with the one man who was fitted to be the passive agent of their crime.

Even the bare doubt that it might be so was more than he could endure. He left his room; resolved to force the truth out of the Countess, or to denounce her before the authorities as a murderess at large.

Arrived at her door, he was met by a person just leaving the room. The person was the manager. He was hardly recognisable; he looked and spoke like a man in a state of desperation.

"Oh, go in, if you like!" he said to Henry. "Mark this, sir! I am not a superstitious man; but I do begin to believe that crimes carry their own curse with them. This hotel is under a curse. What happens in the morning? We discover a crime committed in the old days of the palace. The night comes, and brings another dreadful event with it—a death; a sudden and shocking death, in the house. Go in, and see for yourself! I shall resign my situation, Mr. Westwick: I can't contend with the fatalities that pursue me here!"

Henry entered the room.

The Countess was stretched on her bed. The doctor on one side, and the chambermaid on the other, were standing looking at her. From time to time, she drew a heavy stertorous breath, like a person oppressed in sleeping. "Is she likely to die?" Henry asked.

"She is dead," the doctor answered. "Dead of the rupture of a blood-vessel on the brain. Those sounds that you hear are purely mechanical—they may go on for hours."

Henry looked at the chambermaid. She had little to tell. The Countess had refused to go to bed, and had placed herself at her desk to proceed with her writing. Finding it useless to remonstrate with her, the maid had left the room to speak to the manager. In the shortest possible time, the doctor was summoned to the hotel, and found the Countess dead on the floor. There was this to tell— and no more.

Looking at the writing-table as he went out, Henry saw the sheet of paper on which the Countess had traced her last lines of writing. The characters were almost illegible. Henry could just distinguish the words, "First Act," and "Persons of the Drama." The lost wretch had been thinking of her Play to the last, and had begun it all over again!

CHAPTER XXVII

HENRY returned to his room.

His first impulse was to throw aside the manuscript, and never to look at it again. The one chance of relieving his mind from the dreadful uncertainty that oppressed it, by obtaining positive evidence of the truth, was a chance annihilated by the Countess's death. What good purpose could be served, what relief could he anticipate, if he read more?

He walked up and down the room. After an interval, his thoughts took a new direction; the question of the manuscript presented itself under another point of view. Thus far, his reading had only informed him that the conspiracy had been planned. How did he know that the plan had been put in execution?

The manuscript lay just before him on the floor. He hesitated—

then picked it up; and, returning to the table, read on as follows, from the point at which he had left off.

"While the Countess is still absorbed in the bold yet simple combination of circumstances which she has discovered, the Baron returns. He takes a serious view of the case of the Courier; it may be necessary, he thinks, to send for medical advice. No servant is left in the palace, now the English maid has taken her departure. The Baron himself must fetch the doctor, if the doctor is really needed.

"'Let us have medical help, by all means,' his sister replies. 'But wait and hear something that I have to say to you first.' She then electrifies the Baron by communicating her idea to him. What danger of discovery have they to dread? My Lord's life in Venice has been a life of absolute seclusion: nobody but his banker knows him, even by personal appearance. He has presented his letter of credit as a perfect stranger; and he and his banker have never seen each other since that first visit. He has given no parties, and gone to no parties. On the few occasions when he has hired a gondola or taken a walk, he has always been alone. Thanks to the atrocious suspicion which makes him ashamed of being seen with his wife, he has led the very life which makes the proposed enterprise easy of accomplishment.

"The cautious Baron listens—but gives no positive opinion, as yet. 'See what you can do with the Courier,' he says; 'and I will decide when I hear the result. One valuable hint I may give you before you go. Your man is easily tempted by money—if you only offer him enough. The other day, I asked him, in jest, what he would do for a thousand pounds. He answered, "Anything." Bear that in mind; and offer your highest bid without bargaining.'

"The scene changes to the Courier's room, and shows the poor wretch with a photographic portrait of his wife in his hand, crying. The Countess enters.

"She wisely begins by sympathising with her contemplated accomplice. He is duly grateful; he confides his sorrows to his gracious mistress. Now that he believes himself to be on his death-bed, he feels remorse for his neglectful treatment of his wife. He could resign himself to die; but despair overpowers him when he remembers that he has saved no money, and that he will leave his widow, without resources, to the mercy of the world.

"On this hint, the Countess speaks. 'Suppose you were asked to do a perfectly easy thing,' she says; 'and suppose you were rewarded for doing it by a present of a thousand pounds, as a legacy for your widow?'

"The Courier raises himself on his pillow, and looks at the Countess with an expression of incredulous surprise. She can hardly be cruel enough (he thinks) to joke with a man in his miserable plight. Will she say plainly what this perfectly easy thing is, the doing of which will meet with such a magnificent reward?

"The Countess answers that question by confiding her project to the Courier, without the slightest reserve.

"Some minutes of silence follow when she has done. The Courier is not weak enough yet to speak without stopping to think first. Still keeping his eyes on the Countess, he makes a quaintly insolent remark on what he has just heard. 'I have not hitherto been a religious man; but I feel myself on the way to it. Since your ladyship has spoken to me, I believe in the Devil.' It is the Countess's interest to see the humorous side of this confession of faith. She takes no offence. She only says, 'I will give you half an hour by yourself, to think over my proposal. You are in danger of death. Decide, in your wife's interests, whether you will die worth nothing, or die worth a thousand pounds.'

"Left alone, the Courier seriously considers his position—and decides. He rises with difficulty; writes a few lines on a leaf taken from his pocket-book; and, with slow and faltering steps, leaves the room.

"The Countess, returning at the expiration of the half-hour's interval, finds the room empty. While she is wondering, the Courier opens the door. What has he been doing out of his bed? He answers, 'I have been protecting my own life, my lady, on the bare chance that I may recover from the bronchitis for the third time. If you or the Baron attempts to hurry me out of this world, or to deprive me of my thousand pounds reward, I shall tell the doctor where he will find a few lines of writing, which describe your ladyship's plot. I may not have strength enough, in the case supposed, to betray you by making a complete confession with my own lips; but I can employ my last breath to speak the half-dozen words which will tell the doctor where he is to look. Those words, it is needless to add, will be addressed to your Ladyship, if I find your engagements towards me faithfully kept.'

"With this audacious preface, he proceeds to state the conditions on which he will play his part in the conspiracy, and die (if he does die) worth a thousand pounds.

"Either the Countess or the Baron are to taste the food and drink brought to his bedside, in his presence, and even the medicines which the doctor may prescribe for him. As for the promised sum of money, it is to be produced in one bank-note, folded in a sheet of paper, on which a line is to be written, dictated by the Courier. The two enclosures are then to be sealed up in an envelope, addressed to his wife, and stamped ready for the post. This done, the letter is to be placed under his pillow; the Baron or the Countess being at liberty to satisfy themselves, day by day, at their own time, that the letter remains in its place, with the seal unbroken, as long as the doctor has any hope of his patient's recovery. The last stipulation follows. The Courier has a conscience; and with a view to keeping it easy, insists that he shall be left in ignorance of that part of the plot which relates to the sequestration of my Lord. Not that he cares particularly what becomes of his miserly master—but he does dislike taking other people's responsibilities on his own shoulders.

"These conditions being agreed to, the Countess calls in the Baron, who has been waiting events in the next room.

"He is informed that the Courier has yielded to temptation; but he is still too cautious to make any compromising remarks. Keeping his back turned on the bed, he shows a bottle to the Countess. It is labelled 'Chloroform.' She understands that my Lord is to be removed from his room in a convenient state of insensibility. In what part of the palace is he to be hidden? As they open the door to go out, the Countess whispers that question to the Baron. The Baron whispers back, 'In the vaults!' The curtain falls."

CHAPTER XXVIII

❦❦❦❦

So the Second Act ended.

Turning to the Third Act, Henry looked wearily at the pages as he let them slip through his fingers. Both in mind and body, he began to feel the need of repose.

In one important respect, the later portion of the manuscript differed from the pages which he had just been reading. Signs of an overwrought brain showed themselves, here and there, as the outline of the play approached its end. The handwriting grew worse and worse. Some of the longer sentences were left unfinished. In the exchange of dialogue, questions and answers were not always attributed respectively to the right speaker. At certain intervals the writer's failing intelligence seemed to recover itself for awhile; only to relapse again, and to lose the thread of the narrative more hopelessly than ever.

After reading one or two of the more coherent passages Henry recoiled from the ever-darkening horror of the story. He closed the manuscript, heartsick and exhausted, and threw himself on his bed to rest. The door opened almost at the same moment. Lord Montbarry entered the room.

"We have just returned from the Opera," he said; "and we have heard the news of that miserable woman's death. They say you spoke to her in her last moments; and I want to hear how it happened."

"You shall hear how it happened," Henry answered; "and more than that. You are now the head of the family, Stephen; and I feel bound, in the position which oppresses me, to leave you to decide what ought to be done."

With those introductory words, he told his brother how the Countess's play had come into his hands. "Read the first few pages," he said. "I am anxious to know whether the same impression is produced on both of us."

Before Lord Montbarry had got half-way through the First Act, he stopped, and looked at his brother. "What does she mean by boasting of this as her own invention?" he asked. "Was she too crazy to remember that these things really happened?"

This was enough for Henry: the same impression had been produced on both of them. "You will do as you please," he said. "But if you will be guided by me, spare yourself the reading of those pages to come, which describe our brother's terrible expiation of his heartless marriage."

"Have *you* read it all, Henry?"

"Not all. I shrank from reading some of the latter part of it. Neither you nor I saw much of our elder brother after we left school; and, for my part, I felt, and never scrupled to express my feeling, that he behaved infamously to Agnes. But when I read that unconscious confession of the murderous conspiracy to which he fell a victim, I remembered, with something like remorse, that the same mother bore us. I have felt for him to-night, what I am ashamed to think I never felt for him before."

Lord Montbarry took his brother's hand.

"You are a good fellow, Henry," he said; "but are you quite sure that you have not been needlessly distressing yourself? Because some of this crazy creature's writing accidentally tells what we know to be the truth, does it follow that all the rest is to be relied on to the end?"

"There is no possible doubt of it," Henry replied.

"No possible doubt?" his brother repeated. "I shall go on with my reading, Henry—and see what justification there may be for that confident conclusion of yours."

He read on steadily, until he had reached the end of the Second Act. Then he looked up.

"Do you really believe that the mutilated remains which you discovered this morning are the remains of our brother?" he asked. "And do you believe it on such evidence as this?"

Henry answered silently by a sign in the affirmative.

Lord Montbarry checked himself—evidently on the point of entering an indignant protest.

"You acknowledge that you have not read the later scenes of the 'piece," he said. "Don't be childish, Henry! If you persist in pinning your faith on such stuff as this, the least you can do is to make yourself thoroughly acquainted with it. Will you read the Third Act? No? Then I shall read it to you."

He turned to the Third Act, and ran over those fragmentary passages which were clearly enough written and expressed to be intelligible to the mind of a stranger.

"Here is a scene in the vaults of the palace," he began. "The victim of the conspiracy is sleeping on his miserable bed; and the Baron and the Countess are considering the position in which they stand. The Countess (as well as I can make it out) has raised the money that is wanted by borrowing on the security of her jewels at Frankfort; and the Courier upstairs is still declared by the Doctor to have a chance of recovery. What are the conspirators to do, if the man does recover? The cautious Baron suggests setting the prisoner free. If he ventures to appeal to the law, it is easy to declare that he is subject to insane delusion, and to call his own wife as witness. On the other hand, if the Courier dies, how is the sequestrated and unknown nobleman to be put out of the way? Passively, by letting him starve in his prison? No: the Baron is a man of refined tastes; he dislikes needless cruelty. The active policy remains—say, assassination by the knife of a hired bravo? The Baron objects to trusting an accomplice; also to spending money on anyone but himself. Shall they drop their prisoner into the canal? The Baron declines to trust water; water will show him on the surface. Shall they set his bed on fire? An excellent idea; but the smoke might be seen. No: the circumstances being now entirely altered, poisoning him presents the easiest way out of it. He has simply become a superfluous person. The cheapest poison will do. —Is it possible, Henry, that you believe this consultation really took place?"

Henry made no reply. The succession of the questions that had just been read to him, exactly followed the succession of the dreams that had terrified Mrs. Norbury, on the two nights which she had passed in the hotel. It was useless to point out this coincidence to his brother. He only said, "Go on."

Lord Montbarry turned the pages until he came to the next intelligible passage.

"Here," he proceeded, "is a double scene on the stage—so far as I can understand the sketch of it. The Doctor is upstairs, innocently writing his certificate of my Lord's decease, by the dead Courier's bedside. Down in the vaults, the Baron stands by the corpse of the poisoned lord, preparing the strong chemical acids which are to reduce it to a heap of ashes—Surely, it is not worth while to trouble ourselves with deciphering such melodramatic horrors as these? Let us get on! let us get on!"

He turned the leaves again; attempting vainly to discover the meaning of the confused scenes that followed. On the last page but one, he found the last intelligible sentences.

"The Third Act seems to be divided," he said, "into two Parts or Tableaux. I think I can read the writing at the beginning of the Second Part. The Baron and the Countess open the scene. The Baron's hands are mysteriously concealed by gloves. He has reduced the body to ashes by his own system of cremation, with the exception of the head——"

Henry interrupted his brother there. "Don't read any more!" he exclaimed.

"Let us do the Countess justice," Lord Montbarry persisted. "There are not half a dozen lines more that I can make out! The accidental breaking of his jar of acid has burnt the Baron's hands severely. He is still unable to proceed to the destruction of the head—and the Countess is woman enough (with all her wickedness) to shrink from attempting to take his place—when the first news is received of the coming arrival of the commission of inquiry despatched by the insurance offices. The Baron feels no alarm. Inquire as the commission may, it is the natural death of the Courier (in my Lord's character) that they are blindly investigating. The head not being destroyed, the obvious alternative is to hide it—and the Baron is equal to the occasion. His studies in the old library have informed him of a safe place of concealment in the palace. The Countess may recoil from handling the acids and watching the process of cremation; but she can surely sprinkle a little disinfecting powder——"

"No more!" Henry reiterated. "No more!"

"There is no more that can be read, my dear fellow. The last page looks like sheer delirium. She may well have told you that her invention had failed her!"

"Face the truth honestly, Stephen, and say her memory."

Lord Montbarry rose from the table at which he had been sitting, and looked at his brother with pitying eyes.

"Your nerves are out of order, Henry," he said. "And no wonder, after that frightful discovery under the hearth-stone. We won't dispute about it; we will wait a day or two until you are quite yourself again. In the meantime, let us understand each other on one point at least. You leave the question of what is to be done with these pages of writing to me, as the head of the family?"

"I do."

Lord Montbarry quietly took up the manuscript, and threw it into the fire. "Let this rubbish be of some use," he said, holding the pages down with the poker. "The room is getting chilly—the Countess's play will set some of these charred logs flaming again." He waited a little at the fireplace, and returned to his brother. "Now, Henry, I have a last word to say, and then I have done. I am ready to admit that you have stumbled, by an unlucky chance, on the proof of a crime committed in the old days of the palace, nobody knows how long ago. With that one concession, I dispute everything else. Rather than agree in the opinion you have formed, I won't believe anything that has happened. The supernatural influences that some of us felt when we first slept in this hotel— your loss of appetite, our sister's dreadful dreams, the smell that overpowered Francis, and the head that appeared to Agnes— I declare them all to be sheer delusions! I believe in nothing, nothing, nothing!" He opened the door to go out, and looked back into the room. "Yes," he resumed, "there is one thing I believe in. My wife has committed a breach of confidence—I believe Agnes will marry you. Good night, Henry. We leave Venice the first thing to-morrow morning.

So Lord Montbarry disposed of the mystery of The Haunted Hotel.

POSTSCRIPT

A LAST chance of deciding the difference of opinion between the two brothers remained in Henry's possession. He had his own idea of the use to which he might put the false teeth as a means of inquiry when he and his fellow-travellers returned to England.

The only surviving depositary of the domestic history of the family in past years, was Agnes Lockwood's old nurse. Henry took his first opportunity of trying to revive her personal recollections of the deceased Lord Montbarry. But the nurse had never forgiven the great man of the family for his desertion of Agnes; she flatly refused to consult her memory. "Even the bare sight of my lord, when I last saw him in London," said the old woman, "made my finger-nails itch to set their mark on his face. I was sent on an errand by Miss Agnes; and I met him coming out of his dentist's door—and, thank God, that's the last I ever saw of him!"

Thanks to the nurse's quick temper and quaint way of expressing herself, the object of Henry's inquiries was gained already! He ventured on asking if she had noticed the situation of the house. She had noticed, and still remembered the situation— did Master Henry suppose she had lost the use of her senses, because she happened to be nigh on eighty years old? The same day, he took the false teeth to the dentist, and set all further doubt (if doubt had still been possible) at rest for ever. The teeth had been made for the first Lord Montbarry.

Henry never revealed the existence of this last link in the chain of discovery to any living creature, his brother Stephen included. He carried his terrible secret with him to the grave.

There was one other event in the memorable past on which he preserved the same compassionate silence. Little Mrs. Ferrari never knew that her husband had been—not, as she supposed, the Countess's victim—but the Countess's accomplice. She still believed that the late Lord Montbarry had sent her the thousand-pound note, and still recoiled from making use of a present which she persisted in declaring had "the stain of her husband's blood on it." Agnes, with the widow's entire approval, took the money to the Children's Hospital; and spent it in adding to the number of the beds.

In the spring of the new year, the marriage took place. At the special request of Agnes, the members of the family were the only persons present at the ceremony. There was no wedding break-fast—and the honeymoon was spent in the retirement of a cottage on the banks of the Thames.

During the last few days of the residence of the newly married couple by the riverside, Lady Montbarry's children were invited to enjoy a day's play in the garden. The eldest girl overheard (and reported to her mother) a little conjugal dialogue which touched on the topic of The Haunted Hotel.

"Henry, I want you to give me a kiss."

"There it is, my dear."

"Now I am your wife, may I speak to you about something?"

"What is it?"

"Something that happened the day before we left Venice. You saw the Countess, during the last hours of her life. Won't you tell me whether she made any confession to you?"

"No conscious confession, Agnes—and therefore no con-fession that I need distress you by repeating."

"Did she say nothing about what she saw or heard, on that dreadful night in my room?"

"Nothing. We only know that her mind never recovered the terror of it."

Agnes was not quite satisfied. The subject troubled her. Even her own brief intercourse with her miserable rival of other days suggested questions that perplexed her. She remembered the Countess's prediction. "You have to bring me to the day of discovery, and to the punishment that is my doom." Had the prediction simply failed, like other mortal prophecies?—or had it been fulfilled on the terrible night when she had seen the apparition, and when she had innocently tempted the Countess to watch her in her room?

Let it, however, be recorded, among the other virtues of Mrs. Henry Westwick, that she never again attempted to persuade her husband into betraying his secrets. Other men's wives, hearing of this extraordinary conduct (and being trained in the modern school of morals and manners), naturally regarded her with compassionate contempt. They spoke of Agnes, from that time forth, as "rather an old-fashioned person."

Is that all?

That is all.

Is there no explanation of the mystery of The Haunted Hotel?

Ask yourself if there is any explanation of the mystery of your own life and death.—Farewell.

The Dream-Woman

The Dream-Woman

CHAPTER I

❧❧❧❧❧

I HAD not been settled much more than six weeks in my country practice when I was sent for to a neighbouring town, to consult with the resident medical man there on a case of very dangerous illness.

My horse had come down with me at the end of a long ride the night before, and had hurt himself, luckily, much more than he had hurt his master. Being deprived of the animal's services, I started for my destination by the coach (there were no railways at that time), and I hoped to get back again, toward the afternoon, in the same way.

After the consultation was over, I went to the principal inn of the town to wait for the coach. When it came up it was full inside and out. There was no resource left me but to get home as cheaply as I could by hiring a gig. The price asked for this accommodation struck me as being so extortionate, that I determined to look out for an inn of inferior pretensions, and to try if I could not make a better bargain with a less prosperous establishment.

I soon found a likely-looking house, dingy and quiet, with an old-fashioned sign, that had evidently not been repainted for many years past. The landlord, in this case, was not above making a small profit, and as soon as we came to terms he rang the yard-bell to order the gig.

"Has Robert not come back from that errand?" asked the landlord, appealing to the waiter who answered the bell.

"No, sir, he hasn't."

"Well, then, you must wake up Isaac."

"Wake up Isaac!" I repeated; "that sounds rather odd. Do your hostlers go to bed in the daytime?"

"This one does," said the landlord, smiling to himself in rather a strange way.

"And dreams too," added the waiter; "I shan't forget the turn it gave me the first time I heard him."

"Never you mind about that," retorted the proprietor; "you go and rouse Isaac up. The gentleman's waiting for his gig."

The landlord's manner and the waiter's manner expressed a great deal more than they either of them said. I began to suspect that I might be on the trace of something professionally interesting to me as a medical man, and I thought I should like to look at the hostler before the waiter awakened him.

"Stop a minute," I interposed; "I have rather a fancy for seeing this man before you wake him up. I'm a doctor; and if this queer sleeping and dreaming of his comes from anything wrong in his brain, I may be able to tell you what to do with him."

"I rather think you will find his complaint past all doctoring, sir," said the landlord; "but, if you would like to see him, you're welcome, I'm sure."

He led the way across a yard and down a passage to the stables, opened one of the doors, and, waiting outside himself, told me to look in.

I found myself in a two-stall stable. In one of the stalls a horse was munching his corn; in the other an old man was lying asleep on the litter.

I stooped and looked at him attentively. It was a withered, woe-begone face. The eyebrows were painfully contracted; the mouth was fast set, and drawn down at the corners.

The hollow wrinkled cheeks, and the scanty grizzled hair, told their own tale of some past sorrow or suffering. He was drawing his breath convulsively when I first looked at him, and in a moment more he began to talk in his sleep.

"Wake up!" I heard him say, in a quick whisper, through his clinched teeth. "Wake up there! Murder!"

He moved one lean arm slowly till it rested over his throat, shuddered a little, and turned on his straw. Then the arm left his throat, the hand stretched itself out, and clutched at the side toward which he had turned, as if he fancied himself to be grasping at the edge of something. I saw his lips move, and bent lower over him. He was still talking in his sleep.

"Light gray eyes," he murmured, "and a droop in the left eyelid; flaxen hair, with a gold-yellow streak in it—all right, mother—fair white arms, with a down on them—little lady's hand, with a reddish look under the finger nails. The knife—always the cursed knife—first on one side, then on the other. Aha! you she-devil, where's the knife?"

At the last word his voice rose, and he grew restless on a sudden. I saw him shudder on the straw; his withered face became distorted, and he threw up both his hands with a quick hysterical gasp. They struck against the bottom of the manger under which he lay, and the blow awakened him. I had just time to slip through the door and close it before his eyes were fairly open, and his senses his own again.

"Do you know anything about that man's past life?" I said to the landlord.

"Yes, sir, I know pretty well all about it," was the answer, "and an uncommon queer story it is. Most people don't believe it. It's true, though, for all that. Why, just look at him," continued the landlord, opening the stable door again. "Poor devil! he's so worn out with his restless nights that he's dropped back into his sleep already."

"Don't wake him," I said; "I'm in no hurry for the gig. Wait till the other man comes back from his errand; and, in the meantime, suppose I have some lunch and a bottle of sherry, and suppose you come and help me to get through it?"

The heart of mine host, as I had anticipated, warmed to me over his own wine. He soon became communicative on the subject of the man asleep in the stable, and by little and little I drew the whole story out of him. Extravagant and incredible as the events must appear to everybody, they are related here just as I heard them and just as they happened.

CHAPTER II

SOME years ago there lived in the suburbs of a large seaport town on the west coast of England a man in humble circumstances, by name Isaac Scatchard. His means of subsistence were derived from any employment that he could get as an hostler, and occasionally, when times went well with him, from temporary engagements in service as stable-helper in private houses. Though a faithful, steady, and honest man, he got on badly in his calling. His ill luck was proverbial among his neighbours. He was always missing good opportunities by no fault of his own, and always living longest in service with amiable people who were not punctual payers of wages. "Unlucky Isaac" was his nickname in his own neighbour-hood, and no one could say that he did not richly deserve it.

With far more than one man's fair share of adversity to endure, Isaac had but one consolation to support him, and that was of the dreariest and most negative kind. He had no wife and children to increase his anxieties and add to the bitterness of his various failures in life. It might have been from mere insensibility, or it might have been from generous unwillingness to involve another in his own unlucky destiny, but the fact undoubtedly was, that he had arrived at the middle term of life without marrying, and, what is much more remarkable, without once exposing himself, from eighteen to eight-and-thirty, to the genial imputation of ever having had a sweetheart.

When he was out of service he lived alone with his widowed mother. Mrs. Scatchard was a woman above the average in her lowly station as to capacity and manners. She had seen better days, as the phrase is, but she never referred to them in the presence of curious visitors; and, though perfectly polite to every one who approached her, never cultivated any intimacies among her neighbours. She contrived to provide, hardly enough, for her simple wants by doing rough work for the tailors, and always managed to keep a decent home for her son to return to whenever his ill luck drove him out helpless into the world.

One bleak autumn when Isaac was getting on fast toward forty and when he was as usual out of place through no fault of his own, he set forth from his mother's cottage on a long walk inland to a gentleman's seat where he had heard that a stable-helper was required.

It wanted then but two days of his birthday; and Mrs. Scatchard, with her usual fondness, made him promise, before he started, that he would be back in time to keep that anniversary with her, in as festive a way as their poor means would allow. It was easy for him to comply with this request, even supposing he slept a night each way on the road.

He was to start from home on Monday morning, and, whether he got the new place or not, he was to be back for his birthday dinner on Wednesday at two o'clock.

Arriving at his destination too late on the Monday night to make application for the stable-helper's place, he slept at the village inn, and in good time on the Tuesday morning presented himself at the gentleman's house to fill the vacant situation. Here again his ill luck pursued him as inexorably as ever. The excellent written testimonials to his character which he was able to produce availed him nothing; his long walk had been taken in vain: only the day before the stable-helper's place had been given to another man.

Isaac accepted this new disappointment resignedly and as a matter of course. Naturally slow in capacity, he had the bluntness of sensibility and phlegmatic patience of disposition which frequently distinguish men with sluggishly-working mental powers. He thanked the gentleman's steward with his usual quiet civility for granting him an interview, and took his departure with no appearance of unusual depression in his face or manner.

Before starting on his homeward walk he made some inquiries at the inn, and ascertained that he might save a few miles on his return by following the new road. Furnished with full instructions, several times repeated, as to the various turnings he was to take, he set forth on his homeward journey and walked on all day with only one stoppage for bread and cheese. Just as it was getting toward dark, the rain came on and the wind began to rise, and he found himself, to make matters worse, in a part of the country with which he was entirely unacquainted, though he knew himself to be some fifteen miles from home. The first house he found to inquire at was a lonely roadside inn, standing on the outskirts of a thick wood. Solitary as the place looked, it was welcome to a lost man who was also hungry, thirsty, footsore and wet. The landlord was civil and respectable-looking, and the price he asked for a bed was reasonable enough. Isaac therefore decided on stopping comfortably at the inn for that night.

He was constitutionally a temperate man. His supper consisted of two rashers of bacon, a slice of home-made bread and a pint of ale. He did not go to bed immediately after this moderate meal, but sat up with the landlord, talking about his bad prospects and his long run of ill-luck, and diverging from these topics to the subjects of horse-flesh and racing. Nothing was said either by himself, his host, or the few labourers who strayed into the tap-room, which could, in the slightest degree, excite the very small and very dull imaginative faculty which Isaac Scatchard possessed.

At a little after eleven the house was closed. Isaac went round with the landlord and held the candle while the doors and lower windows were being secured. He noticed with surprise the strength of the bolts and bars, and iron-sheathed shutters.

"You see, we are rather lonely here," said the landlord. "We never have had any attempts made to break in yet, but it's always as well to be on the safe side. When nobody is sleeping here, I am the only man in the house. My wife and daughter are timid, and the servant-girl takes after her missuses. Another glass of ale before you turn in? No! Well, how such a sober man as you comes to be out of place is more than I can make out, for one. Here's where you're to sleep. You're our only lodger to-night, and I think you'll say my missus has done her best to make you comfortable. You're quite sure you won't have another glass of ale? Very well. Good-night."

It was half-past eleven by the clock in the passage as they went upstairs to the bedroom, the window of which looked on to the wood at the back of the house.

Isaac locked the door, set his candle on the chest of drawers, and wearily got ready for bed. The bleak autumn wind was still blowing, and the solemn, monotonous, surging moan of it in the wood was dreary and awful to hear through the night-silence. Isaac felt strangely wakeful. He resolved, as he lay down in bed, to keep the candle alight until he began to grow sleepy, for there was something unendurably depressing in the bare idea of lying awake in the darkness, listening to the dismal, ceaseless moaning of the wind in the wood.

Sleep stole on him before he was aware of it. His eyes closed, and he fell off insensibly to rest without having so much as thought of extinguishing the candle.

The first sensation of which he was conscious after sinking into slumber was a strange shivering that ran through him suddenly from head to foot, and a dreadful sinking pain at the heart, such as he had never felt before. The shivering only disturbed his slumbers; the pain woke him instantly. In one moment he passed from a state of sleep to a state of wakefulness—his eyes wide open—his mental perceptions cleared on a sudden, as if by a miracle.

The candle had burned down nearly to the last morsel of tallow, but the top of the unsnuffed wick had just fallen off, and the light in the little room was, for the moment, fair and full.

Between the foot of his bed and the closed door there stood a woman with a knife in her hand, looking at him.

He was stricken speechless with terror, but he did not lose the preternatural clearness of his faculties, and he never took his eyes off the woman. She said not a word as they stared each other in the face, but she began to move slowly toward the left-hand side of the bed.

His eyes followed her. She was a fair, fine woman, with yellowish flaxen hair and light gray eyes, with a droop in the left eyelid. He noticed those things and fixed them on his mind before she was round at the side of the bed. Speechless, with no expression in her face, with no noise following her footfall, she came closer and closer—stopped—and slowly raised the knife. He laid his right arm over his throat to save it; but, as he saw the knife coming down, threw his hand across the bed to the right side, and jerked his body over that way just as the knife descended on the mattress within an inch of his shoulder.

His eyes fixed on her arm and hand as she slowly drew her knife out of the bed: a white, well-shaped arm, with a pretty down lying lightly over the fair skin—a delicate lady's hand, with the crowning beauty of a pink flush under and round the finger-nails.

She drew the knife out, and passed back again slowly to the foot of the bed; stopped there for a moment looking at him; then came on—still speechless, still with no expression on the blank, beautiful face, still with no sound following the stealthy footfalls— came on to the right side of the bed, where he now lay.

As she approached, she raised the knife again, and he drew himself away to the left side. She struck, as before, right into the mattress, with a deliberate, perpendicularly-downward action of the arm. This time his eyes wandered from her to the knife. It was like the large clasp-knives which he had often seen labouring men use to cut their bread and bacon with. Her delicate little fingers did not conceal more than two-thirds of the handle: he noticed that it was made of buck-horn, clean and shining as the blade was, and looking like new.

For the second time she drew the knife out, concealed it in the wide sleeve of her gown, then stopped by the bedside, watching him. For an instant he saw her standing in that position, then the wick of the spent candle fell over into the socket; the flame diminished to a little blue point, and the room grew dark.

A moment, or less, if possible, passed so, and then the wick flamed up, smokingly, for the last time. His eyes were still looking eagerly over the right-hand side of the bed when the final flash of light came, but they discerned nothing. The fair woman with the knife was gone.

The conviction that he was alone again weakened the hold of the terror that had struck him dumb up to this time. The preternatural sharpness which the very intensity of his panic had mysteriously imparted to his faculties left them suddenly. His brain grew confused—his heart beat wildly—his ears opened for the first time since the appearance of the woman to a sense of the woeful ceaseless moaning of the wind among the trees. With the dreadful conviction of the reality of what he had seen still strong within him, he leaped out of bed, and screaming "Murder! Wake up, there! wake up!" dashed headlong through the darkness to the door.

It was fast locked, exactly as he had left it on going to bed.

His cries on starting up had alarmed the house. He heard the terrified, confused exclamations of women; he saw the master of the house approaching along the passage with his burning rush-candle in one hand and his gun in the other.

"What is it?" asked the landlord, breathlessly.

Isaac could only answer in a whisper. "A woman, with a knife in her hand," he gasped out. "In my room—a fair, yellow-haired woman; she jobbed at me with the knife twice over."

The landlord's pale cheeks grew paler. He looked at Isaac eagerly by the flickering light of his candle, and his face began to get red again; his voice altered, too, as well as his complexion.

"She seems to have missed you twice," he said.

"I dodged the knife as it came down," Isaac went on, in the same scared whisper. "It struck the bed each time."

The landlord took his candle into the bedroom immediately. In less than a minute he came out again into the passage in a violent passion.

"The devil fly away with you and your woman with the knife! There isn't a mark in the bedclothes anywhere. What do you mean by coming into a man's place and frightening his family out of their wits about a dream?"

"I'll leave your house," said Isaac, faintly. "Better out on the road, in rain and dark, on my road home, than back again in that room, after what I've seen in it. Lend me a light to get my clothes by, and tell me what I'm to pay."

"Pay!" cried the landlord, leading the way with his light sulkily into the bedroom. "You'll find your score on the slate when you go downstairs. I wouldn't have taken you in for all the money you've got about you if I'd known your dreaming, screeching ways beforehand. Look at the bed. Where's the cut of a knife in it? Look at the window—is the lock bursted? Look at the door (which I heard you fasten yourself)—is it broke in? A murdering woman with a knife in my house! You ought to be ashamed of yourself!"

Isaac answered not a word. He huddled on his clothes, and then they went downstairs together.

"Nigh on twenty minutes past two!" said the landlord, as they passed the clock. "A nice time in the morning to frighten honest people out of their wits!"

Isaac paid his bill, and the landlord let him out at the front door, asking, with a grin of contempt, as he undid the strong fastenings, whether "the murdering woman got in that way."

They parted without a word on either side. The rain had ceased, but the night was dark, and the wind bleaker than ever. Little did the darkness, or the cold, or the uncertainty about the way home matter to Isaac. If he had been turned out into a wilderness in a thunder-storm it would have been a relief after what he had suffered in the bedroom of the inn.

What was the fair woman with the knife? The creature of a dream, or that other creature from the unknown world called among men by the name of ghost? He could make nothing of the mystery—had made nothing of it, even when it was midday on Wednesday, and when he stood, at last, after many times missing his road, once more on the doorstep of home.

CHAPTER III

❧

His mother came out eagerly to receive him. His face told her in a moment that something was wrong.

"I've lost the place; but that's my luck. I dreamed an ill dream last night, mother—or maybe I saw a ghost. Take it either way, it scared me out of my senses, and I'm not my own man again yet."

"Isaac, your face frightens me. Come in to the fire—come in, and tell mother all about it."

He was as anxious to tell as she was to hear; for it had been his hope, all the way home, that his mother, with her quicker capacity and superior knowledge, might be able to throw some light on the mystery which he could not clear up for himself. His memory of the dream was still mechanically vivid, though his thoughts were entirely confused by it.

His mother's face grew paler and paler as he went on. She never interrupted him by so much as a single word; but when he had done, she moved her chair close to his, put her arm round his neck, and said to him:

"Isaac, you dreamed your ill dream on this Wednesday morning. What time was it when you saw the fair woman with the knife in her hand?" Isaac reflected on what the landlord had said when they had passed by the clock on his leaving the inn; allowed as nearly as he could for the time that must have elapsed between the unlocking of his bedroom door and the paying of his bill just before going away, and answered:

"Somewhere about two o'clock in the morning."

His mother suddenly quitted her hold of his neck, and struck her hands together with a gesture of despair.

"This Wednesday is your birthday, Isaac, and two o'clock in the morning was the time when you were born."

Isaac's capacities were not quick enough to catch the infection of his mother's superstitious dread. He was amazed, and a little startled, also, when she suddenly rose from her chair, opened her old writing-desk, took pen, ink and paper, and then said to him:

"Your memory is but a poor one, Isaac, and, now I'm an old woman, mine's not much better. I want all about this dream of yours to be as well known to both of us, years hence, as it is now. Tell me over again all you told me a minute ago, when you spoke of what the woman with the knife looked like."

Isaac obeyed, and marveled much as he saw his mother carefully set down on paper the very words that he was saying.

"Light gray eyes," she wrote, as they came to the descriptive part, "with a droop in the left eyelid; flaxen hair, with a gold-yellow streak in it; white arms, with a down upon them; little lady's hand, with a reddish look about the finger nails; clasp-knife with a buck-horn handle, that seemed as good as new." To these particulars Mrs. Scatchard added the year, month, day of the week, and time in the morning when the woman of the dream appeared to her son. She then locked up the paper carefully in her writing-desk.

Neither on that day nor on any day after could her son induce her to return to the matter of the dream. She obstinately kept her thoughts about it to herself, and even refused to refer again to the paper in her writing-desk. Ere long Isaac grew weary of attempting to make her break her resolute silence; and time, which sooner or later wears out all things, gradually wore out the impression produced on him by the dream. He began by thinking of it carelessly, and he ended by not thinking of it at all.

The result was the more easily brought about by the advent of some important changes for the better in his prospects which commenced not long after his terrible night's experience at the inn. He reaped at last the reward of his long and patient suffering under adversity by getting an excellent place, keeping it for seven years, and leaving it, on the death of his master, not only with an excellent character, but also with a comfortable annuity bequeathed to him as a reward for saving his mistress's life in a carriage accident. Thus it happened that Isaac Scatchard returned to his old mother, seven years after the time of the dream at the inn, with an annual sum of money at his disposal sufficient to keep them both in ease and independence for the rest of their lives.

The mother, whose health had been bad of late years, profited so much by the care bestowed on her and by freedom from money anxieties, that when Isaac's birthday came round she was able to sit up comfortably at table and dine with him.

On that day, as the evening drew on, Mrs. Scatchard discovered that a bottle of tonic medicine which she was accustomed to take, and in which she had fancied that a dose or more was still left, happened to be empty. Isaac immediately volunteered to go to the chemist's and get it filled again. It was as rainy and bleak an autumn night as on the memorable past occasion when he lost his way and slept at the road-side inn.

On going into the chemist's shop he was passed hurriedly by a poorly-dressed woman coming out of it. The glimpse he had of her face struck him, and he looked back after her as she descended the doorsteps.

"You're noticing that woman?" said the chemist's apprentice behind the counter. "It's my opinion there's something wrong with her. She's been asking for laudanum to put to a bad tooth. Master's out for half an hour, and I told her I wasn't allowed to sell poison to strangers in his absence. She laughed in a queer way, and said she would come back in half an hour. If she expects master to serve her, I think she'll be disappointed. It's a case of suicide, sir, if ever there was one yet."

These words added immeasurably to the sudden interest in the woman which Isaac had felt at the first sight of her face. After he had got the medicine-bottle filled, he looked about anxiously for her as soon as he was out in the street. She was walking slowly up and down on the opposite side of the road. With his heart, very much to his own surprise, beating fast, Isaac crossed over and spoke to her.

He asked if she was in any distress. She pointed to her torn shawl, her scanty dress, her crushed, dirty bonnet; then moved under a lamp so as to let the light fall on her stern, pale, but still most beautiful face.

"I look like a comfortable, happy woman, don't I?" she said, with a bitter laugh.

She spoke with a purity of intonation which Isaac had never heard before from other than ladies' lips. Her slightest actions seemed to have the easy, negligent grace of a thoroughbred woman. Her skin, for all its poverty-stricken paleness, was as delicate as if her life had been passed in the enjoyment of every social comfort that wealth can purchase. Even her small, finely-shaped hands, gloveless as they were, had not lost their whiteness.

Little by little, in answer to his questions, the sad story of the woman came out. There is no need to relate it here; it is told over and over again in police reports and paragraphs about attempted suicides.

"My name is Rebecca Murdoch," said the woman, as she ended. "I have ninepence left, and I thought of spending it at the chemist's over the way in securing a passage to the other world. Whatever it is, it can't be worse to me than this, so why should I stop here?"

Besides the natural compassion and sadness moved in his heart by what he heard, Isaac felt within him some mysterious influence at work all the time the woman was speaking which utterly confused his ideas and almost deprived him of his powers of speech. All that he could say in answer to her last reckless words was that he would prevent her from attempting her own life, if he followed her about all night to do it. His rough, trembling earnestness seemed to impress her.

"I won't occasion you that trouble," she answered, when he repeated his threat. "You have given me a fancy for living by speaking kindly to me. No need for the mockery of protestations and promises. You may believe me without them. Come to Fuller's Meadow to-morrow at twelve, and you will find me alive, to answer for myself—No !—no money. My ninepence will do to get me as good a night's lodging as I want."

She nodded and left him. He made no attempt to follow—he felt no suspicion that she was deceiving him.

"It's strange, but I can't help believing her," he said to himself, and walked away, bewildered, toward home.

On entering the house, his mind was still so completely absorbed by its new subject of interest that he took no notice of what his mother was doing when he came in with the bottle of medicine. She had opened her old writing-desk in his absence, and was now reading a paper attentively that lay inside it. On every birthday of Isaac's since she had written down the particulars of his dream from his own lips, she had been accustomed to read that same paper, and ponder over it in private.

The next day he went to Fuller's Meadow.

He had done only right in believing her so implicitly. She was there, punctual to a minute, to answer for herself. The last-left faint defenses in Isaac's heart against the fascination which a word or look from her began inscrutably to exercise over him sank down and vanished before her forever on that memorable morning.

When a man, previously insensible to the influence of women, forms an attachment in middle life, the instances are rare indeed, let the warning circumstances be what they may, in which he is found capable of freeing himself from the tyranny of the new ruling passion. The charm of being spoken to familiarly, fondly, and gratefully by a woman whose language and manners still retained enough of their early refinement to hint at the high social station that she had lost, would have been a dangerous luxury to a man of Isaac's rank at the age of twenty. But it was far more than that—it was certain ruin to him—now that his heart was opening unworthily to a new influence at that middle time of life when strong feelings of all kinds, once implanted, strike root most stubbornly in a man's moral nature. A few more stolen interviews after that first morning in Fuller's Meadow completed his infatuation. In less than a month from the time when he first met her, Isaac Scatchard had consented to give Rebecca Murdoch a new interest in existence, and a chance of recovering the character she had lost by promising to make her his wife.

She had taken possession, not of his passions only, but of his faculties as well. All the mind he had he put into her keeping. She directed him on every point—even instructing him how to break the news of his approaching marriage in the safest manner to his mother.

"If you tell her how you met me and who I am at first," said the cunning woman, "she will move heaven and earth to prevent our marriage. Say I am the sister of one of your fellow-servants—ask her to see me before you go into any more particulars—and leave it to me to do the rest. I mean to make her love me next best to you, Isaac, before she knows anything of who I really am."

The motive of the deceit was sufficient to sanctify it to Isaac. The stratagem proposed relieved him of his one great anxiety, and quieted his uneasy conscience on the subject of his mother. Still, there was something wanting to perfect his happiness, something that he could not realise, something mysteriously untraceable, and yet something that perpetually made itself felt; not when he was absent from Rebecca Murdoch, but, strange to say, when he was actually in her presence! She was kindness itself with him. She never made him feel his inferior capacities and inferior manners. She showed the sweetest anxiety to please him in the smallest trifles; but, in spite of all these attractions, he never could feel quite at his ease with her. At their first meeting, there had mingled with his admiration, when he looked in her face, a faint, involuntary feeling of doubt whether that face was entirely strange to him. No after familiarity had the slightest effect on this inexplicable, wearisome uncertainty.

Concealing the truth as he had been directed, he announced his marriage engagement precipitately and confusedly to his mother on the day when he contracted it. Poor Mrs. Scatchard showed her perfect confidence in her son by flinging her arms round his neck, and giving him joy of having found at last, in the sister of one of his fellow-servants, a woman to comfort and care for him after his mother was gone. She was all eagerness to see the woman of her son's choice, and the next day was fixed for the introduction.

It was a bright sunny morning, and the little cottage parlour was full of light as Mrs. Scatchard, happy and expectant, dressed for the occasion in her Sunday gown, sat waiting for her son and her future daughter-in-law.

Punctual to the appointed time, Isaac hurriedly and nervously led his promised wife into the room. His mother rose to receive her—advanced a few steps, smiling—looked Rebecca full in the eyes, and suddenly stopped. Her face, which had been flushed the moment before, turned white in an instant; her eyes lost their expression of softness and kindness, and assumed a blank look of terror; her outstretched hands fell to her sides, and she staggered back a few steps with a low cry to her son.

"Isaac," she whispered, clutching him fast by the arm when he asked alarmedly if she was taken ill, "Isaac, does that woman's face remind you of nothing?"

Before he could answer—before he could look round to where Rebecca stood, astonished and angered by her reception, at the lower end of the room, his mother pointed impatiently to her writing-desk, and gave him the key.

"Open it," she said, in a quick breathless whisper.

"What does this mean? Why am I treated as if I had no business here? Does your mother want to insult me?" asked Rebecca, angrily.

"Open it, and give me the paper in the left-hand drawer. Quick! quick, for Heaven's sake!" said Mrs. Scatchard, shrinking further back in terror.

Isaac gave her the paper. She looked it over eagerly for a moment, then followed Rebecca, who was now turning away haughtily to leave the room, and caught her by the shoulder—abruptly raised the long, loose sleeve of her gown, and glanced at her hand and arm. Something like fear began to steal over the angry expression of Rebecca's face as she shook herself free from the old woman's grasp. "Mad!" she said to herself; "and Isaac never told me." With these few words she left the room.

Isaac was hastening after her when his mother turned and stopped his further progress. It wrung his heart to see the misery and terror in her face as she looked at him.

"Light gray eyes," she said, in low, mournful, awe-struck tones, pointing toward the open door; "a droop in the left eyelid; flaxen hair, with a gold-yellow streak in it; white arms, with a down upon them; little lady's hand, with a reddish look under the finger nails—*The Dream-Woman*, Isaac, the Dream-Woman!"

That faint cleaving doubt which he had never been able to shake off in Rebecca Murdoch's presence was fatally set at rest forever. He *had* seen her face, then, before—seven years before, on his birthday, in the bedroom of the lonely inn.

"Be warned! oh, my son, be warned! Isaac, Isaac, let her go, and do you stop with me!"

Something darkened the parlour window as those words were said. A sudden chill ran through him, and he glanced sidelong at the shadow. Rebecca Murdoch had come back. She was peering in curiously at them over the low window-blind.

"I have promised to marry, mother," he said, "and marry I must."

The tears came into his eyes as he spoke and dimmed his sight, but he could just discern the fatal face outside moving away again from the window.

His mother's head sank lower.

"Are you faint?" he whispered.

"Broken-hearted, Isaac."

He stooped down and kissed her. The shadow, as he did so, returned to the window, and the fatal face peered in curiously once more.

CHAPTER IV

⌒⌒⌒⌒⌒⌒

THREE weeks after that day Isaac and Rebecca were man and wife. All that was hopelessly dogged and stubborn in the man's moral nature seemed to have closed round his fatal passion, and to have fixed it unassailably in his heart.

After that first interview in the cottage parlour no consideration would induce Mrs. Scatchard to see her son's wife again or even to talk of her when Isaac tried hard to plead her cause after their marriage.

This course of conduct was not in any degree occasioned by a discovery of the degradation in which Rebecca had lived. There was no question of that between mother and son. There was no question of anything but the fearfully-exact resemblance between the living, breathing woman and the specter-woman of Isaac's dream.

Rebecca on her side neither felt nor expressed the slightest sorrow at the estrangement between herself and her mother-in-law. Isaac, for the sake of peace, had never contradicted her first idea that age and long illness had affected Mrs. Scatchard's mind. He even allowed his wife to upbraid him for not having confessed this to her at the time of their marriage engagement, rather than risk anything by hinting at the truth. The sacrifice of his integrity before his one all-mastering delusion seemed but a small thing, and cost his conscience but little after the sacrifices he had already made.

The time of waking from this delusion—the cruel and the rueful time—was not far off. After some quiet months of married life, as the summer was ending, and the year was getting on toward the month of his birthday, Isaac found his wife altering toward him. She grew sullen and contemptuous; she formed acquaintances of the most dangerous kind in defiance of his objections, his entreaties, and his commands; and, worst of all, she learned, ere long, after every fresh difference with her husband, to seek the deadly self-oblivion of drink. Little by little, after the first miserable discovery that his wife was keeping company with drunkards, the shocking certainty forced itself on Isaac that she had grown to be a drunkard herself.

He had been in a sadly desponding state for some time before the occurrence of these domestic calamities. His mother's health, as he could but too plainly discern every time he went to see her at the cottage, was failing fast, and he upbraided himself in secret as the cause of the bodily and mental suffering she endured. When to his remorse on his mother's account was added the shame and misery occasioned by the discovery of his wife's degradation, he sank under the double trial—his face began to alter fast, and he looked what he was, a spirit-broken man.

His mother, still struggling bravely against the illness that was hurrying her to the grave, was the first to notice the sad alteration in him, and the first to hear of his last worst trouble with his wife. She could only weep bitterly on the day when he made his humiliating confession, but on the next occasion when he went to see her she had taken a resolution in reference to his domestic afflictions which astonished and even alarmed him. He found her dressed to go out, and on asking the reason received this answer:

"I am not long for this world, Isaac," she said, "and I shall not feel easy on my death-bed unless I have done my best to the last to make my son happy. I mean to put my own fears and my own feelings out of the question, and to go with you to your wife, and try what I can do to reclaim her. Give me your arm, Isaac, and let me do the last thing I can in this world to help my son before it is too late."

He could not disobey her, and they walked together slowly toward his miserable home.

It was only one o'clock in the afternoon when they reached the cottage where he lived. It was their dinner-hour, and Rebecca was in the kitchen. He was thus able to take his mother quietly into the parlour, and then prepare his wife for the interview. She had fortunately drunk but little at that early hour, and she was less sullen and capricious than usual.

He returned to his mother with his mind tolerably at ease. His wife soon followed him into the parlor, and the meeting between her and Mrs. Scatchard passed off better than he had ventured to anticipate, though he observed with secret apprehension that his mother, resolutely as she controlled herself in other respects, could not look his wife in the face when she spoke to her. It was a relief to him, therefore, when Rebecca began to lay the cloth.

She laid the cloth, brought in the bread-tray, and cut a slice from the loaf for her husband, then returned to the kitchen. At that moment, Isaac, still anxiously watching his mother, was startled by seeing the same ghastly change pass over her face which had altered it so awfully on the morning when Rebecca and she first met. Before he could say a word, she whispered, with a look of horror:

"Take me back—home, home again, Isaac. Come with me, and never go back again."

He was afraid to ask for an explanation; he could only sign to her to be silent, and help her quickly to the door. As they passed the breadtray on the table she stopped and pointed to it.

"Did you see what your wife cut your bread with?" she asked, in a low whisper.

"No, mother—I was not noticing—what was it?"

"Look!"

He did look. A new clasp-knife with a buckhorn handle lay with the loaf in the bread-tray. He stretched out his hand shudderingly to possess himself of it; but, at the same time, there was a noise in the kitchen, and his mother caught at his arm.

"The knife of the dream! Isaac, I'm faint with fear. Take me away before she comes back."

He was hardly able to support her. The visible, tangible reality of the knife struck him with a panic, and utterly destroyed any faint doubts that he might have entertained up to this time in relation to the mysterious dream-warning of nearly eight years before. By a last desperate effort, he summoned self-possession enough to help his mother out of the house—so quietly that the "Dream-woman" (he thought of her by that name now) did not hear them departing from the kitchen.

"Don't go back, Isaac—don't go back!" implored Mrs. Scatchard, as he turned to go away, after seeing her safely seated again in her own room.

"I must get the knife," he answered, under his breath. His mother tried to stop him again, but he hurried out without another word.

On his return he found that his wife had discovered their secret departure from the house. She had been drinking, and was in a fury of passion. The dinner in the kitchen was flung under the grate; the cloth was off the parlour table. Where was the knife?

Unwisely, he asked for it. She was only too glad of the opportunity of irritating him which the request afforded her. "He wanted the knife, did he? Could he give her a reason why? No! Then he should not have it—not if he went down on his knees to ask for it." Further recriminations elicited the fact that she had bought it a bargain, and that she considered it her own especial property. Isaac saw the uselessness of attempting to get the knife by fair means, and determined to search for it, later in the day, in secret. The search was unsuccessful. Night came on, and he left the house to walk about the streets. He was afraid now to sleep in the same room with her.

Three weeks passed. Still sullenly enraged with him, she would not give up the knife; and still that fear of sleeping in the same room with her possessed him. He walked about at night, or dozed in the parlour, or sat watching by his mother's bedside. Before the expiration of the first week in the new month his mother died. It wanted then but ten days of her son's birthday. She had longed to live till that anniversary. Isaac was present at her death, and her last words in this world were addressed to him:

"Don't go back, my son, don't go back!"

He was obliged to go back, if it were only to watch his wife. Exasperated to the last degree by his distrust of her, she had revengefully sought to add a sting to his grief, during the last days of his mother's illness, by declaring that she would assert her right to attend the funeral. In spite of all that he could do or say, she held with wicked pertinacity to her word, and on the day appointed for the burial forced herself—inflamed and shameless with drink—into her husband's presence, and declared that she would walk in the funeral procession to his mother's grave.

This last worst outrage, accompanied by all that was most insulting in word and look, maddened him for the moment. He struck her.

The instant the blow was dealt he repented it. She crouched down, silent, in a corner of the room, and eyed him steadily; it was a look that cooled his hot blood and made him tremble. But there was no time now to think of a means of making atonement. Nothing remained but to risk the worst till the funeral was over. There was but one way of making sure of her. He locked her into her bedroom.

When he came back some hours after, he found her sitting, very much altered in look and bearing, by the bedside, with a bundle on her lap. She rose, and faced him quietly, and spoke with a strange stillness in her voice, a strange repose in her eyes, a strange composure in her manner.

"No man has ever struck me twice," she said, "and my husband shall have no second opportunity. Set the door open and let me go. From this day forth we see each other no more."

Before he could answer she passed him and left the room. He saw her walk away up the street.

Would she return?

All that night he watched and waited, but no footstep came near the house. The next night, overpowered by fatigue, he lay down in bed in his clothes, with the door locked, the key on the table, and the candle burning. His slumber was not disturbed. The third night, the fourth, the fifth, the sixth passed, and nothing happened.

He lay down on the seventh, still in his clothes, still with the door locked, the key on the table, and the candle burning, but easier in his mind.

Easier in his mind, and in perfect health of body when he fell off to sleep. But his rest was disturbed. He woke twice without any sensation of uneasiness. But the third time it was that never-to-be-forgotten shivering of the night at the lonely inn, that dreadful sinking pain at the heart, which once more aroused him in an instant.

His eyes opened toward the left-hand side of the bed, and there stood—

The Dream-Woman again? No! His wife; the living reality, with the dream-specter's face, in the dream-specter's attitude; the fair arm up, the knife clasped in the delicate white hand.

He sprang upon her almost at the instant of seeing her, and yet not quickly enough to prevent her from hiding the knife. Without a word from him—without a cry from her—he pinioned her in a chair. With one hand he felt up her sleeve, and there, where the Dream-Woman had hidden the knife, his wife had hidden it—the knife with the buckhorn handle, that looked like new.

In the despair of that fearful moment his brain was steady, his heart was calm. He looked at her fixedly with the knife in his hand, and said these last words:

"You told me we should see each other no more, and you have come back. It is my turn now to go, and to go forever. I say that we shall see each other no more, and *my* word shall not be broken."

He left her, and set forth into the night. There was a bleak wind abroad, and the smell of recent rain was in the air. The distant church-clocks chimed the quarter as he walked rapidly beyond the last houses in the suburb. He asked the first policeman he met what hour that was of which the quarter past had just struck.

The man referred sleepily to his watch, and answered, "Two o'clock." Two in the morning. What day of the month was this day that had just begun? He reckoned it up from the date of his mother's funeral. The fatal parallel was complete: it was his birthday!

Had he escaped the mortal peril which his dream foretold? or had he only received a second warning?

As that ominous doubt forced itself on his mind, he stopped, reflected, and turned back again toward the city. He was still resolute to hold to his word, and never to let her see him more; but there was a thought now in his mind of having her watched and followed. The knife was in his possession; the world was before him; but a new distrust of her—a vague, unspeakable, superstitious dread had overcome him.

"I must know where she goes, now she thinks I have left her," he said to himself, as he stole back wearily to the precincts of his house.

It was still dark. He had left the candle burning in the bedchamber; but when he looked up to the window of the room now there was no light in it. He crept cautiously to the house door. On going away, he remembered to have closed it; on trying it now, he found it open.

He waited outside, never losing sight of the house, till daylight. Then he ventured indoors—listened, and heard nothing—looked into kitchen, scullery, parlour and found nothing; went up at last into the bedroom—it was empty. A picklock lay on the floor, betraying how she had gained entrance in the night, and that was the only trace of her.

Whither had she gone? That no mortal tongue could tell him. The darkness had covered her flight; and when the day broke, no man could say where the light found her.

Before leaving the house and the town forever, he gave instructions to a friend and neighbour to sell his furniture for anything that it would fetch, and apply the proceeds to employing the police to trace her. The directions were honestly followed, and the money was all spent, but the inquiries led to nothing. The picklock on the bedroom floor remained the one last useless trace of the Dream-Woman.

At this point of the narrative the landlord paused, and, turning toward the window of the room in which we were sitting, looked in the direction of the stable-yard.

"So far," he said, "I tell you what was told to me. The little that remains to be added lies within my own experience. Between two and three months after the events I have just been relating, Isaac

Scatchard came to me, withered and old-looking before his time, just as you saw him to-day. He had his testimonials to character with him, and he asked for employment here. Knowing that my wife and he were distantly related, I gave him a trial in consideration of that relationship, and liked him in spite of his queer habits. He is as sober, honest, and willing a man as there is in England. As for his restlessness at night, and his sleeping away his leisure time in the day, who can wonder at it after hearing his story? Besides, he never objects to being roused up when he's wanted, so there's not much inconvenience to complain of, after all."

"I suppose he is afraid of a return of that dreadful dream, and of waking out of it in the dark?" said I.

"No," returned the landlord. "The dream comes back to him so often that he has got to bear with it by this time resignedly enough. It's his wife keeps him waking at night, as he has often told me."

"What! Has she never been heard of yet?"

"Never. Isaac himself has the one perpetual thought about her, that she is alive and looking for him. I believe he wouldn't let himself drop off to sleep toward two in the morning for a king's ransom. Two in the morning, he says, is the time she will find him, one of these days. Two in the morning is the time all the year round when he likes to be most certain that he has got that clasp-knife safe about him. He does not mind being alone as long as he is awake, except on the night before his birthday, when he firmly believes himself to be in peril of his life. The birthday has only come round once since he has been here, and then he sat up along with the night-porter. 'She's looking for me,' is all he says when anybody speaks to him about the one anxiety of his life; 'she's looking for me.' He may be right. She *may* be looking for him. Who can tell?"

"Who can tell?" said I.

Achevé d'imprimer sur Roto-Page par l'Imprimerie Floch à Mayenne, le 10 janvier 2005.
Dépôt légal : janvier 2005 - N° d'impression : 61996 - ISBN : 2-84304-284-4
Imprimé en France